A PENNY FOR THE OLD GUY

A PENNY

FOR THE OLD GUY

Gaylord Dold

ST. MARTIN'S PRESS • NEW YORK

Design by Judy Dannecker

Library of Congress Cataloging-in-Publication Data

Dold, Gaylord.
    A penny for the old guy / Gaylord Dold.
        p. cm.
    "A Thomas Dunne book."
    ISBN 0-312-06442-X
    I. Title.
  PS3554.0436P4 1991
  813'.54—dc20   91-21027
                                           CIP

10 9 8 7 6 5 4 3 2

Christmas is coming
The goose is getting fat,
Won't you please put a penny
In the old man's hat?

If you haven't got a penny
A ha'penny will do.
If you haven't got a ha'penny
Then God bless you.

—English Christmas song

LONDON

PROLOGUE

THE old couple strolling so sweetly along the Backs found
Jonathan just as the light was leaving a chilly October sky.
Lamps in the Cambridge shops glowed on across the willow
fens, casting bright spears on the river's surface, where no
waves broke the solid gray cast. There had been a morning
shower, very sudden, and then the sky had become pure delft
blue, only to be swallowed again, later, by a whale's maw
English drizzle, which lay now on the grassy slopes, making
the footing slippery for the old man and his wife, who were
hobbled anyway by age and complaint.

Brian ap Rhys, the old gentleman was called, though his
friends, five or six ruddy town men, retired like him, called
him Lippy for short. The nickname, which he hated, or pre-
tended to, was from the way his red lips, pronounced in their
thinness and color, stood away from the white cast of his face
when Lippy, or Brian, had downed five or six Forest Brown
Ales at the Crow and Corn, his pub. That drizzly October
evening, shuffling along the banks of the river, he thought he
saw floating in the reeds a picnic basket, lost, he thought, by
one of the young punters, left behind in a champagne-and-
pâté haze, which is how Brian thought the students at University behaved on bright October afternoons after Michaelmas.
Twenty-nine years at the Wren Library chit room had made
his eyes weak, sitting there reading cheap Pan editions by the
cool dark glow of an electric fire, tearing at the student chits,

keeping the visitor's record in that bad light—and coddling students for so long with their messes of macs and umbrellas, chatting at them like a friendly Welshman would, hence too his name Lippy. Until he had finally been made to see poorly, forced to squint.

So it was that Brian peered like a rabbit at the basket in the reeds and nudged his wife, who was holding his left arm, herself thinking about other things, the sausage she had in the fridge, her broadcast of the Garden Club on BBC 2. She had known, she told a copper later, that Lippy was daft, crooked as an old drainpipe, she said, and at first she didn't believe him when he told her to look at the basket, but when she felt him bridle, felt his old man's bones grown hard, she stopped with him and studied the basket herself. Both stared hard, and because the light was fading so quickly, and because the slope was so difficult and wet, dared not, at first, walk down to the water until the old man had taken out his unfolding umbrella and had begun to poke it down the hillside for balance.

A swan swam by, and then another, and then the clocks of Cambridge chimed in the city towers and the streetlamps on the High Street by Trinity College whisked on, imparting a yellow glow to the horizon. There was enough light for the old man to lead his wife down to the edge of the water, where he stood in some reeds and shallow backwash, Brian shaky at the knees, stabbing the water for his picnic basket prize, thrusting the umbrella anxiously at the flotsam while the swans circled curiously. The wife begged her husband to quit his foolishness, but forty years of marriage to Lippy had inured her to failure in the business of admonishment, advice, and she knew she was only making noise for the old man to hear and ignore. Ah, she thought, she had been doing so for forty years.

Brian whacked the water with his umbrella. It made a flat sound on the surface and the swans swam farther out, honking as they glided through points of light as delicate as lace. Feeling suddenly cold, the old woman tugged at Brian's coatsleeve, but just then he struck a hollow place on the basket and realized, horribly, that the green wicker he thought he had perceived was not woven rattan at all, but was instead the Lincoln Green of Harlow School, with black piping around the sleeve and collar of a coat, and that below the water line, twinkling on the front pocket above the breast, three beaver, a stand of oak—a heraldic shield. Under water, it was like a cluster of stars.

He was aghast. The old woman could feel his panic, grabbed him, thinking he was going into the drink. Later, a solicitous chap named Clannahan let Lippy sip some brandy, though it was Spanish, not French, and on the way to the station house in Ipswich Lippy had brightened a little, though he still felt awful inside.

At the first *plock* from his umbrella, Brian had nearly fallen, but being saved by his wife from a broken hip or worse, he had slowly pushed the wooden tip of the umbrella into the water, and had drawn forth the coat breast and had clearly seen the shield of Harlow School, which he knew plainly from his years at the Wren Library. Harlow children, boys they were, were often brought to the library by their masters, or by bigger boys on duty, where they would run among the book-shelves like billy goats. It had fallen all these years to Brian to insist repeatedly in hushed tones on absolute silence from these billy goats. It was a task he disliked when he was a younger man, partly because he was ashamed, and partly because he knew that insisting on silence from a billy goat was silly, but one he relished when he grew older, knowing in fact that most of the boys were quite decent, and that their cheeki-ness had all the outward aspects of good humor. Really, Brian knew, the Harlow boys were a well-behaved lot, good chaps, he told Clannahan, and he was surprised to find one of the little fellows face down in the river Cam. And wearing his school uniform too.

Giselle, the wife, had pleaded with her husband to quit the riverbank and call the constable, but the old man persisted until from the slate-colored water he had heaved the body over and had viewed the pale face of a boy upturned from the surface, and until he had studied the ashen features, the sprinkle of freckles, one eye closed, one open, and the delicate floating hair, which in the dark was like pictures he had seen of plants swaying in coral gardens undersea. Giselle saw the face as well, but was too shocked to bother the old man as he tugged at the coat with the tip of his umbrella, pulling the boy toward shore while the swans continued to honk.

Farther up the bank were willows and some coarse-leaved sedge. While the old man fiddled with the boy, Giselle stumbled uphill and squatted beside the trunk of one of the willows. The sedge scratched her legs and she shuddered as the whole body appeared slowly, the delicate hair matted out of the water, sticks and leaves plastered to the boy's face. She saw a dreadful stare from the open eye. Brian ap Rhys had been an air raid warden in London during the war, and he had seen the Face of Death, had even seen children maimed and burned, and so he hesitated and then steadied to his task, telling Giselle in his best air raid warden voice, now, to run and fetch the constable, that he would stay with the boy, who was drowned, poor lad.

FRIDAY, NOVEMBER 22

KENSINGTON Park was nearly black with rain, though above the rim of chestnut trees there had appeared a razor edge of blue. Amanda cried as she told Roberts about her son Jonathan, her lovely son, and as she cried and talked, Roberts watched the sun sink into the edge of the razor and sprinkle a haze of color on the low clouds. A keeper was in the park below, bowed beneath his mac, shaking a broom at the wet leaves that clung to a stone walking path leading to darkness. The keeper's beard shone like silk in the rain, and he was being watched by two girls in yellow rain gear and public-school skirts who marched mercurially around and around a huge puddle, splashing themselves gloriously, pausing to watch the keeper as he waltzed his broom around the wet stones. Cabs cruised down Kensington Road, hissing, throwing deep cones of white ahead like tusks, like elephants goring the rain, the Occupied signs inside aglow like yellow orbs.

"That's what I know," Amanda said finally.

She was sitting on the sofa with her head between her knees, abjectly, whimpering softly, pausing to wipe tears from her face with the sleeve of her robe. "My lovely Jonathan."

Mitchell Roberts sipped iced Kir and studied the effect of the rain on the latticework, where drops worked down the Georgian frame in squiggles. A few pedestrians walked downhill to Portobello, where already an organdy glow was spreading from the cinemas and pubs in a smoky aurora, as if

7

bonfires were ablaze where Kensington Road disappeared into the alleys and cul-de-sacs. The Kir made his teeth ache.

While the girls watched, infinitely amused, the keeper stowed his broom in a hutch beside the park entrance gate and took out his set of keys. The girls marched to his side and together the girls and the keeper left the park, the keeper locking the gates behind them, taking their leave, the little girls skipping unhindered uphill, oblivious of the rain, while the keeper marched in a halting gait downhill, headed no doubt home to his shilling fire and his bacon and egg. Notting Hill had taken shape like a dark bulb, and the coal fires of Shepherd's Bush tinted the clouds an inky red.

All Roberts knew about Jonathan's death he had learned from a short note Amanda had written to America. The Harlow School choir had sung for Jonathan at the Anglican Chapel in Cambridge. There had been a funeral, and the boy had been buried beside his stepfather in the Soldier's Cemetery across the Vauxhall Bridge in Battersea, a peaceful white necropolis towered over by copper beeches and tended by the Fusiliers, who had done service in the Colonies. The Fusiliers had planted irises everywhere on the grounds. Each spring the grounds were convulsed with pinks and lavenders and carbuncle blues, violets too, and among the white tombstones you could often see the Fusiliers moving about in their starched red-and-gray outfits. It had been Amanda's custom to write to Roberts, keeping alive their friendship, usually a Christmas letter about the boys, and to invite him to England for the holidays, which were always quite splendid, a time of tipsy evenings by the fire while the boys played imaginary tennis games or roughhoused and mused about their gifts like kittens at a ball of string. Jonathan would have been twelve years old on Boxing Day. Jocko, her other son, was through his O Levels, hard to believe, nearly seventeen and shaving. Roberts always sent gifts and made promises, feeling the hopefulness of distance bridge. Now, sitting there on the sofa watching the rain, he felt only a weariness, a heartsickness at the death of his godchild, whose life had barely begun to be lived.

Amanda sighed and tried to smile. Shadows crawled up the walls and the room turned cold. On the wallpaper were scenes of Irish castles and fox hunting on the Downs, and between the scenes ran a lilac wreath to the plaster molding around the ceiling. Amanda busied herself with the fire, placing a piece of coal in the stove with a pair of silver tongs. Flames popped in the stove and a tinge of warmth emerged. The room was lined with bookshelves, carved busts of Locke and Hobbes on the mantel, and on the bar a photograph of Captain Reece, who had married Amanda during the Battle of Britain. Next to that was a small picture of the boy named Smitty who had married Amanda before the invasion, and who lay in Normandy beneath rye grass, glazed by salt air.

Amanda leaned back and sipped at a glass of whiskey. Roberts observed her, noticing the gray streaks in her hair, where before he only remembered an auburn wave. Her eyes, beautifully hazel, were red rimmed, circled by black pouches.

"I'm such a bloody crybaby," Amanda said.

"Nonsense," Roberts muttered helplessly. He was utterly exhausted, but his thought was as tireless as the rain. He was remembering his war buddy, Smitty, Jonathan's father, an age and a world ago.

He was feeling a little dizzy from the Kir too, from the fatigue of chasing Jocko around Holland Park all afternoon while a dank drizzle pushed at the kites they were trying to fly. Jocko had limitless energy, or so it seemed to Roberts that afternoon, though he knew the boy was breaching his horror and the sadness of his half brother's death by romping in the Common, watched by portly workingmen from Fulham and the squires on their penny benches. Later, they had gone up the Church Street and had drunk four ciders at the Bung and Barrel. Jocko had tried to be cheery, but had cried for his brother and his mother, and Roberts had brought him home with tears streaming down his face, which he tried to hide from his mother, who had met them at the stoop, Jocko pretending that his tears were rain. Roberts had helped him with his wet clothes, the boy nearly limp in his grief, the bright red-and-blue jersey pasted to his skin, Roberts stripping him of his woolen trousers until he had stood before the mirror, skinny and pale and choked by cider. When Jocko had gone to sleep, Roberts went downstairs and made himself a Kir, and sat beside Amanda while she told him about Brian ap Rhys, about her lovely Jonathan. And then the long day was finally ending.

"I'm bloody well finished," Amanda said between sips of her own Kir.

"You've some more crying to do," Roberts said. "Then we'll go to the cemetery, and then you'll start your life again."

Roberts was drifting in the memory of Smitty. They had met in the hold of a rusty troopship halfway across the Atlantic. Smitty had been squatting beside a boiler in its hellish glare with a baseball mitt on his right hand, bouncing a ball off the boiler and onto a cold-water pipe overhead, so that the ball caromed perfectly from the bulkhead back to his waiting mitt. He had done it with such grace and with a nonchalance that had impressed Roberts immediately and belied the strength in Smitty's huge red-knuckled hands. Smitty had freckles and tawny hair and an innocent look which said he did not believe in death, that war was a lark, and that luck was on his side. Now that Roberts remembered it, they had all felt that way then.

They became shipboard friends, and were assigned to train at High Wycombe with the Engineers. It was a base just north of London, where Smitty had met Amanda, and where, in spite of the odds and common sense, they had married. Amanda was older, she had lost her first husband to the English Channel and the Germans. But she had bucked the odds, they all had, and now Smitty was dead, and she had lost her youngest son as well. "Finished," Roberts heard her say, softly.

10

"Nothing is ever finished," he said. "You have Jocko, you have me."

"I've been such a mess these weeks."

Amanda finished her drink and leaned her head back against the sofa. She looked very tired, her hair sheenless, her face taut and miserable. "Every time," she said, "I think of my little boy I go to pieces. It's so terribly unfair, so bloody unfair and awful."

Roberts set down his Kir on the windowsill. Some more people had taken to Kensington Park Road now, and a line of red buses chugged along Ladbrooke Gardens. Black cabs smoldered down the hill, raising tiny halos of water behind them. The sun had gone down entirely, leaving a purple smudge among the crooked outlines of Richmond suburb. Roberts touched Amanda's hand, feeling it cold against his skin. Her fingers were narrow and very delicate.

"I'll stay in England until you're back on your feet. We'll get through this thing together."

"You Yanks are so noble," she said, without a trace of irony. "But Mitchell, this isn't your burden. I haven't worked since Jonathan died, and I haven't stopped drinking my whiskey either."

Just then Jocko came down the stairs and halted on the landing across the room. He stood there wrapped in a dressing gown, looking across at his mother. He seemed older now than his years, his sandy hair tousled from sleep, wiping his eyes. "Please, Mum," he said, "please don't cry."

"Go back to bed, darling," Amanda said, smiling as gently as she could.

Roberts was looking at the photograph of Captain Reece on the mahogany bar, realizing how much Jocko resembled his father, the darkly intelligent stare, the pronounced Norfolk jaw stamping them both as coming from the sea and the wetland estuaries. Jocko was grasping the banister, trying not to cry himself. "Mitchell will sit up with me, darling," Amanda said.

11

"I'll see to you, Mum," Jocko said. Now the shadows were turning up the stairs like snakes.

"I know," said Amanda. For an instant they were locked together in their trance of grief, and then Jocko turned and went back upstairs to his room. They heard his bed creak as he lay back down. Amanda looked at Roberts while the wind whispered at the windows. "I'm surrounded by such brave men," she said. "I wish I could take some courage from that, but I can't."

Roberts saw that some color had come back to her face, or maybe it was the glow of the coal fire, he couldn't tell which. He went over to the bar and got the Teacher's, and some ice from the bucket. They sat in the dark and drank whiskey and watched the rain. Roberts felt his consciousness drift away, across the city of London and out over the Irish Sea, and then across the great Atlantic Ocean, to another world, this long sighing collapse of time where death had deposited itself, soldiers' deaths in the war, his own father abed at home, his face sunken with the effort of dying, the grandmother he had loved. All this familiar death, and none of it so terrible as the death of a child.

SUNDAY, NOVEMBER 24

THE men of the 56th Combat Engineer Battalion celebrated their twelfth annual reunion with a formal sit-down dinner in the elaborate ballroom of the Ennismore Hotel on Prince Ennismore Street, a striking Queen Anne structure located on Embassy Row, across the wide avenue from Hyde Park. Roberts had taken a weekly residence room on a back street across the Cromwell Road, a fashionably poor stone building without benefit of sunshine and fresh air, but cheap and clean and friendly. He could walk to the Serpentine, the Natural History Museum, and two or three Indian restaurants. In stark contrast to the Ennismore, Roberts's Dunsmore residence had leaky water closets and worn carpets and a collection of oddball inhabitants who could have stepped out of a Dickens novel.

Roberts and the other engineers had gone ashore in France at Omaha Beach in the predawn murk of June 6, 1944. They were covered by darkness and a pounding surf, and set about blowing tank traps, clearing mine fields for the approaching infantry, and chartering pillboxes in advance of the main invasion force. Four hundred and sixteen men had waded through the cold water from about two hundred yards out in a low tide, then began to place satchel charges around the X-shaped tank traps, sweeping the beach with mine detectors, clipping barbed wire, the men accompanied for their safety by only a platoon of riflemen, and by three dogs, a Dalmatian named Ernie, for Ernie Pyle, the revered war correspondent, and two other mongrel types named Hal and Barney, who were assigned the duty of barking if either saw Hitler or Goebbels.

The invasion itself was followed by two weeks of almost constant combat, terrible raw fighting in support of the First Army under Eisenhower. Roberts's outfit had suffered fifty-one dead and seventy-five seriously wounded, and among the dead was Joseph Smith, the boy named Smitty who had just married Amanda Trench, a civilian nurse from High Wycombe who was pregnant with their first child. Two hundred of the survivors and their families had come to London for the reunion, and before the formal dinner had stood in the lobby of the Prince Ennismore swapping stories and studying battle photos compiled by the Signal Corps.

That afternoon Roberts had met with twelve special guys, men with whom he'd shared battle, each with a reason to be thankful for being alive, groping for a fondness in the experience of war. They were mostly married, persisting in their lives as best they could, selling insurance and cars, building tract houses, sitting at their stateside desks with their memories studded down deep by the explosions and the burning metal and the pictures of villages in rubble, people starving. After the reunion dinner, Roberts had walked the silent London streets, his mind still in turmoil, and then had retired to his tiny room off the Cromwell Road, where he slept fitfully, disturbed by his memories of Joseph Smith, by the death of Smith's son, Jonathan, whom he had never even seen. Early the next Sunday morning, Roberts got up and ate some jam and rolls, then went outside for the four-mile trek to Kew, the huge gardens in Richmond suburb, established by Queen Anne herself.

He found the gardens magnificent under an opaque gray sky. Fall mist was rising from the Thames, imparting to the oaks and chestnuts a silver veneer, as if the massive trunks and slender branches had been fashioned by a smith. Church bells tolled across the nearly immeasurable silence, ravens squawked in the trees, and out on the Richmond Road some diesel trucks chugged back and forth. He walked around to the museum grounds and bought tea from a roughish-looking Irish chap with no teeth and a wicked piercing stare. After rambling in the gardens for an hour on his own, he left Kew by a back gate and trudged south along the Thames embankment on a concrete path, the river lapping gently against the wooden docks built for small boats, pleasure craft and oaring sculls. The Owl Tavern crouched on a knoll above the river, a queer gingerbread construction, part Tudor, its windows ablaze with a maple-hued light, waiters scurrying around the small tables set willy-nilly on a patio outside, drinkers leaning at all angles around the bars and windowsills.

Amanda was sitting at one of the outdoor tables looking down at the river. She moved, sipped her tea, staring then at the Twickenham sky, back at the tiny figures on Fulham Golf Course, small slashes of tweed on the green background of fairway. The Thames was being ruffled by a chop, exuding a slightly metallic smell, and some white houses across the river reflected their windows onto the water. Roberts walked up the steps and touched Amanda's arm, gently, hoping not to startle her, she seemed so specially vulnerable and silent. She flinched a bit in surprise, but when she turned Roberts could see some real color in her cheeks for a change, and he knew that being outside, even on a dull Sunday, was probably good for her. She had washed her hair, and she had tied it back behind her head with a lavender silk scarf, so that it lay on her shoulders in a pillow, with only a few wisps escaping from behind her ears. She tried to smile, and caught herself being artificial, and sipped her tea, looking back at the figures on the fairway, these surreal ciphers, plaid swatches of color.

"You look much better," Roberts said. He sat down and studied a menu, wanting desperately to say just the right thing, finding himself empty to the task, not really prepared to deal with such a disaster. After all, he had wanted to come to England for his reunion, to see Amanda, her sons. The air was damp, he was glad he had worn a woolen muffler, his leather bomber jacket, he thought he looked like a tough American, he even thought that people were looking at him from across the stone wall of the pub fence. "This air should help," he said.

"I'm going to work tomorrow," Amanda said. It was clear to Roberts that she was going to try to be bright. She had put on some makeup too, it looked like maybe she had gotten some sleep.

After the war, after all the rottenness, Amanda had taken a job as an assistant editor for a tiny literary review and periodical, a poetry and arts journal supported by a few wealthy patrons and some government grant money. She solicited material and funds from universities and scholarly groups, selected type for chapbook editions of esoteric verse, and went to cocktail parties at which poets and their admirers traded drunken compliments, all very British and civilized. Her income was from insurance, and a small sum from her father's estate in trust. He had been a wealthy solicitor in Ipswich, but Amanda had worked hard for herself, and she enjoyed her place on the literary staff, and was greatly admired for her dedication and her good taste. She loved literature truly, and the hurly-burly of magazine life. She was fond of saying that she had met Ezra Pound, and that she had driven a drunken Robert Lowell to his hotel one night after a party.

"I'm glad for you," Roberts said. "I don't think you could have made a better decision." He took her hands as if they were a bouquet of flowers, and they sat that way with the wind coming off the river, blowing Amanda's hair, until a wispy Pakistani waiter appeared with an order pad. He was a tightly bunched fellow with a wad of wet black hair under a turban, the back of it held in a net. His double-breasted serving jacket was far too large for his small frame, he had surprisingly delicate wrists, which you could see when he stretched out his arms, rolling up his sleeves to write down the order. His white stained jacket was the kind of coat that men passed through, on their way up or down. He emitted a titil-

16

lated laugh, recommending cucumber sandwiches, something quite out of place in late November. With his hands drawn to his lips, as if he had overheard some outrageously funny joke, he watched while Amanda and Roberts studied the menu. They ordered ham sandwiches and fish soup, with apple crumble for dessert.

Only a few of the outside tables were occupied, because of the cold and the damp November breeze. From the Owl came the din of drinking Englishmen on Sunday afternoons, a-shouting for more ale, gin, a glass of bitters, voices above the clipped adagio of the mandolin and fiddle, the clink of glasses. Gulls wheeled above the river while some scullers rowed downstream toward the City, the thin hulls skipping above the water, throwing spray, the college lads shouting and grunting in the effort. Above Twickenham the sky was dim rose. The waiter brought the fish soup, and the two ate it, pausing to look at the river, the ragged clouds over Richmond suburb.

"You know, don't you," Amanda said, looking up from the table, pursing her lips gently while she studied Roberts's face, "that we're going to talk about our dead sooner or later?"

"Yes, I know," he replied. "But I still think it's wonderful that you're starting back to work. No matter what else happens, one has to find one's place in the world and dig in."

"That sounds like American army talk."

"When someone is shooting at you, grab a shovel and dig a goddamn hole. Don't come out until the shooting stops."

"You think that's good advice?"

"Sometimes. For you, right now, I think it is."

Amanda touched her mouth with a napkin, a gesture that he thought was wonderfully delicate, very womanly and English. He wished he had that kind of manners, he was more likely to wipe his mouth with his sleeve. She had worn a smart Scotch plaid sweater, a lavender scarf, it all worked with the hazel in her eyes, the two emerald slashes for an iris. She had folded her hands together, tucking two thumbs under her chin, the repose of someone waiting for an answer, but Roberts wasn't sure of the question. "I want to know about Joseph," Amanda said, matter-of-factly. It was odd, Roberts had just been thinking about Amanda as she was before the invasion, this young woman walking down a row of benches in an ankle-length gray skirt, a smartly tailored blue cotton blouse buttoned to the neck, the peaked nurse cap tilted jauntily on her head. In his mind's eye, he could see her across the years, passing out candy and decks of playing cards to the boys who had gathered for an evening of English musical comedy in the metal Quonset hut on base, the room a smoky caricature of itself, smell of cigarette smoke, dense clouds of it, the rosy-cheeked nurses, the band up front, piano, fiddle, some drums. It was no wonder, he remembered, thinking now, that they had been so drawn to the English nurses, but it was Joseph who had been overwhelmed. He had courted Amanda instantly, suddenly, it was volcanic. Amanda was living near the camp with her child, the very epitome of English reserve, cheeks like June roses, a smile of pastoral simplicity, but down deep, bawdy and humane too.

"Of course we will," Roberts said. "I want to know about Jonathan too. If you can talk about it now, I'm ready and willing. But I'm willing to wait for you."

"I've made my first peace. I've cursed God and I've prayed to him. I'm afraid my friends are next."

Roberts was thinking, starting to feel the cold through the bomber jacket, watching the gulls dart down over the Thames. After the war, on his way home, he had seen Amanda only briefly on the train platform at Victoria, this woman he knew part of a milling humanity. They had kissed and made some promises, and Amanda had given him the baptismal certificate for Jonathan Trench Smith, Roberts standing in absentia as godfather for the boy.

"This is difficult for me," Roberts said. "I'll try to tell you what happened to Joseph, but I don't think I can go on about it for very long."

"Please don't worry," Amanda said, nibbling her lower lip. "I feel ever so much stronger today. Perhaps having you near has made the difference, but I feel as if the night is over, and I'm going to survive. I don't really know how I'm going to do it, but I don't have the bloody courage to kill myself—believe me I've thought about it."

"As they say in the American army, thumbs-up."

"Thank you anyway," Amanda said, suffering a smile. "Please just tell me about Joseph. I've waited twelve years to hear, and now I think I'm ready."

Roberts was trying to ready himself, his heart was beating, it was as if he were back on the beach, under fire; it was a terrible memory. Nobody knew who hadn't been through it, it was the worst nightmare you could imagine, something you can't talk about with anyone.

"Joseph and I went ashore about two hundred yards out," he said, noticing that Amanda was not looking at him, but out at the golfers on Fulham Course, her eyes glazed and wet, as though she was fighting off the tears. "The surf was bad," he went on, "and we had to swim with our equipment part of the way in. Joseph was carrying the satchel charges, and I had the metal detector, and all the wire. Joseph had a map of the beach area and inland as far as the first village, but all we were supposed to do was to blow up all the tank traps we could find. Joseph handled the charges, and I wired the detonators. You couldn't believe how silent and gray it all was at first, until later when the Germans opened up on the landing craft. Once in a while you could hear the men working up and down the beach, and then there would be an explosion, some machine gun fire, then quiet again, a little rain, just a drizzle, everything muffled by the sand and the waves. We were just kids, I can't believe I was out on a beach with Germans above me firing machine guns and howitzers, nineteen years old, and we were scared as hell. I suppose if they had wanted, the Germans could have come down on the beach and killed every one of us, but they stayed up on the cliffs and waited for what they knew was inevitable anyway. Just before the sun came up, the main force appeared on the horizon, you couldn't believe how many ships, and all hell broke loose. Smitty and I waited under the cliffs, hell, all we had were sidearms anyway."

The waiter came out of the Owl and stood beside the table with a tray of sandwiches and tea. While he served, Roberts watched a tour boat plunge noiselessly north on the river headed for Greenwich. A few couples were lined on the prow of the boat, and in that moment Roberts saw Amanda exactly as she had been on the station platform, this burst inside his head, his brain ticking along and then, crack, it hit something and he was staggered by the fissures in reality, there was Amanda. The linen tablecloth was rippling in the breeze, it made him think of the wind in Norfolk long ago when the three of them, Amanda, Smitty, and Mitchell Roberts, had toured Norfolk on bicycles. It had been in May just before the invasion, these three young people in love with life, and each other, running around like young deer in the resplendent green countryside, through the ruined churches, drinking ale in country pubs on the shore of the North Sea, all the white-caps and gulls, the sound of the tugs coming into harbor. Suddenly, the waiter had gone, the memory abandoned him, Roberts was alone with himself.

"Tell me," Amanda said. "We've avoided this for twelve years. I've had my bloody whiskey, and I've had my cry." She touched Roberts's hand across the table to reassure him.

"After the first wave came ashore Smitty and I found a ravine in the cliffside and bivouacked for the day. In the late afternoon we went up the ravine with our group and worked inland along the country roads ahead of the battalion. We made it through three or four villages. As I recall there was terrible fighting all the way. It was the road to Paris, the Germans were giving it everything. There was still a chance the invasion would fail. You couldn't believe the confusion, booby traps everywhere, snipers in the trees, all the villages burning. Bridges blown, and roads dug up, tanks destroyed. On the seventh day after the invasion Smitty and I were walking down a country road between rye fields. It was the first day we'd had a break, it was almost like being home, you didn't even know the war was going on, it was that quiet. I remember the grass, the new rye, green as an ocean. There were some Jersey cows, and some Guernseys too, bright sunshine, and a breeze off the sea behind us. I guess we stopped for a smoke, something like that, down in a ditch full of daisies. There was a village away down the road, a white church with a steeple and a bell tower, you could see it in the sunshine, white and peaceful. Smitty was standing behind me, he tapped me on the shoulder for a light. I turned around and lit his cigarette, cupped my hands, and stood there while he leaned over and got his cigarette going. The sun was on his face, and I could see he was looking at the church over my shoulder. I guess the sniper's bullet came right over my shoulder, it had to. It hit Smitty in the head. He was still for a moment, looking at the church, then he slumped into my arms. He was dead right then, Amanda, right there in my arms."

"He didn't suffer?" she asked, tears in her eyes.

"He died looking at the church. There was no pain, nothing. I cradled him until a medic came up the road and took him to the camp hospital. I had to keep going, they wouldn't let me go back. I went on into the village with the battalion."

"I'm glad," Amanda whispered. "I'm glad it was quiet. I don't think I could stand it if he had been hurt, torn up. I want to remember him the way he was."

The waiter was clearing the soup dishes. Another tour boat steamed by, trailed by gay streamers. The sky was tearing up into blue patches, clouds hazy puffs like cotton. Roberts ate some of his sandwich and waited.

"Jonathan was a lovely boy," Amanda said at last. There was a long tear rolling down her cheek. Roberts knew she wasn't going to touch it, she wanted it there.

"You don't need to do this now," he said.

"But I must. Waiting won't do me any good. We've got to get this out in the open." She paused, gathering her courage while the tour boat went past. "He was a lively boy who could gather people's affection. Everyone loved Jonathan. He was devoted to Jocko, and Jocko to him. But he was also very independent, you wouldn't think of him as a mummy's boy. He had insect collections, and stamps, and he played football and I'm afraid he pulled girls' pigtails too. He was also very smart."

"I'm sure he was," Roberts said.

"Had an American streak in him too, his father's son. Very foolhardy sometimes, and naive, but very brave." Now that the wind was coming up stronger, Amanda had taken up her coat from the back of the chair and was belting it around her waist. Much of the Owl was empty after the first rush, and now the silence of Richmond suburb was everywhere, in the ornamental roofs of Hampton Palace far away, in the filmy distance which shimmered in the soft gray Kew light. "I was home on a Sunday six weeks ago today when Master Glenville called from Harlow School and told me that Jonathan had drowned in the Cam. Bloody sorry and all that, could I come to Ipswich and see about him?"

"Why Ipswich?" Roberts asked.

"He didn't say. Master Glenville runs the student digs there and I was in no state to inquire. The school physician, a fellow named Martin Brooke, called from the hospital in Cambridge to tell me he was sorry. We've know Martin for years, he loved Jonathan, he was very upset."

"Did Brooke tell you how it happened?"

"He said only that an old man named Brian ap Rhys had found Jonathan in the river and had called a constable. I took the evening train from Liverpool Street Station to Ipswich and spent the night on a bench in the municipal building. Somebody named Clannahan was in charge and they let me see Jonathan. I stayed there that night, and in the morning took Jonathan back to Cambridge with the help of Martin Brooke."

"What was Jonathan doing in Ipswich? That's another county entirely, isn't it?"

"Yes of course, Sussex. I didn't have the wit to worry over it at the time. Do you think that means anything?"

"I'm just wondering. Who examined Jonathan?"

"Brooke. He's the boys' doctor at Harlow School, as I said, has been for his whole life. He tended to Jonathan once when Jono had come down with a terrible fever. Single-handedly pulled him through a terrible spell. There was a doctor in Ipswich who signed the death certificate, but I hardly had a chance to speak with him during my night in the municipal building. I'm sure I was nearly hysterical, I don't really remember much of anything. Just grief and exhaustion. Martin was good enough to come and fetch me back."

"Did you speak to the old man who found Jonathan?"

"Brian ap Rhys?"

"Yes."

"Once, briefly. He came to the chapel with his wife to pay his respects. The boy's choir sang, and I guess the old man had worked for years at the Wren. Said he'd been walking by the river on a Sunday evening—what he thought was a picnic basket turned out to be Jono. Said he thought he must have been playing beside the river and had fallen in accidentally. He stayed with Jonathan until the constable came. He seemed very nice, really, and upset at what had happened."

"And the constable? Did you speak to him?"

"Oh, briefly. He's a young fellow named Miles. He was the only copper on duty at the shire station that evening. Oh, dear God," Amanda sighed, "I don't know, Mitchell, honestly. Everything those first few days is a jumble, it didn't seem as if it were really happening. I think I was in a state of complete nervous collapse, at times I could hardly catch my breath. I think Miles made some inquiries, that's all I know. Martin collected Jonathan's things, or some of them, from Harlow School and took them to his office in Cambridge. Most of Jonathan's clothes and books are still at his digs."

"I'm sorry to ask this," Roberts said.

"Oh, go ahead," Amanda said, touching his hand again. "Another thing about Yanks, they are thorough."

"Did they do an autopsy?"

"Good God no," Amanda said. "I couldn't bear the thought."

"But Brooke examined the boy?"

"Yes, he looked at him once we'd gotten him back to Cambridge. You don't think anything could be amiss, do you?"

"Not really," he said. If he had looked inside himself right then, Mitchell Roberts would have found a great anger, this rage against the world. "It's just my nature acting up, that's all."

"I suppose," Amanda said, "it is a bit odd, Jonathan being taken to Ipswich."

Roberts closed his eyes, and when he opened them it seemed that the sky had filled with blue dust, as though crushed diamonds were falling through the clouds, the light had a filmy unreality to it. Matins had ended long ago, and the Owl publican was calling time. When Roberts looked over, he could see the man, big and tubby, standing in the open doorway of the pub, hale-built with a flood of red hair and a black, unbuttoned vest over his stomach. The Pakistani waiter was beside him, ready to go home for the day.

Amanda was starting to get up, gathering her coat around her shoulders. There was a white cloud of gulls over the river, moving. "I need your help," Amanda said.

"Anything, you know that."

"I'm going to work tomorrow as I said. I want to get Jonathan's things from his digs in Cambridge, but I can't bring myself to go up there just now. Master Glenville is holding his room the way it was, just so I can come up, but I don't have the strength. I don't suppose you could run up to Cambridge and get his things for me?"

"Oh, Amanda," Roberts said. "Of course. You know I'd do anything in the world for you. Anything at all."

"Of course you would," Amanda said, coming around the table, kissing him on the cheek. The Pakistani had come over to collect the bill from Roberts. "Talk to Martin Brooke, would you? I'd feel ever so much better if you would do that."

"Naturally," he said.

24

It seemed just then that all the church bells in Richmond and in Twickenham began to ring. The gulls rose, then fell again, like paper blowing in the street. The two people walked down some stone steps to the river's edge, then along the Thames all the way through Richmond and Chiswick, through the gorse fields of Barn Elms, as far as Hammersmith Bridge. At Hammersmith they fed the pigeons and didn't talk any more about death.

TUESDAY, NOVEMBER 26

JOCKO skidded on the clay, sneakers whisking up small pieces of gravel, leaned down hard on his right hip and whipped a shot crosscourt that darted down past Roberts, nicked the net and the sideline and was gone into the fence, bouncing, *plop, plop.* Roberts looked up to see Jocko smiling shamefacedly. He ambled back to the baseline and stood, after he had retrieved the bouncing ball, and then tossed it back across the net. Jocko was standing still in the hazy light of early morning with the dark mass of Lincoln's Inn behind him. He rocked back on his heels and shot another serve across the right corner of the service line, the ball bouncing chest high to Roberts, who took a crazy, uncoordinated swing, ticking the ball as it went by. There was an attendant sitting on a stool in the corner of the courts who clapped politely and kicked the ball back into the court. "Set," Jocko called, taking off his cricket cap, wiping his hair with one hand.

Jocko had dressed in gray wool cricket pants and a white school shirt, white tennis sweater bulked around his shoulders. Roberts could see him standing there, breath rising in the cold air, he looked like a young colt in a field, something intent in his expression. His cheeks had taken on that peculiar English redness, especially pronounced on pale skin in the cold air. The boy's movements around the court seemed casual to Roberts, almost laconic, but he realized they were calculated, uncoiling almost in slow motion with a certain torque that fooled him, maybe it was his age. Jocko struck the ball squarely and with great energy, picking the low skipping shots off the clay like an expert, sending the ball back across the net with a combination of timing and strength. To Roberts, Jocko appeared skinny enough to pass through a keyhole, yet he seemed to have an enormous reserve of energy. The boy stood in the gloomy gray air, slightly hesitant about beating Roberts, you could tell, he was glancing down at the court, away to the law offices, the great chestnuts dripping rain. "I'll be needing a shilling," the attendant said from his stool. "And you'll be needing to return the lad's serve."

"He's too good," Roberts called to the attendant, to Jocko too, and to some young girls watching the game, and perhaps Jocko, through the green wire fence. There were a few men from the Strand strolling around the concourse of Lincoln's Inn, carrying black umbrellas and the *London Times*. Roberts had worn some dark blue waterproof pants which he'd brought to England in the hope of fishing the Test and Itchen, famous chalk streams in Hampshire. Now he was playing tennis, having ventured into Oxford Street for some sneakers.

"Just good luck," Jocko said. He was smoothing down the clay on the baseline, looking embarrassed by the ease of his game. The attendant began to shuffle around, fixing his kit bag, his sandwiches and tea. Black elms around the court were dripping rain too, and you could smell chestnuts roasting in the alleys and streets around High Holborn.

"Where on earth did you learn this game?" Roberts shouted. The attendant broomed the court while he caught his breath.

"Jono and I played all summer, every summer."

"Jonathan was good?" Roberts asked, walking over to the net.

"Bloody good," Jocko said.

"As good as you?"

"Quite. For his age, Mr. Roberts. He wasn't at all awkward, you see." Jocko had walked to the net now, and they were standing facing each other across it while the attendant continued to broom. Jocko looked at the girls, who giggled. "Nobody was like Jono," Jocko said. "He could take care of himself. We went to town together in the evenings from school at Cambridge. We would play tennis or fish in the Cam. Every summer Mum would take us to Holland Park where they have such awfully good courts."

"What do you mean?" Roberts asked. "Jonathan wasn't like the other boys?"

"Oh," Jocko said. He was looking down at his clayed sneakers, probably feeling bad again. "I loved Jonathan, you see. A lot of the other lads had brothers in lower forms. Just like Jono and me. I don't know if you know this or not, but at Harlow, and most other public schools in England, torment is a kind of sport. A fellow is expected to mistreat his brother, and all the younger boys. When I say Jono wasn't like that, I mean he didn't torment younger boys, and I didn't torment him either, not like so many other boys do. A fellow is expected to torment his brother. Terrible things are done."

"You mean hazing?"

"Is that what you call it in America? I just know I wouldn't torment Jono, and some of the other boys resented that. Really, it's a terrible thing to grow up in an English public school. But I didn't treat Jonathan that way, and I wouldn't let anybody treat him like that if I could help it."

The girls had come through a gate onto the court with expectant looks. Roberts and Jocko walked to a bench and sat down to watch the girls exchange some indistinct forehands. Then as the morning passed, Lincoln's Inn became nearly deserted and a fine mist began to descend. You could hear the Underground rumble past High Holborn. Roberts and Jocko cooled down and walked around the corner of the courts to the London School, and went down a flight of dark stairs to a basement gymnasium, which had the locker rooms. They sat on some cold benches and took off their sneakers. There were some schoolboys kicking a football around the gym floor, scurrying in the murky light. There was a smell of must and sweat in the air, and to Roberts it seemed unnaturally cold.

"Was Jonathan bothered by any boys at Harlow?" he asked while Jocko was unlacing his shoes.

"No more than usual."

"For example."

"For example, some older boys held him down once and ducked him in the bloody water closet. Jonathan didn't tell me, but I know it happened."

"For God's sake," Roberts growled.

"For Harlow's sake. For the sake of England."

"Anything else?"

"Some of my own mates toweled shut Jono's door."

"Toweled shut his door?" Roberts said, frowning, wiping some sweat from his face. "What is that?"

"It's an old trick. On examination day, the lads tacked a towel over Jono's door on the outside. They had smeared it with dung."

"My God," Roberts said.

"Another time they roped him in. The small chaps live on one wing with their doors directly across from one another along a hallway. On examination day, the older boys had tied a towel to one doorlatch, then secured the other end to the door on the opposite side of the hall. Since both doors open inward, neither would come open when pulled on. When the examination was coming up, Jonathan couldn't get out of his room. Neither could the chap on the other side of the hall, for that matter. If I hadn't happened by to walk with him to the classes, he would have missed the examination. Would have been bloody too bad."

"And what if he had missed the examination?" Roberts's shirt was damp through, though he could see that Jocko was fresh. He was starting to feel a chill and he knew there wasn't any hot water in the showers. Right then it seemed as if all England were freezing.

"He would have become a shoemaker," Jocko said.

"I don't follow."

"Simple," Jocko said. "Every few years an English schoolboy takes an examination. If he passes, he moves to the next form. If he fails, he's shunted out to a vocational school. Even passing your forms isn't enough, if your marks are low. You see, if you fail an examination you become a shoemaker, clerk, something like that." Jocko tossed his shoes away, stripped off his wet socks. "You get one chance to join the club, Mr. Roberts, and if you fail you become a shoemaker."

"The club?" Roberts asked.

"You know," Jocko said, half smiling. "The old boy's club. The school tie. Fleet Street or the City. The civil service, maybe a knighthood. You go to public school, then get a scholarship to University. Then you spend your bloody life carrying an umbrella and a paper, like those chaps we saw this morning at Lincoln's Inn."

Roberts leaned back against one of the lockers, trying to relax, finding his muscles sore, overworked. He sniffed the wax smell from the floors, he could hear the football being kicked around the gym, it brought back memories of his own youth.

"I'm sorry, Mr. Roberts," Jocko said. "I don't mean to be such a blighter. Harlow School isn't such a bad place. Some schools are much worse, the private schools particularly. In some schools, a small chap is lucky to survive. The English raise such monsters."

"A lot of education is like that."

"Perhaps so," Jocko said. From where they sat, you could hear the sound of traffic coming from the Strand, cars honking, buses chugging past. "But when I went to Harlow School I was six years old," Jocko continued. "The smaller boys are put on the top floor. As you get older, you move down. You climb stairs. There isn't any heat beyond the second floor, so at night it gets so cold in the rooms that you wake up in the morning and your glass of water is frozen solid. You have chilblains on your fingers. The main thing I remember as I got older is the sound of the little lads crying." Jocko stopped suddenly, it looked to Roberts as if he might cry.

"I know you miss Jono," Roberts said.

"Bloody hell," Jocko muttered into his sweater sleeve. "It's Mum who hurts most."

"I know, Jocko. But she's strong. You have to hang in there. Give her the support she needs."

"Still, it's terrible for her."

"We can show her the way through. I'm going to stay in England until everything gets cleared up. If we stick together we can help her, Jocko."

"Perhaps so," Jocko said. "But I was one of the little boys who cried. And there were plenty of others. Waking up in the morning with a sheet over the door covered with human muck."

Roberts put an arm around Jocko's shoulder. Water was dripping from a shower head, plopping onto the tile floor. There was some sunshine slicking into the gym from outside. "Come on, Jocko," he said. "We've got to meet Amanda for lunch. She's just gone back to work and she'll need some cheering up. Suppose we do that."

"You're right, Mr. Roberts," Jocko said. He stiffened up and banged shut a locker door behind him.

They showered and left the London School and walked down Portugal Street and skirted Tavistock Square and the Strand. Pigeons rose above Trafalgar Square and there were smoke trails along the Embankment, above the turrets of Westminster. Black umbrellas bobbed in the streets, slick with rain, and the shop windows were yellow with light. They window-shopped at the antiquarian book stalls on Charing Cross, and stopped at one in Hunt's Court, standing under an awning in the drizzle, leafing through used books while the noon crowds milled about. Jocko was reading some poetry, Roberts a book about Lord Kitchener.

"Tell me about Glenville, the master," Roberts said.

"Kind of a cretin, but not a terrible chap," Jocko said without looking up from his book. Roberts saw it was a Manley Hopkins volume bound in leather. "He believes in the club, but I'm afraid he's a bit shabby around the collar, never quite made it in. I suspect he resents being a schoolmaster at a public school, made to live in the dormitories. All that."

"Is he hard?"

"Some. Tries to be, but fails."

Roberts laughed. He went over to the shopkeeper and paid a quid for the Manley Hopkins. Jocko was watching with wide eyes. Roberts handed the book to Jocko. "Oh, thank you," the boy said, looking genuinely pleased. Roberts was feeling a little embarrassed, but good nonetheless.

They walked again, picking their way through the crowds, down Newport Street and past Leicester Square, the theaters and cinemas just coming open for business, red buses and cabs plying the streets, knots of people heading to Soho for lunch. They jostled their way up Greek Street amid the garlic and cardamom smells, meeting up with the meat and vegetable stalls along the edge of Soho, the Chinese restaurants, all color and sound. For a while they lingered outside a music store and studied the brass instruments in the window, rings of orange and dark gold on wet glass.

"Tell me more about Glenville," Roberts said. "Where are his rooms? How does he live?"

"I think he has a dormitory flat on the walk along the Cam. Most of the time he's in his office, the Administrator's Room at Harlow School, on the main floor, just near Trinity College. He's been at Harlow ever so long. One of those chaps with long fingernails and dandruff on his collar."

"Will he be at school during the holiday?"

"Likely," answered Jocko. It occurred to Roberts that he'd like to speak with Glenville, just for a minute. There was something eating at the back of his mind and he thought Glenville might clear it up.

"Married?" Roberts asked, knowing the answer.

"That wicked thing? I should hope not."

"Who were Jonathan's mates?"

"Schoolmates, you mean?" Roberts nodded. They were just nearing the restaurant where they were going to meet

Amanda. "His dig mate is a Dutch chap named Wim van Euwe."

"Anybody else?"

"Lads on the cricket team. Allan Barker. Lots of chaps like that. Jonathan was well liked."

"But his best friend."

"Oh," said Jocko, "that would be Wim. They were best of chums. Couldn't be separated. Wim often came to London for the holidays, when he couldn't go home to Amsterdam." Jocko stopped to catch his breath. They had been hurrying up Greek Street in a heavy crowd. "What are you thinking, Mr. Roberts?"

"Just American curiosity, Jocko. Something terribly odd about Jono being found in his good clothes in the Cam. Your mother called to Ipswich, where they had taken Jonathan. That's halfway across the country in Suffolk. There wasn't any autopsy. The local constable and Martin Brooke weren't consulted. Your mother tells me the death certificate was signed in Ipswich by a doctor she never talked with. It just sounds funny, that's all. I don't think anything is wrong, mind you, and I don't want to worry Amanda."

"So, you'll be making inquiries?"

"Not really, Jocko. I'll be getting your brother's things from Harlow. I thought I might chat with Glenville just to ease my own mind. Your mum needs to get back to work, and if it helps her to know, I thought I could do that at least."

They stopped at a place called Luigi's, a noisy literary knockabout in upper Greek Street, across from Soho Square. It was dense with smoke inside, and they saw that Amanda had gotten a table near the front, next to the window so they could look outside at all the people going by. She was poised over the red-checked tablecloth, there was a vase and a plastic rose on the table, and she was wearing a full-length woolen dress, a shepherd's coat of white fleece, and a rhinestone butterfly pin on her lapel. When they had joined her around the table, sipping some wine, they talked about the release of Ezra Pound from an American insane asylum, about the

Queen's horse set to go off at Epsom at odds of five to one. Amanda was chain-smoking, stubbing the ends out in her lasagna. Roberts ordered some clams and linguini, and had had a glass of Chianti. They were talking around and around, knowing they weren't going to say anything of importance, it was like everything was too painful, every sentence had such danger, it might draw blood. Jocko was sitting right next to the window, looking out at the people, hardly eating, every so often glancing at his Manley Hopkins. Roberts saw there was an old duffer outside on the street fiddling for coppers and he had drawn an audience.

"How is the reunion going?" Amanda asked.

"It's over," Roberts replied. He was finishing his clams, his Chianti. He felt languid, drained by the smoke. "We had a memorial service last night at Victoria and Albert. Speeches and an invocation. That sort of thing."

"I know it's a strain for you," Amanda said. "Being here now. With all these memories."

"It isn't."

"Will you fetch Jono's things?"

"Of course I will," he said, patting her hand. "I've made arrangements to meet Martin Brooke tomorrow at his London place. I tried to call him in Cambridge yesterday, but his office said he would be in London for the school break. They gave me his telephone number. He has some of Jono's toys, some of the clothes he was wearing that night. I'll see him, then I'll get up to Cambridge. Don't you worry at all."

"That's awfully good of you, Mitchell," Amanda said. Roberts paid the bill and drank some coffee the waiter had brought, staring out at the old beggar playing a fiddle. "I've got to go back to the office," Amanda said after a while. She kissed Jocko, and they watched her put on her coat and go out into Greek Street, into the crowds. Roberts and Jocko went outside, tossed some coins in the old man's hat, then walked down Soho Square to Saint Martin's. They were standing on the church steps in a cloud of pigeons.

"There is something," Jocko said.

34

"What's on your mind?" Roberts asked.

"Jono was a fine swimmer," Jocko said slowly. "Once he swam the bloody tidal river in Ipswich where Grandmum lives. And I know the Cam where they found him, too. It can't be more than a few feet deep along the bank, and no more than five or six feet deep in the middle." They had begun to walk again, heading for the Underground at Leicester Square. "A porpoise he was," Jocko said. "Swam like a porpoise."

WEDNESDAY, NOVEMBER 27

JOCKO was watching a giraffe munch eucalyptus leaves suspended from a basket above its enclosure. The giraffe nodded, or seemed to, as if it were exchanging a glance with Jocko, peering down with its liquid eyes, batting long black eyelashes, hypnotic, unconcerned, its mouth gyrating as the pear-shaped leaves disappeared. Traffic streamed around Regents Park, tiny Fords and blue Caravels, and a few French imports darting in and out like bees. Somewhere beyond the roundabout, a train pounded north with a wisp of smoke trailing in the rubble of Saint Pancras, an etch on the glass of gray sky. Macaws and parrots were yakking in the middle distance.

Roberts had spent the night walking under a twisted sky, circling the Serpentine in Hyde Park, followed by swans. In his mind he had been somewhere else—on the Isles of Scilly, engulfed in flowers; in Penzance; in some rubbish-smelling port on Barbados where young women ducked through ovals of bright sunshine. Early the next morning he had called for Jocko, and they walked the three miles to the zoo, stopping for some eggs and bacon, each of them wrapped in their thoughts.

They bought some peanuts at a vendor's, then toured the insect house, studying African twig crawlers, the huge Malay caterpillars, poisonous spiders from Sumatra. Jocko remained very quiet, though he seemed to be enjoying the zoo, but as the morning passed, Roberts began to sense his ultimate impatience, his own dissatisfaction with the delay that kept them from an interview with Martin Brooke at his London place on Gloucester Court, just off Oval Road, a place the giraffe probably could see from his height.

They sat down on a park bench across from the rhino park. The rhino was a huge black beast standing stock-still on a hump of red earth, his tiny ears working spastically, the eyes gaps of red in thick hide.

"Mum will be all right, won't she?" Jocko asked. He was eating peanuts, tossing the shells into a dustbin. He sat there, fidgeting on the bench without another word, his Queen's Park Ranger muffler curled around his neck, trailing on the grass. The boy looked a little pale to Roberts.

"Of course, Jocko, don't worry. She's back at work. She's seen her doctor, and she's sleeping again. The whiskey is temporary, take it from me. You'll be home until after Christmas, and once she finds herself, gets back to the poetry, things will get back to normal. You can trust your mother."

The rhino flicked its tail, this short stumpy blade on the rump. Jocko tossed a peanut over the fence, the rhino didn't move. "Did you have a good time at the reunion?" he asked.

"You bet I did," Roberts said.

There had been a rousing American drunk for the twelve in an Indian restaurant in Chelsea. Near closing time, the owner, a sallow Indian from Biswah with a wispy black beard and two shiny opals for eyes, had pleaded for closing time and the bill. The Americans had been awash in good cheer and refused to heed the call.

"But I couldn't find a taxi at one o'clock this morning. Had to walk home three miles in a freezing rain. Nearly lost my way twice and not a soul about to ask directions from. In one of the largest and most sophisticated cities in the world, I nearly froze to death on a public street. Twelve million souls, and every one of them asleep. I've been stranded in Arkansas with more chance of rescue."

Jocko leaned away, balancing his chin on his hands, a stud-

37

ied pose of meditation, hands on knees then, the wind ruffling his hair.

"I hope you never go home," he said.

"Not soon anyway, Jocko."

"I'm glad," the boy he said pensively. The noon chimes were echoing from Saint Paul's, fine convergent notes. The rhino sniffed the air, skuffed some dirt. "But what are you going to do?"

"Come on, Jocko. Don't worry. We're going to be late for our appointment with Brooke." Jocko smiled, then pulled up his football muffler, beginning to rise when Roberts tugged him gently back down on the bench. "You're entitled to know what I'm thinking," he said.

"I wouldn't mind."

"But please don't speak with your mother right now. I don't want to keep secrets from her, especially between you and me. But I want her to be free to concentrate on her own life, and the work she needs to do, rather than worrying about me and what I'm doing. Besides, we can't bring Jonathan back and her own life is very important right now."

"I understand," Jocko said, placing a finger on his coat. "Cross my heart, I won't say." Now that Roberts was looking at Jocko in the clear liquid light he seemed hardly old enough to be on his way to Trinity at Cambridge, hardly old enough to read the *Times* and its news of war and famine. Something deep inside Roberts filled him with the desire to preserve Jocko from life itself, to save him from the gashes and great rends that Being inflicts. Really, though, he knew Jocko would sail away into the Sea of Trouble, he'd face it as very nearly everybody else did. You set out with the best equipment you could find and the rest was simple luck and courage.

"We have to go," Roberts said.

"Please," Jocko said. "Tell me what you're thinking."

Roberts ate some peanuts, trying to organize his thoughts. He looked at the stolid rhino, motionless, at the ring of oaks around Regents Park, at the dark planks of cloud on the shell of horizon. "First," Roberts said, seriously, "tell me what you know about what Jonathan was doing Sunday night, the night he drowned."

"Like all the boys," he answered, "he had Sunday night free. The youngest boys stay at school to eat and study. Jono could go where he wished for a few hours, and we always ate fish and chips together at a shop on the Cambridge High Street. We usually met at Round Church. Jonathan was at field sports that afternoon, and I watched him play some football with the lads. He was bloody good at that too, he played midfield. He was fast around the pitch. I went back to my rooms to study mathematics, but we'd made a date to meet for fish and chips. It was like every Sunday that way. When I got back to my rooms, I stayed there, then went out to Round Church. He never came."

"You waited."

"I thought he must have lost track of the time, so I went to the shop just in case. When he wasn't there, I thought he might be playing with Wim. They often play chess. I waited almost an hour and then went back to my digs. I tried to find him in his room after a while, but Wim was there and said Jonathan had left much earlier. Wim hadn't seen him since showering up after football. I wasn't worried because Jonathan was a clever lad. He was beating me at chess and backgammon. So, I went back to my room and studied some more."

"What happened then?"

"Master Glenville came to my room and fetched me to his office downstairs. Mum was on the phone. She was in London and told me she was on her way to Ipswich and that Jonathan was dead. She was crying and she couldn't speak well at all. Master Glenville was decent to me, he let me stay with him for a time."

"What did Glenville tell you?"

"Only that Jono had been found by an old couple that evening. He said Jacob Miles, the constable, had called him. He mumbled a lot of rot and stood around with his hands in his pockets, and I finally went back to my room later. There wasn't much Glenville could do really, but he looked in on me. I sat alone in my room until morning. Mum came then and fetched me and we went to see Jono at the chapel where they had him. A lot of the boys were there too, they were singing for Jono."

"Did you speak to Wim?"

"Wim was at Chapel. He was crying as well and everybody was very broken down. Brooke was there. He said he'd looked after Jonathan, but Wim was with the other boys and I didn't see him again. Mum and I took the train to Liverpool Station and were home that night."

"Tell me about the stretch of Cam where your brother was found."

"Just a slow bit of water between Trinity Bridge and Clare Bridge. There are some willows on the bank and a punt house near Trinity. The Backs are beyond the river and the country opens out from there."

"The Backs?"

"A long stretch of little hills with willows and oaks."

"What about the river itself?"

"Shallow banks, not very steep. Sunday afternoons the river is full of punters. The colleges are along the east bank. The other bank is empty with the Backs. The middle channel isn't very deep. You can wade way out, and lots of people do in the afternoon, knickers rolled up, you know. I don't see how Jonathan could have drowned in water like that, Mr. Roberts. I just don't understand. How could it have happened?"

"I don't know, Jocko," Roberts answered. The rhino had clambered laboriously up a red hill and was gamboling beside some water pools. It looked as though he was chasing some pigeons from a pot of grain and vegetables. People shoot these beasts, Roberts thought, just for devilment. Jocko had started to look fretful, staring at the rhino, Roberts hoped he wouldn't break down before it was time to go. "I want to ask you something," he said, hoping to untrack Jocko. "Just thinking out loud now."

"Go ahead," Jocko said.

"Could there have been a school prank involved? You've told me about some bullies. Sometimes in American schools people are hurt during hazing. It happens. Could one of the other boys have caused this accident?"

"I don't think anything like that ever happened at Harlow School. Jono was bullied by a fellow named Gerald Marseden, but I've heard nothing from him in a long time."

"But he bullied Jono?"

"On occasion. It's possible, but I really couldn't say for certain."

"All right," Roberts said, sighing, getting up from the bench. "That's enough for now. I'm going to Cambridge and I'll make some inquiries, as you say. I'm not here to make things worse, only to make them better. I know your mum feels uncomfortable about the way things were handled in Cambridge, but I think it would be silly to stir up some trouble where none exists. That's why I don't want you to say anything to her about our conversations."

"I won't breathe a word," Jocko said. He had walked a way up the stone path. Roberts could tell he was trying to look over the Regents wall, straining to see into Hampstead, the green waving expanses of the heath. Beyond the rhino moat, Roberts could see monkeys swinging through some trees, chattering high up, exercising their diurnal rights.

The Oval Road was knuckled by barren sycamores. They crossed Regents Road and were walking past a row of Georgian houses toward Gloucester Court where there were shadows of towering stone edifices with classical motifs, wide steps to narrow front stoops, iron gates. The houses were surrounded by iron fences and each had a postage stamp of green garden with some tulip trees and hydrangea plants. All of the windows were huge pools of gray glass grown pinkish in the sun. Expensive cars were parked on the street, and it was very quiet and removed. They went up a flight of sand-colored stairs and stood under one of the porticos, Roberts ringing the bell in the middle of a maple door.

The woman who opened the door was a dowdy matron type with a red face and white hair, slightly feeble, but feisty. She was wrapped nearly entirely in a brown shawl and was looking at the two visitors through a pince-nez. She ushered them into a parlor filled with knickknacks and army souvenirs, pictures, insignia, citations. Jocko gave her his muffler and she hung it on a peg near the door and gazed at Roberts as if he were a thief. Martin Brooke appeared around a corner from his den, holding a *London Times*, breaking a slight smile. "Jocko, my boy," he said, striding into the parlor, folding the paper. He shook hands with Jocko and looked at the old woman. "That's fine, Mum, thanks," he said, squeezing her shoulder. The old woman scurried down the hall, climbed the stairs slowly and disappeared at the top of the landing. Roberts was looking over Brooke's shoulder into the study, a fireplace, some leather-bound books on shelves on either side, cool white decanters of liquor on the sideboards. "I'm terribly sorry about your brother, Jocko," Brooke said, touching Jocko lightly on his shoulder, patting him while Roberts stood still, the doctor looking at Jocko with his heavily lidded eyes. He was portly and going bald and he was wearing a sloppy wool sweater misbuttoned in front over a white shirt. Some tobacco ticks had caught in the wool and Roberts noticed his blotched skin, how rings of white hair circled his ears. "Well now," Brooke went on, trying to be good-natured, "you must be the American, Roberts. Please come in. Do make yourself at home, gentlemen."

They followed Brooke into the study. Jocko walked over to the big windows and stood looking down at Gloucester Court, one elbow on an ancient harpsichord. The doctor poured some sherry into crystal glasses and handed one to Roberts. They sat down in some wing chairs beside a roaring fire. Brooke handed over a paper parcel tied by string.

"Jonathan's things," he murmured. "His clothes, the ones he was wearing, what was in the pockets. I understand you'll fetch his things from Harlow School."

"I'll be going soon," Roberts replied, trying to concentrate, but unable to keep from glancing at Jocko, who seemed slumped in the window.

"I'll help you in any way I can. Terrible shame about the lad. He was special, one of the best. I've been his physician since he was a baby. And how is Amanda?"

"As well as can be expected. She went back to work."

"Well and good. Nothing like work." The doctor sipped some sherry and took up a meerschaum, sat fiddling with a huge twist of tobacco, spilling some on his sweater. Roberts was instantly transfixed, the England he loved, all this terror, the huge log banked by coals, flames. "Lost my own boy at Dunkirk. Couldn't bloody move for six weeks. Sat in a haze drinking sherry and thinking about the past. Finally, got out of my chair and went back to work. Tried to forget for a time. When the wife died, did the same bloody thing." Roberts had noticed a photograph on the mantel, a young soldier in brown standing on the steps of a church. Roberts felt warped, like a part of his past had suddenly structured itself to be just outside his vision but still there. He could hear Jocko striking one of the harpsichord keys, the trill echoing in the room. "One other thing," Brooke added, handing Roberts a cigar box. "These are the boy's toys. They found them near the bank." Roberts mumbled his thanks and took the box.

"Tell me about the night Jonathan died," Roberts said.

"Amanda want to know?"

"She wants to lay it aside eventually."

"Of course, quite right. Can't blame her," Brooke said. "My boy Steven was lost at sea. Awful really, waiting alone for word. Couldn't even carry my own son to the churchyard. They never found him." He paused, sipping his sherry, looking at the fire. "Amanda sleeping?"

"I think so, now."

"She'll be fine," Brooke said. "She's a trouper. I've known her boys since they came to Harlow."

"Would you mind going over the evening?"

"Of course not," Brooke said, trying to light his pipe. He got up and stabbed at the fire with a poker. "Miles called me

43

around six that evening. He's the constable, you know, bloody good chap. Asked me to come over to Clare Bridge, didn't say why, only sounded upset and anxious. It sounded urgent, so I put on my mac and left right off. Went there direct, it's only about five minutes. Saw Miles on the opposite bank across the river and when I went across the bridge and up the bank, I saw Jonathan there. Miles had covered him. I took a look at the boy, tried to revive him, but it was far too late for that. He was dead, I'm afraid, not a thing anyone could have done. Nothing for it."

"Anyone else around?"

"Not a soul. Just the old man and woman who found the boy. It was getting cold, so I stayed with the boy while Miles and his men walked up and down the river as far as King's Bridge and Bachelor's Walk. Then two of Miles's men brought a litter and we covered the lad again and took him to hospital on Christ's Pieces. I undressed the boy and looked him over as best I could. What I've got here, and those things in the cigar box, are what I collected. Some time later that night, Miles came over to the office and told me he and his men had checked the colleges along the river and nobody had seen or heard a thing. It wasn't likely, Sunday night and all, awfully quiet along there about then. He asked my opinion and I told him I thought the boy had drowned. Some water in his lungs when I tried to revive him."

"How did the boy get to Ipswich?"

"Bloody good question," Brooke said, poking some tobacco into his meerschaum, which had gone out. Jocko had turned and was watching from the window, Roberts could see him, the pain on his face. "I telephoned Glenville and he telephoned Amanda while I was busy with the boy. I did phone Amanda later as well, but by then she was on her way to Ipswich. All I know is a chap named Clannahan had come from Ipswich to take the boy back there to the Scotland Yard."

"But you kept Jono's clothes and his toys?"

"Quite so," Brooke said. "I'm the Shire Examiner. At the

time I thought it was my duty to make the examination as to cause of death, all that. Still don't know why Clannahan had the boy moved. There wasn't any suspicion of foul play of course, so you'd think Miles could handle the situation well enough, thank you. Still don't know why Clannahan stuck his nose in, you know these bloody civil servants. Not that it matters for Jonathan, but it's bloody odd."

"So you'd ordinarily handle the situation."

"Indeed. I've been Harlow School physician for twenty years now, and Shire Examiner for nearly that long. I know my bloody job."

"Could you tell me about your examination?"

"You'll not say anything to Amanda? It really wouldn't do to upset her." Roberts nodded and finished his sherry. Jocko had turned back to the window. The doctor poured another sherry. "Normal lad twelve years old," Brooke said. "Simple as that. A bruise on his neck behind the right ear, and a puncture wound on his calf above the left ankle, probably from football. Morbidity was plain, the boy had been alive in the water, and had drowned." Roberts saw Jocko turn and put his head against the glass. "Jonathan's clothes are in the parcel," Brooke said. "Green school coat, Queen's Park Ranger muffler, some woolen pants. Few bob and some coppers. He had his toys spread out on the bank beside a willow. Those are in the cigar box. I'd go easy on Amanda if I were you. It might set her back, seeing her boy's things like that."

Roberts rose and went to the window, leading Jocko back to the fire. He thanked Brooke for the sherry and they all walked out to the parlor, getting on their mufflers, bomber jackets, while the doctor watched in silence. Roberts had the cigar box under his arm, the other arm around Jocko. They shook hands and the doctor opened the front door to Gloucester Square. It was strange standing there in the thin English light, all the swaying green up in Hampstead, the roar from a lion in the Zoological Gardens across the way. Roberts and Jocko walked down the stairs and across the square, then through Regents Park to a Wimpy Bar and had some tea.

When he opened the cigar box, Roberts found a beeswax honeycomb about the size of a deck of cards. There was an ivory-hued sliver of pelvic bone from a small animal, and three pearlescent cowrie shells strung together on fish wire. He found three black pebbles worn smooth, one a perfect circle, the other two shaped like fishhooks. Lying on top of the other toys was a flat piece of hardwood stained moss green, shaped like a puppet, featureless, with a triangular head, arms and legs hinged with tiny coral spikes.

SATURDAY, NOVEMBER 30

THE Downs were sun-bathed, with green flanks rolling away to quilted fields. There was a flush of gold in the sky and the clouds had turned a sugary brown, and on the race grounds umbrella tents had begun to flutter in the wind. The Epsom crowd milled, drinking Pimm's and champagne, tasting fresh cider, eating sausages and browned kidney pie. Roberts was watching the Queen's horse, a nice filly named Fox Hunt, make the far turn, leading the race with her breath streaming back, lunging through the soft green turf course, as the crowd began to roar. She leapt a hedge, her rider bouncing once in the saddle, and she hung on to the lead and began to make for the water jump, followed by a dozen other horses, huge clods of turf flung up from the wet grass. Then she was up and over and the crowd was roaring its approval and a few of the blokes down the finish line were unfurling a banner while others pushed forward against the wooden rail. Martin Brooke had his arm around his mother, studying the race through a pair of dainty opera glasses, his face flushed, his mother's white hair over one of the lenses. The sound of the horses, a deep rhythmic thunder, came slowly across the sedge, the water.

"I've got a fiver on the goat in last place," Brooke muttered, dropping his glasses on the clubhouse table. Through his field glasses Roberts could see Fox Hunt really stretched out now, her roan flanks white with foam as she glided past the quarter pole, up and over a water jump with her back heels clicking

47

in the water, pounding down on the wet turf just like the good girl she was. And she was sleek, very muscular for a filly, with a fine confirmation and a shapely head, tawny with a yellow streak between her eyes, and he was glad he had a fiver on her, not the goat in last place, even if Fox Hunt was the favorite, the Queen's horse, because now she looked unstoppable, happy. Roberts was thinking, How could anyone bet against a girl that lovely? He knew that Amanda had a quid on her too, and he had made a bet for Jocko as well. He strained over the edge of the box to see Fox Hunt as she roared past the concourse, the sound of the crowd swelling, the finish just a furlong away, partly hidden by a hedge, a jump, and a wing of the paddock.

Amanda began to squeeze Roberts's arm in excitement. "You've just won five pounds," he told her, having to speak in her ear because of the noise. Brooke's mother was beaming, looking at him with a glint. She had turned out to be a lively old lady with a solid wit, even though she was wearing a dowdy blue suit with a low slouch hat that reminded Roberts of something that Margaret Rutherford might have worn in a movie. She had a jolly look about her, the wrinkled face with so much expression once she got going, stopping to lick some spittle from her lip, take a drink of her double Pimm's, announce her next wager. It occurred to Roberts that Martin Brooke's mother drank just like a sailor on leave in Singapore.

Brooke fingered his opera glasses, patted Jocko's arm across the table. The box was halfway up the grandstand, deeply in shadow, though the course itself was deep in sunshine. Roberts saw Fox Hunt clear the last jump cleanly, the crowd really roaring now. He could see the Queen Mother in her box by the finish line, the crowd surging around her, shouting, trying to get a glimpse of her. He had been drinking Irish whiskey all afternoon and he was beginning to feel abstract and nice, like someone had shaved off part of his brain and he was getting his sensations directly on a raw line to his head. He was enjoying the pale oolong color of his sensations, it was like being buried in a cup of nice sugary tea. He heard Jocko and Amanda tell him good-bye, they were going down to see Fox Hunt, to collect their winnings, and he could see flash-bulbs popping somewhere in the crowd and then he thought that suddenly it was very still, like someone had flipped a switch, and then he heard "God Save the Queen" and every-body was standing up.

Brooke grinned and tore up his tickets and threw the pieces all over the table, like confetti. "Glad you could come up today," he said to Roberts. They were alone in the crowd, except for the mother who was trying to get another Pimm's from a distracted waiter.

"It's very nice of you to have us. I think this trip is doing a world of good for Amanda's outlook. I don't mind telling you what a kick it is to have a private box at Epsom."

"Nothing to it, my boy," Brooke said, genuinely pleased. "Best time of my life was right here before the war. The Germans had invaded Poland and everybody was having a final fling before the darkness. My boy Steven came, and my wife. It was a warm September day, and there wasn't enough champagne in France to supply this corner of England. Women were kissed, my boy, women were kissed. Kissed dozens myself. Didn't know it at the time, but the men were walking dead, most of them, the women walking widows. It seems a bit sad that it takes a war to make people pull to-gether. You'd bloody think that they'd drink champagne and kiss each other when there was peace, get grim when there was war. Suppose the bloody populace can't have a good time until it stares death right in the bloody face." Brooke picked up his glass of gin and drained it. Roberts couldn't understand this English mania for pink gin, he thought it tasted like aftershave. "What?" Brooke said, gulping.

"You do go on, Martin," said his mum, whose name was Celia. She had gotten her Pimm's and was busy studying the racing form. Roberts was surprised she was paying any atten-tion, but then he had been surprised by her all along.

"Steven and I," Brooke said, "spent all day together. Not long after that he was killed. Put up a stone for him at Cambridge, in the cemetery for the war dead. Three thousand American stones there too. Don't you think we'll ever forget you American boys either." Roberts felt his throat swell, he thought he might cry, maybe it was the whiskey, but he choked it down. On the lower concourse he could see Fox Hunt in the winner's circle, a bushel of roses around her neck, the jock raising a silver cup. Applause.

"Here now, Brooke," said Celia. "Don't go on so. You know how you are when you've had too much gin."

"Right you are, Mum," Brooke said. "Right you are."

Roberts finished his glass of whiskey. "Now that Amanda is gone, there's something I've been meaning to ask you."

"Thought you might," Brooke said.

"I'm here as a friend. Jonathan was my godchild. His father was my best friend in the service."

"Right you are," Brooke said. "Amanda's told me all about it. The boy Amanda married."

"He was killed in the invasion."

"Bloody tragic, that."

Brooke flagged a waiter and ordered another gin and a whiskey for Roberts. There was another race to come, and it was going to be a good finish to a fine day. Roberts was pleased that Amanda had seemed so lively; she had even cheered some horses down the stretch. Brooke was tucking a shawl around his mother.

"I looked at Jonathan's coat," Roberts said.

"So you opened the parcel I gave you."

"Yes," Roberts said. "You had the coat cleaned?"

"Laundered, you mean? Indeed. Chinese place in Camden Town. I hope nothing is wrong." There was a gentleman in a black frock coat pounding Brooke on the shoulder, looking very stimulated and tipsy. Brooke chatted with the man and then turned back to Roberts.

"Nothing wrong," Roberts said.

"It was a filthy mess," Brooke said. "Soiled with muck and reeds and whatnot. Didn't want to send it back to Amanda that way. Seemed a shame for her to see it looking like that.

50

Might just remind her of the accident, and do no good at all. No need, no use."

"That's right," Roberts said.

"Why do you ask?"

"Did you examine it at the hospital?"

"I did. Miles and I cleaned out the pockets. Found that bloody awful puppet."

"And the shirt and pants?"

"Found the lad's room key. There was a quid balled up like lint in the front shirt pocket. Probably his money for fish and chips. Found his other toys on the riverbank." The waiter brought their drinks and Brooke paid him. Celia was immersed in the race program. Brooke looked pensive and said, "Don't see how the boy could have drowned like that. But stranger things have happened in my time. An Australian rugger played a match once in Cambridge. On tour they were. Chipped a bone in his ankle during the match. A piece of it got in his bloodstream, went up the leg, lodged in his heart. Two hours later he walked into the locker room and died. Handsome ruddy lad, weighed ten stone, chest like an Afghan camel. Died on the spot. Sad, that."

Celia rolled up a fiver and passed it to Brooke. She whispered to him and Brooke smiled and put the fiver in his vest. He winked at Roberts.

"Was Jonathan taking medication?" Roberts asked.

"Thought of that already, old man. Checked his records and didn't find a thing. He wouldn't have been taking anything without my knowledge. I'd have known. The lad was as hale as a ruddy blacksmith."

"But you didn't check his blood?"

"Here now," Brooke said. "I had no cause. Are you meaning to imply that there was something else involved in Jonathan's death?"

"No, I assure you, Doctor. I'm just trying to think this thing through because I promised Amanda I would. Jocko told me Jonathan could swim like a fish. Well, he said a porpoise, but it set me thinking."

"Well, he was seaworthy, that's a fact. I would bet my stake on that, all right. And you couldn't drive a stake through the lad's constitution."

"His shoes," Roberts said.

"What about his shoes?"

"Were they tied?"

"Yes of course they were. Took them off him myself."

"Any mud or muck in them?"

Sunshine caught Brooke's face, an instant of clarity just as the last rays angled down past the hills. Brooke seemed transfixed in the moment, Roberts could see that he was thinking, he drank some of his gin, called over the waiter and gave a fiver to him to make a bet. "I'd say not," Brooke said softly, "but I didn't look very closely. It was evening and I was shocked. I can see what you mean, though."

"Where are the shoes?"

"Quite right," Brooke said. "Must have left them at my Cambridge office. Seemed unnecessary to send along the shoes. Thought Amanda might want the school coat and the school pants, his uniform, you know."

"Perhaps we could take a look at the shoes."

"Of course. Whenever you wish."

Some horses were coming out of the paddock, commencing their exercise before the race. There was a flintstone tower way out on the Downs, a slash of gray on the green backdrop, Roberts could see it turn fiery red as the sun sank. He had his eye on a large gray named Hobnail, the horse swishing its tail, no sign of lather, a good bet, he decided, about eight to one.

"You know Harlow boys, don't you, Doctor?"

"Right well I do."

"Would a Harlow boy wade out into the Cam with his good shoes on, with his school coat and pants on too? On a Sunday evening on his way to meet his brother for fish and chips like they always did on Sunday night? Would a Harlow boy do that?"

"Never thought he did," Brooke said.

"Then how did this happen?"

"Perhaps he stumbled and fell. The banks were wet and slippery. It occurred to me that the lad may have been playing on one of the bridges, fell over, stunned himself, and drowned. The old couple came along and found the lad where the current had taken him."

"From where they found the body, how far is it upstream to the Trinity Bridge?"

"Likely fifty meters or so," Brooke said.

"That far?"

"Every bit," he said.

"And Jacob Miles talked to the old couple," Roberts said. Brooke nodded, sipping some of his gin, leaning forward over their table. "As I understand it, they found Jonathan just near the bank in some reeds."

"That's right, I believe."

"Do you have an opinion about the flow of the current in the Cam?"

"I see what you mean," Brooke muttered, clearly starting to become confused. "I'd say there isn't much current at all. The Cam has been dammed and channeled until it doesn't move very much. But move it does, especially near the center of the channel. Still, I'd wager if the boy fell from Trinity Bridge, near the middle, he could have been stunned from the fall. Depending on how long he was in the water, he may have floated that far. It is possible. After all, we don't really know how long he'd been in the water. From my examination I'd say about forty-five minutes."

"That brings me to something else," Roberts said. The horses began to trot around the far turn, making for the starting gate. He was thinking, watching the starter raise his green flag, his pistol. The horses went into the gate and the starter fired, and they were off, thundering down the back stretch on the turf.

"Last race of the day," Roberts said, watching the horses go. "I hope I go home winner for a change."

"Right you are," Brooke replied, leaning forward and looking at the horses through his glasses. "What was it you wanted to say?"

"Had you planned to do an autopsy? Were you going to suggest that one be performed?"

"Heavens, no," Brooke said, turning to Roberts. "It never occurred to me."

The horses went around the back turn, Hobnail in front by five. Roberts watched the race while Celia grabbed the opera glasses and began to giggle. The air above the Downs was growing dark, and there was a definite chill in the breeze. "I'm puzzled by the boy's toys," Roberts said after watching the horses for a while.

"Gibble and gabble, boys will collect," Brooke said. "Collected beer caps when I was a lad."

"But the puppet," Roberts said.

"That ugly green thing? Found it right in the lad's pocket. Tucked away." Brooke began to wave at a bloke, the one who had pounded on his shoulder. The man waved back, lifted a silver flask. "Sorry, old man," Brooke said, standing. "Seen an old chum. Think I'll hop down and share a drink. Take care of Mum, would you?" he said, starting away.

When Brooke was gone, Celia said, "Don't mind Brooke, he's the devil of a fine doctor." She licked her lips and drank the last of the Pimm's. She had powdered her face to clown white, her cheeks red rouged. "But he doesn't know a horse's hock from a horse's rump. And bless you me, there is a considerable difference." She grinned and adjusted her floppy hat. "Now my husband, Rupert, was the horseman of the family. Rode like an absolute prince. I could have told Martin he'd lose his fiver on the last race, but would he listen?"

"Who do you have in this one?" Roberts asked.

"Rosemont. Solid bet, that." She paused, folded her hands on the table. "You mustn't think that Martin is a fool."

"I don't think that at all," Roberts said. "I know Amanda loves him, so does Jocko."

Roberts watched Brooke share a flask with the gentleman in the frock coat, doublet and vest. "This awful thing with

Jono has Martin terribly upset. He was very fond of Jonathan. My grandson Steven went to Harlow as well. I think Martin went up to Harlow from London after Steven's death in order to have boys like Steven around him. He treats the lads as if they were his own sons, you see. Trying to make up for what the years have done. Especially after his own Lucy died so unexpectedly. Now, it's he and I alone to play cribbage on the weekends. Nasty thing, getting old without anyone of your own to love." Celia squinted at Roberts through her pince-nez. Brooke was waving up at them, pointing at the tote board, Rosemont had edged Hobnail at the finish, paid ten pounds at three to one. "Mind you this," Celia said, hushed now, leaning over to Roberts, "I was a House Mother at Harlow for many years myself, took care of the lads. No Harlow boy like Jonathan would play with seashells and puppets, no Harlow boy would fall into the Cam in his best clothes. It just isn't done. Don't you bloody believe it. Not a boy of the Beaver and Oak. Not on your royal life."

Down on the concourse, Amanda and Jocko had joined Brooke, all of them waving up from the crowd, Amanda looking slightly tired, but waving nonetheless. Roberts helped Celia down the stairs and they all stood in the lower boxes, surrounded by windblown refuse, torn tickets, programs, the stuff of dreams. Amanda was showing Roberts her fiver, the one she had won on Fox Hunt, trying to smile. He thought Jocko looked weary. They took their time leaving the grounds, going down to the train station, getting on the London train, about an hour ride to Euston.

They were sitting in the compartment, industrial suburbs going by the train window, gray warehouses in the glare, tiny bits of cadmic blue, brick-red streaks, the row houses stretched out mile after mile. The pubs had opened, and at the crossings men stood drinking ale on street corners. Jocko was asleep, Brooke nodding, Celia deep in thought. Amanda was sitting across from Roberts, in the second-class carriage that smelled faintly of cheese and urine.

"Thank you for fetching Jono's things from Brooke," Amanda said, above the clickety-clack.

"I'm going to Cambridge," he responded.

Amanda said, "I wanted to be an actress," staring out at the night, tears in her eyes. "Never mind," she said to herself.

In the window were five images in an embrace of steam, the dark day done.

CAMBRIDGE

MONDAY, DECEMBER 2

THE noonday express from Liverpool Street to Cambridge was noisy, crammed with soldiers and clergy and the curious English traveling man, shiny blue or brown suit, sample case between the legs, black umbrella. In the cold and the smoke, Jocko tried to doze as the countryside sped past, but in all the hubbub he was having a hard time getting comfortable. They had ridden cramped in a full compartment nearly three hours, and when they got to Harlow School, Jocko had gone to his digs and had fallen immediately asleep on one of the twin maple beds, one arm cocked over his forehead, a puff of black hair escaping from his brow, and his breath pacing evenly, metronomic and calm. Roberts was sitting slouched in an old Indian rattan chair, watching Cambridge turn gold and copper in the winter sunshine, the old city reflected in the panes of the French-style windows. He could see Trinity Street, its warren of bookstalls and flower carts, the river Cam down the way like an icicle in the heart.

Jocko's room at Harlow was a square of freshly painted white, cold as bone, lighted by a row of mullioned windows above two study desks. The windows were set off by a granite parapet that looked down on the Harlow quadrangle, slate walks intersecting crisscross fashion. A pigeon was walking along the parapet, awkwardly, gawking at Roberts, showing dull gray feathers, ruffled by the breeze. Jocko was moving his arm and Roberts could see his eyes opening.

"How long have I been asleep?" Jocko asked. There was an edge of dusky sleep in his voice, and bright red rings around his eyes, and he was rubbing them. He placed his two bare feet on the floor and sat wiggling his toes. Above his head on the wall there was a map of Afghanistan, its provinces and mountains in ocher and red, and beside the map a black-and-white team picture of the Queen's Park Rangers. Jocko had piled a stack of mathematics books on the nightstand beside his bed. He turned on a lamp and studied his clock.

"Not too long," Roberts answered. He had plugged in an electric coil and was brewing tea. Jocko pulled on his socks and shoes, stood in front of a mirror beside the bed, combing his hair. The ceiling was beamed and the light rippled through the mullioned windows as if a school of fish were trapped inside it. The paint was fresh and smelled of lead. Jocko finished with his hair and pulled up a study chair and sat down beside Roberts, facing the windows. They were watching the Fens in the distance of central England fading to pastel, a green bourn of sedge rows and hamlets and the light brown of hay fields and rye. Roberts dunked a tea bag in hot water, smelling the burnt orange aroma. Below in the quad some Harlow boys were playing football. The school composed a stone rectangle around the quad, opened on four sides by portals through to the city, the river, and the Backs. He relaxed finally, listening to the sound of the boys playing, the echoes of their voices, the tick of Jocko's clock. Ravens circled the gables and spires of the city, riding invisible currents, these huge black birds falling slowly through the air. Jocko took some tea and Roberts could hear him savor it.

"What are you going to do now?" he asked Roberts.

"Right this moment?"

"Today, tomorrow."

"Oh," he said. "I've got an entire agenda. Not only for tonight, but for several days. There is enough to keep us busy."

Jocko's cheeks were turning red. He was sitting stiffly in his chair, looking out at the Cam, sunshine falling on the bridges, where some mist was burning up from the water. The sky had turned a navy blue.

Roberts gestured outside. "Which is Jono's room?" He asked. There were four stories of stone across the quad, a slanted gray slate roof. Jocko pointed to a place near the juncture of the east and south wings.

"Top floor on the corner," he said, sitting back. Roberts could see the room, its windows heavily draped, the wing now in deep shadow and a wedge of light escaping under the drapes. He sipped his tea, thinking about Jono. There was a red double-deck bus steaming up Trinity Street, stopping near Clare Bridge to let off some students. The bus went down the street followed by a stream of exhaust. "Do you mind if I get a bit nosy?" Jocko said. "I'm rather curious about something."

"We have no secrets," Roberts said.

"I'm just wondering," he said, pausing. "Mum told me all about your horse training. What's it like?"

"Most of the work is very hard," Roberts said. "I have a small place in Colorado. I raise some horses, work irrigation, try to keep busy. I'm afraid it doesn't keep me very flush, if you know what I mean, so I have to take jobs in town, especially during the winter. You know, Jocko, sometimes it gets boring too. You have to fight through that to what's really worthwhile."

"Oh, it must be wonderful. You wouldn't do something boring. Americans don't do boring things. And I know you wouldn't especially."

Roberts laughed. "Americans don't do boring things in the movies. But we do boring things for a living. For me, my town job lets me keep my ranch. And I'm basically a selfish type. I simply wouldn't be any good with a career, a time clock strapped to my neck. I've done that once or twice when I was younger. At my time of life I don't have the strength to wrestle with the clock." Roberts rubbed his chin, finished his tea. Jocko had curled a leg under himself, waiting, probably fantasizing about Americans. "Well," Roberts continued, "there is something comforting about a salary. But there is something insidious about it too. The clock tends to level things out too much for me. So, I board and train horses, try to raise enough vegetables to last the winter, and when I get in a jam I take a town job." Jocko poured himself some more tea, and the two were sitting close now. "The boss always did get under my skin. He sees every muscle, every sinew, every move you make. And the clock is like his voice, telling you he's got his eye on you. No Jocko, I'm afraid the time clock is one of those objects that defeats a man by its very existence. Like a prison, like rotten governments." Roberts sat back, slightly embarrassed. "There, you've got me going," he said.

Jocko took the kettle off the ring. "Would you do anything different? I mean if you had it to do over again."

"There's the rub," Roberts reflected. "God forbid."

"No, really," Jocko insisted.

"Jocko, the chance of doing it again is the sole reason I profess a belief in God. If there is a God, then there is a devil too. If there is a devil, then there is a slight chance His Majesty the devil may come to me and offer to buy my mortal soul in return for the chance to do it again. If he does, I'll accept."

"And what would you ask?"

"Jocko, the devil could have my soul if he would give me fifteen good years playing third base in the major leagues of American baseball. The devil would have to promise me strength and speed and a good heart. An iron will and strong legs. A rifle arm and good eyes, the eyes of a falcon. The heart of a lion. He would have to give me the dumb luck and humor of Falstaff, the whimsicality of Icarus. And I would need a dark side as well. I would be dangerous with women, like Bogart. With men I would be strictly honorable. For those fifteen good years I would tear the cover off the baseball, fly around the bases like an angel with a jet engine. I would never ever be injured, and would be routinely admired for playing on the hottest day of the year without complaint. The fans would love me, but I would not be their darling. They would know I was too tough to love, but they would give me

their respect. When my career was over, I would retire grace-
fully and learn to fish. I would do some coaching of kids in the
spring. I would have an adobe house somewhere in the desert
where I would brew my own beer and keep bees."

"The devil has his work cut out for him."

"I suppose he does."

Jocko was pouring some tepid water over his old leaves.
Roberts studied the Fens, now obscured in the gathering
dark, shards of aqua dusting the towers, the chestnut trees
along the river. In the limned outline of the fields far away a
train passed, trailing a wake of tiny lights like a necklace.

"And a wife?" Jocko said suddenly. Roberts was frozen by
the words, he thought he knew that Jocko was talking about
Amanda.

"That's another thing entirely," Roberts said. He was trying to head off his anxiety. "The devil isn't allowed to trade
in women and children. One must address oneself to God in
those matters." He could see Jocko's eyes well, he leaned over
and put his arm around the boy. "Here now," he said, "I've
gone too far."

"No, Mr. Roberts, it's all right."

"Of course. And you know what?"

"What?"

"I don't think the devil will have any truck with you either,
Jocko. You seem to have the heart of a lion without his help,
and strength and determination, and all the rest. Why don't
you tell me what you'd like to do?"

"Ah," Jocko whispered. "I'd like to see America."

"Cowboys . . ."

"Oh yes," Jocko said playfully. "I want to see Dodge City.
Frightfully so. And I want to visit California. It must be ever
so nice. And after that I want to go to New Zealand and climb
the mountains on the south island. I want to ride a camel in
Afghanistan and I want to go down the Nile in a canoe and I
want to sail and see the northern lights and I want to read all
the books Jack London ever wrote."

63

"Just a minute," Roberts joked. "That last wish is absolutely impossible."

"Perhaps." Jocko chuckled. "But you probably think I'm a bit daft."

"I don't think you're daft at all. I still dream about all those things you just mentioned. I want to fish every mile of the Salmon River in Idaho. I want to kiss Sophia Loren right on her lips and live to talk about it. I want to work in a South American carnival. I suppose we know we're through as men when we stop dreaming."

Jocko smiled. "My grandfather was a barrister in Ipswich. He wanted me to join his firm in Lincoln's Inn. He wanted me to move to the City and carry an umbrella and a newspaper. He wanted me to wear a black suit and go to court."

"And what about you? What do you want to do?"

"Jono dying has changed everything. I feel like I have to live for him as well, use my eyes for Jono and see everything he won't see. I'm going to use my heart for him too, and my heart is going to be his." Roberts could see real tears had come back, Jocko fighting them down. "I don't think Jono would like it if I worked in courts, walked around Lincoln's Inn carrying an umbrella and a newspaper."

"I've got an idea," Roberts said. "Why don't you come to America next summer? I'll take you to California. We can drive to Oregon and I'll show you a dead volcano full of blue water. I'll teach you to ride a horse. We'll find some cowboys and Indians. We'll watch steelhead trout come up the Rogue River."

"Oregon," Jocko said, pronouncing it "Or-e-gone." "Do you think Mum would let me?"

"Of course. I'm sure she would."

"It's done then," Jocko announced. Then he said, "You don't think Mum would be lonely? America is terribly far."

"Listen, Jocko, your mother is going to be fine. She's strong, Jocko, just like you. I don't believe she is capable of defeat. I'm sure of it. I'm afraid she's better than most all of us in that last way. And she's well supplied with hope, don't you worry.

All of this is terrible, and I don't doubt how she feels, but she won't let you down by behaving badly. She'll expect you to leave home. She'll want you to live." They were quiet then, Roberts lost in reflection, seeing Amanda at Victoria Station on the day he'd left England, her bright face shining in the unfocused light on the platform, the brittle London mist gradually enveloping her as the train had moved away. It was as if he were dreaming, but then the pipes knocked in the room and some heat hissed away from the radiator, and he could see the pigeons walking along the parapet, they were cooing, he could hear the boys shouting down below on the quad. He looked over, across the quad, at Jono's room, still the dull yellow glow under the drapes, and he found himself thinking about clocks and corridors and dreams, the way children dream them, how people seem to go down the corridors of life, doors on either side, later the doors grow fewer, the corridors more stuffy, and then suddenly they've come to the end of the corridor and there is only one door left, what had seemed that glorious human freedom reduced to a single musty room full of photographs, locks of hair, the implements of remembrance. Roberts remembered childhood, thinking about Jono, how it had all seemed so shiny with possibility and promise, like a bubble hovering in the barely ambent air, where cynicism and rancor, and even death, were nothing, just the murmur of birdsong, the silky rustle of a curtain in summer. It seemed then to Roberts that Jocko was helping him more than he was helping Jocko, if that were possible, and then the pipes knocked again and he shook himself awake. He could see that the drapes had parted slightly in Jono's old room, there seemed a small form at the window. "What's the light in Jono's old room?" he asked Jocko, who was finished his tea.

"It's Wim," he said, stretching out, standing and moving over to his bed. "He hasn't gone home for the holidays yet. I think his parents are abroad."

"Where does he live?"

"Amsterdam," answered Jocko. He was sitting on his bed

across the room with his feet drawn up underneath himself, looking tired. "His father is very rich. They had asked Jono to come across and spend last Christmas. Jono told me that Wim's father has a country estate near Delft. They have an old house on one of the canals in Amsterdam too. Jono was thrilled to go, quite."

"They were good friends," Roberts mumbled. He was wondering about the little boy, alone in the room across the quad, what was he thinking?

"Very good friends indeed," Jocko said. "Jono told me they went ice skating on the Amstel last year. They skied cross-country and hiked in the snow. I think Wim's mother liked Jono, because she sent him a present after the holiday visit. Quite nice, actually. She wrote Mum a lovely fine letter as well. I'm afraid Wim is very lonely now without Jono." Roberts had been watching the drapes move, trying to catch a glimpse of the Dutch boy. It was as though he was there but Roberts couldn't discern him, he could only see the window glass blink, the blue-and-gray sky circled in the panes, all of Cambridge turning sepia. It made Roberts cold inside, as if someone had filled his heart with ice.

"I'd like to talk to Wim," Roberts said. "Do you think he'd be up to that? I don't want him upset, but then he might be able to tell us something about the night Jono died. You don't know how long he'll stay at Harlow during the holidays?"

"Surely another week. His father travels on business and much of the time he takes Wim's mother along. But I could find out easily enough."

"Good, do that." Roberts tried to relax again, fixing himself in the rattan chair. "By the way, what does Wim's father do for a living?"

"Don't actually know for sure. Wim says his father explores for oil. You know boys. Whatever it is, it must be exceedingly important, because Jono told me they have a Mercedes."

"Well then"—Roberts chuckled—"we can assume that he isn't familiar with the time clock."

"Hardly," Jocko said.

"Well, let's not worry about it quite yet. You have cowboys and Indians to meet, and I've got to kiss Sophia Loren on the lips and live to speak of it."

"I could get Wim now," Jocko offered.

"No, not now. But it might be good if you'd run over and ask him if he'd speak with me. Don't make it sound too serious. Just run across the quad and tell him I'm here to collect Jono's things from the room, and that I'd like a moment with him when it's convenient. I'll be busy most of the day tomorrow, but perhaps we could go on an outing together during the day anyway. Make it something pleasant. Try to take our minds off the work at hand. Perhaps we could have some tea, fish and chips."

"That would be lovely," Jocko said.

"But look," Roberts added after some thought, "perhaps it would be best if you'd keep Wim away from his room while I collect Jono's things. After tea why don't you suggest a film? I'll go back to the room then. I wouldn't want to subject Wim to any more hurt. There's been enough of that already."

"I'll try," Jocko said. "And what will you do tomorrow?"

"Somehow I have to speak with Glenville. It isn't likely he knows very much, but I'd like to settle it in my own mind nonetheless. Then I want to take a long walk along the riverbank, get a feel of the land. Intuition is a terrible thing, Jocko; but mine tells me something isn't quite right about the way your brother died. I don't want to upset you, but I'm telling you how I feel. If nothing comes of it, then we can tell Amanda and the matter will be finished. And I don't want to upset the boys at school, and take advantage of Brooke's kindness to cause trouble. I've already taken advantage of one person as it is."

"What do you mean?" Jocko asked, his eyes wide.

"I've made a date with Brian ap Rhys to speak with him. I telephoned his home and spoke with his wife. She told me to meet them at the Crow and Corn when it opens. After that I'm going to pay a call on the Marsedens. Brooke told me the family has a farm about five miles out in the Fens. Brooke gave me some general directions, so I thought I'd make a surprise visit. The family will probably be upset, but I think I can smooth it over."

"You think Gerald is involved?"

"Don't know. Perhaps the lad was involved in a prank with Jono."

"Forgive me, Mr. Roberts, but you might be a bit careful out on the Fens."

"How so?"

"I'm afraid Gerald's dad is a bit of a bruiser. I've seen him at school football matches and he's been tipsy every time. He has a temper too. So, I do hope you'll be careful."

"I'm not much of a fighter, Jocko," Roberts said, trying to smile and ease the tension. He could tell that Jocko was agitated, his eyes shiny. "I'm just an old philosopher who can't be easily provoked. Don't you worry, I'll be very diplomatic." Jocko got up from his bed and stood beside Mitchell, looking out over the quad with a sad face. Roberts said, "Tell me something, Jocko. Do *you* think young Marseden could have been playing pranks and caused the accident?"

"I couldn't say," Jocko said. "I know he did some terrible things to Jono during school. He boasted of it at suppers, and I warned him to stop. He cuffed Jono once or twice, and when I heard tell of it I warned him again. But you can't protect your brother too much without the other boys noticing. Just makes it worse. I knew there was no reason for Gerald to torment Jono, but the things bullies do just don't make sense anyway. So, I tried to let Jono fight his own battles, even this one. I knew sooner or later Gerald would give it up, find someone else to torment. If I'd really stepped in, they would have been calling Jono a baby, and that would have been worse than Marseden's antics. It just wouldn't do."

"You're probably right," Roberts said. "It wouldn't do at Harlow, or anywhere else in the world for that matter. There's a Gerald Marseden in all our lives, and we generally survive him quite well. I just want to know that Jono survived this Gerald, this time."

"Still," Jocko said, "do be careful. Old man Marseden has knuckles like a pig."

"I'll be careful," Roberts said. "I've had some experience myself with brutes. You get these two-thousand-pound broncs after you on the ranch." Roberts put on his bomber jacket and muffler, laced his boots. He gave Jocko a hug. Roberts thought of all the things he wanted to talk to Jocko about, wondering if he'd ever have the opportunity, the time. He wanted to talk to the boy some more about dreams, their efficacy, their power, how an honest dream is better than the devil. But he was late for his meeting with Brian ap Rhys, and so he left Jocko in the darkening room and went out to find the Crow and Corn.

MONDAY, DECEMBER 2
EVENING

THE Trinity Street pubs and cafés were filled with milling students, young men and women, hunched around shiny tables and mahogany bars, discussing philosophy and politics, drinking lager and ale, gin and tonic, smoking cigarettes like adults. There were staid professors too, in tweed, loitering at the bookstalls, the antique markets, all the canvas awnings bumping in the wind and the red buses wheezing up the High Street in clouds of fume. Roberts had walked all the way through Trinity Lane, its upper end a narrow confine of haberdashers and tailor shops, then through Green Street and down Sydney, amid the stone and glass of commercial Cambridge, now shuttered and silent. A gray moon was shattering the clouds and a few stars had appeared against the black. Everyplace, though, Roberts could discern the sound of music, a low moan as if it were being made by whales singing, but it was the mandolin and the fiddle, pianos tinkling in the pubs, and when he stopped beside Christ's Church for a time he could hear a choir singing an evensong, which made him sad, and so he hurried on across the Magdalene Bridge and strolled around the docks and quays along the river.

The Crow and Corn was on a corner near the Quayside between a shoe repair shop, the Old Cobbler, and a window full of used band instruments. The pub sign swung over the cobbled street; it showed a scruffy raven with a shiny beak circling the ground for corn. The boards were weathered and

Roberts could hear them creak in the breeze. There were bodies pressed against the pub's window, tightly massed in the half-gray light, and it seemed to him as if the window might press out and shatter at any moment, the place seemed so filled, as if human beings might pour out of a sea of broken glass and beer. When he looked inside, he could see way in the back, beyond all the bodies, all the waiters hustling trays carefully above their heads, men throwing darts, a band playing mandolins and a squeeze box, their gruff sounds barely audible above the noise of the crowd. Dark vertical shadows had climbed the walls. It reminded Mitchell of medieval England, sickness, the smell of gin, as if the pub were a battle field.

He stood in the open doorway looking at the bar, which was angled to the street, European-style, its high bank of glasses shining against a yellowed mirror, images of workingmen and ladies in the flare of cigarettes. There was no room at the bar, so Roberts stood for a time in the doorway looking for Brian ap Rhys, whose wife had told him to find a smallish gent dressed in a red sweater onto which had been sewn the Welsh lion. Roberts was breaking a sweat when somebody clapped him on the back. He turned and saw a ruddy face staring at him from an amazing pair of twinkling blue eyes, this small man with bad teeth but superbly able in his bearing, straight across the shoulders with a narrow waist that reminded Roberts of a jockey. His hair was very black, swept back from the forehead and held there with pomade. As able as he looked, though, there was still something ill-kempt about him, as if he had just tumbled from a washing machine and had not been properly dried off. Perhaps, Roberts thought, it was the gray evening stubble, the yellow teeth, or the fact that he was holding a huge pint glass of porter in his left hand, a cigarette in his right, his old man's lips wet with beer, on the way to being tipsy. "Brian ap Rhys," the old man said, high-pitched voice, very hearty though, with some of the throaty bearing of a mountain man, someone used to speaking loudly. Roberts could barely hear the man even so, because of the noise.

"Thanks for meeting me," Roberts shouted, leaning over to be heard. Drinkers shuffled past, tankards caught in hands that also held cigarettes, making pardons as they brushed by. Roberts noticed that Brian had large hands. The man drank some of his porter, leaving a white mustache on his lip, which he licked, smiling. Roberts noticed the band moving around on the stage, one young fellow in a great cloth coat in green, blond hair with freckles and red cheeks. "Your wife said you wouldn't mind," Roberts said.

"Right you are," Brian shouted.

Together they fought their way through the crowd to a table and a narrow bench at the back of the pub near the stage. There were two men and a woman sitting over beer. The men were named Buck and Timothy, and both had huge goblets of gin. They were brothers with fat jolly faces, both bald-headed. The woman was Brian's wife, Giselle. "Good Welshmen," Brian brayed, sipping his porter while the musicians finished a tune that sounded to Roberts like a reel. Giselle was taller than her husband, she smiled constantly, though she said very little. Roberts thought she was homely, but solid, and when Buck and Tim got up to play some darts a waitress brought her some gin, one for Roberts. The musicians had climbed down from the stage.

Brian said, "Sad about the boy. It was an awful shock to the wife here. How's the lad's family?"

"They've had a tough time," Roberts said, tasting the gin, the burning juniper smell in his head now.

"Not too many Yanks in the Crow," Brian said. "You stand out like a highwayman in church. Bloody tourists make the rounds of the churches and libraries." He swigged some porter, his Adam's apple ducking up and down. "Nor any harm meant," he said. "Yanks are fine by me. It's the bloody English I don't like."

Roberts tried to drink his gin even though it had a raw, overpowering quality that made him gag. He asked the man to tell him about the night in October when he'd found the boy, and Brian frowned, clearly pained, and told the whole story while Roberts listened, adding nothing new to what he knew from Brooke's recounting of the same thing, Amanda's understandings, what he had pieced together already. He asked Brian a few questions, but was certain nothing would happen, the old man couldn't think of anything unusual in the events, except that he was surprised to find a poor Harlow lad like that. Somebody scored a triple in darts and there was a noisy cheer, Roberts saw that the band was getting ready to go back onstage, the noise was getting loud again. His head was already buzzing, and Brian was finishing his porter.

They stood and went back through the crowd. Some Welshmen wearing sheep's coats had come in, crowding about the doorway. Brian was on Robert's arm. "I'm curious about you," he said to Roberts, clapping a fellow on the back who had gone by. "You seem a man with suspicions." Roberts gulped for fresh air at the front entrance. He could hear the band tuning up, the crowd starting to roar again. The sky outside had turned a misty gray and black.

"Jono was a good swimmer," Roberts said. "He was a good boy and was going to meet his brother, Jocko, for supper that night. He was wearing his good clothes. You tell me what a good Harlow lad would be doing wading in the Cam, a cold river on an October night."

Brian seemed dazed, looking out at the river. He stayed that way for a long time. "Right you are, Yank," he said. "Right you are," half whispered. "I've worked at the Wren Library for most of me adult life. Knew young Jonathan as well. All the Harlow boys I knew one time or the other. There's good and bad boys as always, but Jonathan was one of the good ones. It does seem odd that he'd mess his good clothes that way. Perhaps he took a tumble."

"That's what Martin Brooke thinks."

"A shame it is," Brian said.

"I'm taking a taxi to the Marseden place," Roberts announced. It was getting late and he wanted the thing done. "It seems Jono had some trouble with the boy named Gerald.

I thought I might ask a few respectful questions and be on my way. It's the least I can do for the family."

"You mean to bother old Ambrose Marseden?"

"Yes. His son had been tormenting Jono. I just wanted to see if the boy knew anything about that night. I don't expect to learn anything, but you can't pick fruit without shaking the tree."

"Bloody right," Brian snapped. "I've had a run-in with Gerald a time or two meself. Caught him destroying some library books. Stopped up the water closet and it took me an hour of work to unplug the damned thing. If you ask me, Gerald Marseden is a bloodthirsty young bat. I don't ordinarily say that of a lad, but in this case it's true. Even for the son of an Englishman, he's a special rotter."

"Well, that's where I'm going."

"You'll find old Ambrose an armful, mind you."

"I'm told," Roberts said.

"I've seen him in his cups, at football matches. Him supposedly a bloody squire. If he's a squire, then I'm the Queen's prize pig. If he's a squire, then I'm the Archbishop of Canterbury, and a sop to boot. He has money, which is what made the lot of the Englishman." An odd old couple had come out of the pub, brushing by the two men. They hobbled down the street. Brian had watched them go, thinking. "Listen, Yank," he said, "it's a right good piece out to the Marseden place. Let me drive you out there."

"You needn't bother. I'll hire a cab."

"No trouble at all," he said. "Even if you could find a taxi, it would cost you a bloody fiver. No need for that, I don't mind at all. Save your money for gin." Brian turned before Roberts could protest, disappearing inside the pub, then returning with his coat. "I've fetched the keys, and told the old woman," he said, walking down the lane, motioning for Roberts to follow.

They went through New Park Street, where Brian found his battered Morris under a streetlamp. They got in the car and drove south along the Cam and then through the hedgerows until they had come out on the Backs, where the night was suddenly dark and windy. The car was so cramped that Roberts was forced to ride with his knees tucked nearly under his chin, the clatter of the engine enormous, fumes and oil smell ripping through the passenger stall, filling it until he thought he would suffocate. They were driving very fast down the narrow lanes, almost no light, like tunnels.

Brian steered sitting nearly cock-right, looking at Roberts, barely paying attention to the road. "You'll not get much out of old Marseden, I'll wager," he said, shouting because of the engine noise. "He's none too bright as it is, but he thinks his only son is coin of the realm. If you ask me, his son is as big an oaf as he." Brian grinned and said, "But then you've not asked!" He was pounding his palm on the steering wheel, laughing, crazy with porter and the dark night, it seemed to Roberts that they were like moths banging against a light bulb, it was wild and unpredictable. "And that's the thing," Brian shouted again, "these snotty Englishmen have been squires and shopkeepers since bloody creation. Now Welshmen are different."

"How so?" yelled Roberts.

"Different," said Brian. The Morris Minor was rocking in the wind. "The Welshman," he said, "is a poet first, then a fighter. The Welshman walks the hills with a song in his breast. Defender of the marches. Friend to the cloud and the rain. And what have the bloody English done?" He paused for effect. "I'll tell you. Made us dig coal from underground, that's what!" The Morris Minor hopped over some railroad tracks and Roberts saw a whitewashed post office on one corner and a petrol station, a narrow-fenced lane slipping uphill. There were some sheep in the fields, browsing under a fog. Roberts could smell wet hay and dung; it reminded him of his ranch.

Brian worked the Morris Minor uphill, Roberts felt the floorboards shudder, his feet were hot from the exhaust. They reached a rise, and there was a farmstead, stone house, thatched roof, the chimney pouring white smoke. It had recessed windows full of dull light. They rolled to a stop in a circular drive and sat with the motor running while Brian rolled down his window.

"You're here, Yank," he said. The front door to the farmhouse was recessed, like the windows, a heavy oaken plank with a boar's head knocker and a tiny window glass covered by bars. Roberts noticed horses on a hill behind the house, while down the road the way they had come he could make out the smoky glow of Cambridge. He got out of the car, Brian stepping out at the same time, they looked at each other over the roof. "It might do if I came to the door with you. You'll not be such a stranger then."

"That's fine," Roberts agreed. He walked up some stone steps and used the knocker. The door flew open and Ambrose Marseden stood in the entryway, dirty corduroy pants and black lace-up boots, face roiled with sweat. The room behind him was low and grim, and stank of cooking fat and tallow. Two skinny whippets stood nervously beside the squire, dappled black and white like harlequins, both munching bones, ribs heaving.

"Who will this be?" Marseden growled, pausing to run a finger across his lips.

"Brian ap Rhys here," the old man said from behind Roberts. "And an American who'd be wanting a word with you."

Marseden stepped through the portal, looking out at the sheep on the hillside. Roberts thought he looked like an appalling dullard, thick knot of skin on his neck, flat gray eyes, red hair speckled with gray. Marseden took a walnut from his coat pocket and crushed it in his palms.

"My godchild was Jonathan Trench Smith," Roberts said. He was amazed by the girth of the man, this fellow who looked like a Defoe villain. "I believe your son Gerald knew him at school."

"What of it?" Marseden said. He was chewing the walnut meat. He kicked at the whippets and the dogs scampered back into the room as Marseden stepped aside. The room was only a vestibule to the main house and had a roughshod, confining feel to it. The house spoked away from the vestibule, open doors back through a hall to the kitchen. Brian followed Roberts inside, and they stood as Marseden kicked the door shut. "Say what you have to say," Marseden said, sucking at the walnut meat. He had blotchy skin, like that of a blacksmith.

"I'd like to talk with Gerald. I'd like to know if he can tell me anything about the night Jono died."

Brian was standing beside Roberts, trying to take off his coat. Marseden leaned back against a maple stand, watching both with a cold stare.

"Let me be honest," Roberts said.

"That would be nice," Marseden replied sarcastically.

"Gerald had been teasing Jonathan—"

"Ho," Marseden said. He dropped the walnut shells. He puffed himself out, Roberts could see his dirty white shirt, the brown stains on the cheap cotton and the black hair around his neck. "Now I am sorry about young Smith, but who says my boy done it?"

"Nobody is saying that."

Marseden stared at Brian, who fidgeted slightly and clutched the lapels of his overcoat. The whippets had sneaked back into the room, standing just inside the kitchen portals, bones in their mouths, wet eyes.

Marseden said, "If a man were to accuse my boy of doing anything to Jonathan Trench Smith, then that man would be a bloody liar. Name the man."

"I told you I just wanted to ask Gerald . . ."

"My boy is as innocent as Jesus himself." Marseden laughed unpleasantly, a messy roar that came from the throat. Brian nudged Roberts from behind, but Roberts kept looking at Marseden, who had moved away from the maple stand, frowning.

"If I could speak to Gerald," Roberts began.

"Like bloody hell you will," Marseden said. "You'll not come into my own house with your lies." He took off his vest and stood in the middle of the vestibule, swinging the garment in his right hand, the whippets mesmerized by the motion, around and around. "My boy," Marseden said, "is as sweet as one of my own lambs."

"Wait now," Brian said, coming around Roberts, his eyes on the vest, Marseden swinging it around and around.

"I'll wager I do know you," Marseden said, smiling.

"I'd be Brian ap Rhys," the old man said. Roberts tried to nudge him back, but he held ground. "I'm the chit attendant at the Wren. I know your boy Gerald. It's not that I know of him. I know him directly."

"And what of it?" Marseden asked.

"I've seen your lamb destroying books in the library. Badgering the younger lads. Jonathan Smith included."

"You've carried these tales," Marseden said to Brian. Suddenly Marseden took a step forward and struck him on the left ear with the vest. The old man sagged back against the door, and before Roberts could move Brian had been struck again, leather popping against an ear, the bottom button breaking skin.

"That's enough," Roberts shouted. He put an arm around the old man, holding him upright. There was a trickle of blood already on Brian's collar and Roberts could see that water had come to his eyes, it must have hurt terribly. But Marseden was smiling, showing his teeth. Roberts extended his hand to keep Marseden away, opening the doorlatch with the other. He pushed the old man out the door and followed him down the path, watched by Marseden and the whippets from the portal. Roberts got him around to the car and put him in the driver's seat.

Brian looked up. "I told you he was a sod."

"I'm sorry I got you into this."

Brian pulled his feet inside the car and sat there in silence. Roberts could see his face redden with shame, he felt terribly sorry for the old man. "If I were younger," Brian said, "it would be different." Roberts dabbed at the old man's ear with his handkerchief.

"Wait here," he said. Brian nodded, too hurt to say much.

Roberts made certain the old man had his coat around him and that the bleeding had stopped. There was a slash right on the lobe, but he didn't think it was too bad. While he worked over the old man, he noticed some medium-size cedars near the front door. He walked over and stripped one of the bigger branches from the trunk, making a nice-size club once he had taken off the needles. He went up to the door and knocked on the boar's head again and Marseden came out instantly, throwing wide the door and glaring.

"I'll thank you to leave," he roared.

"I'd like another word," Roberts said.

When Marseden came through the door Roberts hit him on the left ear with the branch, throwing his weight into the blow, feeling the club break skin, crack. Blood flew from the ear and Marseden went down to his knees without a sound, his hands on the stone steps, on his knees there while he fought to stay conscious. Roberts stepped closer and hit him again, not quite so hard, just a solid tap on the ear again, to make it hurt. One of the whippets was whimpering, backing away inside the house. Marseden went to his elbows.

Roberts said, "Let this be the end of it." He had leaned down to the squire, and he could smell whiskey and horseflesh on the man. The ear was swelling nicely. "Understand?" he whispered. "Tell me you do."

"Yes, yes, all right," Marseden muttered.

Roberts walked down to the Morris Minor and got in the car. They drove downhill past the post office and down the way they'd come across the Fens and the Backs, through the narrow lanes and hedgerows while Brian brooded silently. He had belted his overcoat and was watching the dark, driving slowly now. "I wish I could have done that," he said when they crossed the bridge into the city. They drove down to New Park Street; Brian lived in a row of stone houses there. Roberts got out and helped the old man inside his house, which was dark. Giselle had come to the door in hair curlers and nightgown, flowsy slippers. She watched her husband go inside the house and turned.

"Trouble?" she asked.

"No, not at all. I'm afraid your husband is just a bit tired. He'll be all right."

"To be sure," she answered. "Perhaps he'll tell me himself tomorrow."

"Thank him for me, will you?"

She nodded. "This is about the boy?"

"In a way," Roberts said, turning to go.

"Nobody asked me," Giselle said. "But I saw the lad Jonathan in the water of the river as well. He was wearing his Harlow coat, he was. And the back of it was bright green. It hadn't gotten soaked at all."

"Are you sure?" Roberts asked.

"Of course I'm sure. Not a one of them stopped to ask me what I'd seen. But that boy's school coat was dry on the back. It was as if he'd laid down and gone to sleep, it was. Just as if he'd gone to sleep." She pulled up the hem of her housecoat and went inside. Roberts could hear some town dogs barking. He walked back up the riverbank where the swans were pooling in the moonlight.

TUESDAY, DECEMBER 3

WIM van Euwe was a wispy shy Dutch kid. Roberts marveled at his wonderful smile, the hub of dark blond hair that ended on the back of his head in a rooster-tail cowlick. He was sitting in full sunshine, watching Jocko slug a tennis ball back across the net, between shots studying absentmindedly from a mathematics text, pausing to appreciate the tennis match, how badly Jocko was trouncing Roberts in the set. They were in the second set, Roberts having lost the first almost too easily, and now Jocko was lobbing up soft shots, trying to keep the rallies alive a little longer. They were playing on courts of cracked asphalt laid down under the shadow of the Museum of Ethnology, on Tennis Court Road. Wim hadn't wanted to play, and so he sat there dressed in jaunty cricket pants and a white school shirt, retrieving Roberts's errant shots with a gracefulness that surprised him. The traffic along Sydney Street created an invisible hum, and the pigeons were walking around the cornices of all the buildings.

After the match, the three walked down to a tea shop on Drummer Street and found a window table. Wim and Jocko ordered traditional ham sandwiches and tea, while Roberts tried the corn soup and an orange soda. The shop was full of glass cases and the air smelled of yeast and day-old pastry. Probably because he was frightened, or a foreigner, Wim said very little, though he had a pleasant voice and a nice clipped accent. In between sips of corn soup Roberts said, "Wim, I'm going to be fetching Jono's things today." The boy was nibbling a bread crust, his blue eyes downcast, looking very sad and pensive.

"Jocko has told me," he said precisely. His oval eyes were covered by long lashes, silky, in the sun his cheekbones very sharply defined, like porcelain. He and Jocko had worn green jackets and theirs were matched by other students in the café. In the midafternoon, professors and university students wandered in and out, to drink tea and eat rich cake. The waiters were bustling around, scraping chairs against the highly polished floor, outside the sound of the traffic. Jocko leaned over and said, "We'll be taking a walk along the river. Perhaps go to the cinema." Wim smiled at Jocko.

"Before you go," Roberts said, "can you tell me about the night Jono died?" Wim bit his lip, eyes filling. They were about fifty meters from the church in Christ's Pieces where Jono had been taken that night, Roberts wished they had chosen another spot. The afternoon was rose-colored, some leaves in the streets.

Wim said, "We had come in from football. Jono was our midfielder, very good too. We went up to the room and Jono took his shower first while I stayed behind to study. Then he took his study things and got on his bed while I took my shower. Like always, he was going to have supper with Jocko. At the fish shop, he said."

"How did he seem to you, Wim?"

"How do you mean, sir?"

"Well, did he seem nervous, preoccupied, upset? Was he out of sorts, or was he normal? Did he say anything that evening that made it appear he was bothered?"

"Nothing, sir. Honestly." Wim looked at Jocko, who smiled gently and nodded, as if to say "Go ahead."

"I want to ask you about Gerald Marseden."

"Oh," Wim said, dully.

"Had Jono been having recent trouble with him?"

"Not recently. Oh, there had been some trouble in the fall,

82

but most of that had been set aside. He didn't say anything to me about Gerald."

Jocko was eating his sandwich, sipping tea. The waiter refilled the cups. Roberts didn't want more orange soda, which he thought tasted like dishwater, terrible and flat, he wanted some good American soda fountain soda. Wim's eyes had glazed from grief, this remembrance he had, so that Roberts felt terribly sorry for the boy, he could see him tremble slightly. "Do you think Gerald did this to Jono?" he asked finally.

"I don't know, sir. Do you think something was wrong with Jono?"

"Wim, I don't know either. But yes, I do think something was wrong that night. I don't know what it was, but if you can possibly take me through every instant of that evening, it might help. Everything you can remember. I'll only ask you to do this once."

Wim sighed. "I'll try, sir," he said bravely. He took a deep breath, like a boy standing on a high dive in front of all his friends. "As I said, we had practiced football. We do that every Sunday afternoon when there isn't a match. After Jono showered, I undressed and went down the hall with my soap and towel. When I left, Jono was sitting on the bed, putting on his socks. I was in the shower for about five minutes when he peeped inside the washroom and said something about the telephone—I couldn't hear him very well because of the water running and the noise from the lads out in the quadrangle. I think he was talking about a phone call, a message he needed to take, but that he would go down to Glenville's room and take it. I finished my shower and it was getting late. I went back to the room and put on my clothes and started to study. I always have dinner at Harlow on Sunday nights, so I didn't go anywhere but down to the dining hall. Jono didn't come back to the room, but nothing seemed wrong in that. I decided he must have gone on to dinner with Jocko. It was only later when Master Glenville came to the room that I knew what had happened."

"Did you hear anyone outside your room? In the quad, or by the river? Perhaps a commotion. Some sound that was out of the ordinary?"

"No sir. Not a thing. It was a very quiet evening."

Jocko looked at Roberts. "It was as he says. I don't think Jono mentioned any trouble with Marseden at all. To me, or anyone."

"That's enough for now," Roberts announced. "You boys run along." When they had left, he paid the bill and went down Sydney Street. He could see Wim and Jocko strolling along the Cam in the low sun. He crossed Green Street to the Harlow School buildings and went up to Wim's room on the fourth story of the school and began to pack Jono's things in pasteboard boxes. The room was an exact replica of Jocko's room, dusty in the afternoon light, filled with the ineffable sadness of Jono's absence. He worked quickly among the things, volumes of mathematics texts, some English classics, Greek primers, all the muddy football shoes, the boy's winter coats, Harlow jackets, football uniform, mittens, and the muffler he had worn to the Queen's Park Ranger games when he was home in London. There were the usual odds and ends for a boy, chess pieces, an old cribbage board, letters from home, and, on the nightstand, breaking Roberts's heart, a picture of Smitty in his American field uniform. He walked the boxes one by one back to Jocko's room across the quad, labeled them for shipment on the train, and tied each with string.

He was exhausted, sitting silently in Jocko's room at the end of a long day, watching the birds rise from the Gothic towers while the air covered Cambridge with a wind-washed gold. A few stars powdered the eastern horizon above the Fens and the city was coming alive with lights in the shops and pubs. He was aware that a lamp had been turned on in Wim's room, and then later Jocko came in through the door behind him, waking Roberts from a doze, taking off his Harlow jacket and muffler. They heated some tea on the electric ring and sat together in their rattan chairs. Wind was blowing papers

84

around the quad and Roberts listened to the sounds of the swans honking down on the river. Jocko was looking at the boxes piled on the floor, as if he expected them to say something. An abstract intensity.

"You all right, Jocko?" Roberts asked.

"Quite," the boy said sadly.

There was a knock on the door, and Jocko answered it to find Martin Brooke standing in the hallway, smoking his meerschaum, carrying a tweed coat over his left arm. He had on a neat tweed suit that matched the coat, his hair slicked down with pomade. He gave Jocko a long hug and came inside the room to shake hands. Jocko retreated to his study desk and began to play chess in the light of a small lamp. The two men sat down in the rattan chairs, watching Cambridge grow dark.

"So," Brooke said, "you've collected Jono's things, I see." He was lighting his pipe again, studying the night outside. They could hear an evensong from Christ's Church far away while tea heated on the electric ring. When it boiled, Roberts poured two cups and they sat drinking it while he told Brooke about his visit to Ambrose Marseden, about what he'd learned from Brian, Wim van Euwe. He told Brooke what Celia had said at the race course, and what old Giselle had whispered on the stoop of her row house on New Park Street. The doctor was thinking quietly, his forehead creased. Jocko was busy with his chess game.

"I want to know some pathology," Roberts said.

Brooke sucked the amber stem of his pipe. "Very well," he said. "Let's talk pathology."

"I'm interested in your medical conclusions, and I'm interested in the way you use physical evidence when you reach them."

"Etiology," Brooke said.

"If that's what you call it. I want to know how you draw conclusions in the absence of an autopsy."

"I see what you mean," Brooke said.

"Please, Doctor," Roberts said gently. Brooke was balanc-

85

ing his teacup on a knee, a worried look on his face. "I'm not questioning your methods at all. Far from it."

"Think nothing of it," he said. "I understand you quite precisely. You think young Jono may have gone into the water against his will? Perhaps foul play."

"Perhaps so. Perhaps he was harmed before. What goes on in the medical mind when confronted with a death like this? How does it work? What is going through your mind when you make an examination like the one you made of Jono?"

The doctor leaned forward and placed his cup and saucer on the recessed sill. Below, there was the stone quadrangle burning in the moonlight, Roberts could hear the wind whisper against the flint, voices from another place and time, anonymous, mournful, he thought. While he spoke, the doctor's voice itself seemed to change in tone, husky, as if he were exerting great effort. "All death is *circumstantial*," he said. "There is a grotesquerie about science that places a cage of objectivity around the events, you want to look at them one way but you can't because your emotions would lead you astray. Place a dead man in water, and his lungs show signs of water. You may conclude that he has drowned. The workings of gravity and wave will cause these effects, you look at the man in the water, so calm, you conclude he has drowned. The fact that the man is dead before he goes into the water will make no difference to that basic physical fact."

"And when you say death is circumstantial?"

"Perhaps I should explain," Brooke said, picking up his cup and saucer. "Find ten perfect doctors in a perfect world. Give them some time, and perfect instruments, and the cooperation of the authorities, and they will still conclude that the death of our man was caused by drowning."

"But the world isn't perfect."

"Not nearly so, and that is precisely the point. Perhaps I should say that death is existential. Circumstantial in every respect, but existential in its most important respect. You have to know all the facts," Brooke said, looking at Roberts, spilling some tea on the saucer. Brooke looked tired, too bundled up, the tweed suit, heavy brogan shoes. "And the facts are every-where, all around us."

"And what if there were an autopsy?"

"The etiology is the same. The instruments change but the variables remain the same. Even in a perfect world, five of the ten doctors would likely still conclude that the cause of death was drowning. If the man had a knife in his back, a wife who hated him, perhaps five others would conclude that he had been murdered by an angry spouse."

"Meaning?" Roberts asked.

"Meaning," Brooke said, pausing over tea, "that death and its etiology are like all science. You make a reasonable guess gleaned from a multitude of circumstances, observations, measurements, calculations. If a toxicologist had examined young Jonathan, and fairly soon after he was found, we might not be having this discussion. One of the circumstances we are currently dealing with is that Clannahan came and took the body of the boy to Ipswich. My own conclusions were based upon the available evidence. There was no witness to the event, a most important item, no signs of violence, no motive for another conclusion. Under these circumstances, he was presumed to have drowned. And now, as a doctor, and as an etiologist, I am back to the same conclusion. This is not a perfect world."

"Well, Doctor," Roberts said. "Assume you live in the kind of world in which you have a second chance to examine Jona-than. What would you do with this second chance?"

"I would call for an autopsy, of course." Brooke had taken out his meerschaum and was tamping at the tobacco in the bowl, furiously, as if he were nervous. Roberts noticed that the tamping tool was a small ivory elephant and pedestal. "But I've been thinking about some other things too," Brooke added, red-faced. "Celia is right about those bloody toys, now that I think about them. I suppose I've gone a bit dotty with the years, living in a boy's school, drinking my bloody tea, worrying about my Virginia twist tobacco, how is the supply? Some old codger out of Beatrix Potter. The whole thing is terrible. Without so much as a second thought, I believed whole cloth that young Jonathan fell off of the Trinity Bridge and drowned in three feet of water, floated forty bloody meters and snagged in some reeds, all on a quiet Sunday night with his best school clothes on, him being a champion swimmer, and all that rot. At the same time, I believed those bloody toys belonged to him. Simple Aristotle, learned it before I learned to pee. Two bloody propositions cannot be both true and false at the same time in the same way. Bloody swimmer drowns in three feet of water, playing on the Trinity Bridge, Sunday best. Well, it won't do for a Harlow boy, no sir. And now Celia, my dear old mother in her eighties, sees that those toys don't quite fit into my picture of a Harlow boy, especially one of Jonathan's age." Brooke got his pipe lit, letting off a huge cloud of smoke, smiling now. "My own mother, you know she won four races at Epsom, don't you?"

"She's a superb horse judge," Roberts said. "I've studied horses myself and she can pick winners. I'm afraid you and I were studying whiskey bottles and pretty girls more than horses."

"Right you are," Brooke said. "But I'd much rather handicap a pretty girl, what?" He dipped a finger into his tea, which had gone cold. "But I tell you," he said, quietly now, "that I still conclude the boy drowned. Only now I'd have to say I have reservations of how he did so." Roberts balanced his feet on the windowsill, watching the evening.

"Did you meet Marseden?" Brooke asked.

"I went out to see the boy's father last night."

"Lusty fellow."

"Very lusty."

"How did it proceed?"

"I knocked him down and popped his left ear."

"Good show!" Brooke exclaimed. He struck another match and lit his pipe again, plainly amused and intrigued. Roberts supplied Brooke with a short version of the events.

Roberts said, "But Brian ap Rhys has a wife who says she

saw Jono in the water that night. Said nobody talked with her about the death."

Brooke reflected. "That's true," he said.

"She claims when she saw the boy floating, his coat was dry on the back. Said she was close, saw it plainly, and that it was green, not soaked through like the rest of him."

"I say," Brooke muttered through clenched teeth. "I think we'd best talk with Jacob Miles, the constable. He is a good chap, reliable and intelligent" Brooke turned his head, stole a glance at Jocko, who was immersed in his chess book, growing drowsy. Brooke turned back. "This will call down more pain on the family, I'm afraid."

"It has to be that way," Roberts acknowledged.

"Yes," Brooke said, "yes, I suppose so."

Jocko got up from the desk, leaving his chessboard, rubbing at his eyes. He walked over to the two chairs, beside the window, looking tired. In one hand he was holding a red chess pawn, turning it over and over as he stared out across the quadrangle at what was now Wim's room only, once had been Jono's too, a bright patch of light covered by drapery. The doctor finished his cold tea with a grimace and gently placed a hand on Jocko's sleeve, Jocko looking down at him with doleful, somnolent eyes, pausing to brush back a wisp of hair from his forehead, tossing the chess piece, catching it with his other hand. The heat pipes rattled again, far away another train was hooting across the Fens, heading north toward Yorkshire.

"Tell me, Jocko," Roberts said. Jocko looked somewhat curious, waking up. "Had you ever seen any toys like those Dr. Brooke found with Jonathan, the ones we looked at in the cigar box? Ever seen anything like that before, in Jono's room?"

"No sir, never," Jocko said sternly. He closed a hand over the pawn.

"I just went through his things, as you know. I found nothing at all resembling those items, the puppet, the bones, the cowrie shells. There was his cricket equipment and his clothes. His books. No beeswax, no puppets."

"I think I would know about something like that."

"Brooke doesn't know about them," Roberts added.

"Doesn't make sense," Brooke said.

Roberts asked Jocko to sit on the windowsill. He did and crossed his legs, looking at Brooke, then Roberts, clutching his pawn, trying to stay awake again. Roberts studied the boy, thinking that he would make a serious and intelligent adult, a good wanderer—whose interest in people wouldn't wear thin, or waver, or turn into exploitation, a good boy now, unpeopled by meanness or greed, and who, like every good wanderer, could stroll into a strange culture, leaving behind blinders and crutches, and take his fill of the sights and sounds, use the currents of alienation like a dolphin in the Gulf Stream. He was a boy of movement and goodwill. He would transform strangeness, it was breaking Robert's heart, looking at him against the backdrop of the night sky, but he had Amanda's hazel eyes, the black wavy hair of his father, Captain Reece. Roberts felt an almost irresistible urge to protect Jocko from the awful uncovering that he felt was about to occur, but he knew, just as well, that Jocko was too wise for all that. He was going to see and understand.

"You remember Wim telling me Jono had received a phone message the night he was killed?" Roberts asked Jocko, who nodded. "When you two went walking this afternoon, did Wim add anything to that?" Jocko thought, shook his head no. "Did your mother say she called Jono that night?"

"She didn't say, but then I didn't ask her either."

"You didn't telephone your brother?"

"Oh no. We were on for fish and chips."

"So—who telephoned for Jono?"

The three studied each other, the dark arrangements in the room, the quadrangle and the stars. The heat pipes clanked again, in the walls.

"Never mind," Roberts said, flicking his wrist, trying to break the spell. Brooke seemed to start, Jocko uncrossed his legs. "Glenville is coming by in a few minutes. I thought he'd be more comfortable if we were all here, very friendly. I'm sure he feels terrible about what's happened."

"Likely," Brooke said.

Roberts suggested that he and Jocko play chess, and they went back to the study desk while Brooke brewed tea. A moon rose above the Gothic towers of Cambridge, it seemed like a white rose, shedding petals on the slate roofs, on the river Cam. Roberts stood above the board, stretching his legs, while Jocko set up the pieces and began to play, pushing Roberts into a strange variation of a game he didn't know. Brooke paced the room, smoking his pipe, tamping it furiously, the way a Moslem worries his beads. Moonlight streamed in the windows and Roberts found himself lost in dreams, about Amanda, the war, all the light and dark colors in the room swarming around him like ghosts.

They heard a scratch at the door, like a cat wanting in, and when Jocko pulled it open Glenville was huddled forlornly in a wedge of light, his eyes darting around the room. Roberts thought he looked like a beaten scholar, itinerant, with his bones barely filling his cheap black suit, the cuffs frayed, wearing pointy black shoes and shiny nylon socks. He had the appearance of one of those poor English humanists, an administrator, a civil servant, a man of latent invisibility. His nose was as pointy as his shoes, lending his appearance a slightly comic aspect, the wart on his cheek adding to it. He began to crack his knuckles, one after the other, up and down his hand. It was making Roberts wince, the pathos of it.

"For God's sake, come in, man," Brooke said.

Glenville shuffled inside and shook hands with Roberts, nodded at Jocko, Brooke waving. Jocko went back to the chess game and Roberts offered Glenville some tea. It had been an embarrassing few moments.

"Thank you for coming," Roberts said, trying to be cheery. Glenville's shoulders slumped slightly, a wry smile on his face. In the light, Roberts could see how thickly the man plastered down his hair, how beady his eyes seemed. He appeared the kind of man whose reputation for meanness was justified, he was probably considered a sissy among the men.

"Have you collected young Jonathan's things?" Glenville asked, fidgeting.

Roberts pointed to the boxes in the corner, tied with string. "Yes, thank you," he said.

"Oh, yes, I see," Glenville said, taking the tea Brooke had offered. Brooke sat down in the rattan chair and stared out the window, his back turned.

"I have only one thing to ask," Roberts said.

"Anything I can do."

"A person telephoned for Jonathan the night he died. I'm told the telephone is in your room, or near it in the hall."

"Yes, quite."

"Do you know who called Jono?"

"No, I'm sorry I don't."

"Man or woman?"

"Hard to tell on that phone."

"Young or old?"

"A husky voice, very low. Though it could have been a mature woman, I'd wager it was a man. Just a wager, mind you."

"Do you recall the exact words?"

"Just asked for Jono. The boys receive many telephone calls, especially on Sunday nights. It is a very popular time among parents, friends." They fell silent. "Is that all?" Glenville asked.

"Yes, thanks for coming," Roberts said. He could tell from looking at Glenville that the man wasn't going to be much help. His jellybean eyes, the blanched skin, like a poached fish, Roberts thought. Glenville smiled and backed out of the door, which Jocko hadn't bothered to close. He pulled it shut.

"Quite a ferret," Brooke said from his chair. Roberts discerned a trail of pipe smoke roiling over the chair, the head of white hair, wings around the ears. Jocko laughed and came to the chair and stood beside Roberts, both of them behind the doctor. They were watching the dark creep into Cambridge,

92

the high stone buildings of Harlow, across the quadrangle the wedge of light under Wim's drapes. Roberts thought he saw something move, a slash of undraped brilliance, curious, some shadows gnashed.

"Something Glenville said—" Jocko said, quietly.

Roberts saw a body push through the drapes. Brooke had grappled up, grabbed his sleeve, staring at the moon-flooded scene, drapes moving as the figure of a boy darted through an opening in the fabric, staggered near the parapet, groping at stone. Brooke spilled tea on the floor, they could hear the clatter of the china, Jocko quiet, frozen, Roberts feeling the twitch of his muscles, behind the neck, a finger of cold on his spine. Jocko was staring at him with a wide-eyed terror. They could see a small form tumble over the parapet and fall in silence, arms fluttering like broken wings, one leg stretched straight out, the other under his body, an unusual broken pose.

"My God—" Brooke said.

"Wim!" Jocko screamed. "Wim!"

They watched the boy strike ground; there was an eerie silence.

"Jocko, listen," Roberts said. He could feel the boy tremble, his shoulders moving. "Run downstairs straight to Glenville and telephone for Jacob Miles and an ambulance. Do it quickly. Don't hesitate, don't be frightened, just do it now." Jocko was still staring at Roberts, his eyes full of tears. Then he jumped and ran through the door and was gone.

"I'm going to the boy," Brooke said. He had already started for the door, Roberts behind, both of them going down the stairs, bounding two at a time. They went out the double doors in the stone wall and stood in the quadrangle. Roberts watched the doctor cross the stone paths, then he himself ran west through a stone portal. Behind him, he could hear Brooke puffing across the quad, toward the fallen boy.

Roberts hurried up a grassy hill, the river before him in blade silver. He waited for his eyes to adjust, it was very dark, the moon hidden behind some towers, and then he could see all of the river, the bridges, the elaborate film of the trees across the way in the Backs. He rested against the stone Harlow walls, feeling the coldness on his back, moving slowly down the river in the shadows, toward Trinity Bridge. He felt as if every nerve were on fire, this burning rage of sensibility, he could hear himself draw breath, all the bridges parabolas, configurations in black, the Backs full of willows in dark motion, wavy grass, the river rippled by the trails of swimming swans. He strained forward, still moving south, more stone walls, it became something that collected around him like a shroud—low crouched, then running, a faint slash in the dark. Roberts could sense that something had moved on the bridge and he began to run, gaining the first incline of the Trinity Bridge, stopping to hold on to the buttresses for support, he could hear his heart. Then he knew, he could see a figure running between the willows out on the Backs, maybe forty meters ahead, this dark comma.

Roberts knew there was someone running. Something was vibrating against his perception, it was like he had become a binary, a collapsed star, something sucking his energy, something *there*. He could smell the river now, he could feel it move, he was sweating, but he felt the calculus of attraction, as if there were a thin wire connecting him to the figure. He had just reached the apex of the bridge when he felt the connection break, it cracked, and a tiny web of pain swelled in his head, his arms grew heavy, it was as though there was a fluid swelling inside himself that made him stagger against the stone railing. It was peaceful then, and he paused to gaze down at the water, he could hear the swans honking clearly, some of them swimming in circles while events became fringed and uncertain, as if a film were covering everything. It reversed, the feelings of peace, and he felt then as if he were being crushed by centrifugal motion, a force that threw him away from his center. His head held flashes, his mouth felt dry, without saliva.

Roberts gulped deep breaths, supporting himself with two hands on the bridge rail. He felt nauseated, his body numb.

He groped back across the bridge, down the grassy slope, trying to act from recent memory, feeling his way down the Harlow walls until he staggered back through the portal, toward Brooke, who was huddled over the fallen boy.

Brooke had made a pillow for Wim's head from his tweed coat, and he was working over the lad, looking up, touching the boy's face. Roberts sat down on the grass, Indian-style, trying to support himself with an arm. "What's happened?" Brooke said, gasping, peering at Roberts through the dark. Roberts could see Wim on the ground in the moonlight with one leg twisted under him, one eye open, a terrible gleaming vacancy in it.

Roberts followed his own vomit to the ground. He looked up at Brooke's face in moonlight, a sky filled with moths, green puppets dancing. Brooke said something, faraway syllables, but in Robert's dreams cities were aflame, hailstorms of fire, Brooke saying, "What's happened, what's happened?" Roberts falling into a single open eye.

WEDNESDAY, DECEMBER 4

WHEN he found that his son had been lost, presumed killed in the war, Martin Brooke concocted an arrangement with Death. He would not have likened it to a rapprochement, old enemies suddenly becoming allies as they glared at one another across the shiny surface of the conference table; nor, in his medical manner, had Brooke either accepted or understood Death. But in those long cold moments when he stood shaving before his mirror in the quarters he then held at Harlow School, steam clanking in the pipes and the old room smelling only of himself, sweat and leather and pipe tobacco, and the unwashed bedclothes in a lump, he knew he had not surrendered either, nor had he even sailed around Death as a helmsman might steer around a threatening squall. The telegram, commencing, "THE WAR OFFICE IS SORRY . . ." had convinced him that he and Death were two wary companions whose friendship no longer worked, perhaps because one had married a woman the other did not trust, but, no matter, both the friendship and the hurt were too deep to forget. At Harlow, Martin Brooke treated sprained knees, bronchitis, maladies requiring a few stitches, some words to calm a boy who was frightened, doses of castor oil. Martin Brooke had walked away from Death, toward the children whose imaginations had not even begun to contemplate an End, who had not even an intimation of Mortality. He and Death were friendly strangers, each caught up in a there-was-a-time haze, mates who

96

must have wondered, across the crowded room, how things were going, if there had been successes, failures perhaps, but unable to ask.

And then his lovely wife had died. Suddenly, the arrangement, as he called it, no longer worked. Brooke, alone in his rooms, in his bachelor sitter near Christ's Pieces, was haunted and tortured by Death. He had been felled like an old beech in the forest and he came crashing down with his rings exposed. Thereafter, Martin Brooke conceded the supremacy of Death in all things, with good will, and fortitude, his Englishness unrepentant, and he affected a *professional* attitude, as if he were a barrister nodding to another of his profession in the courtroom after a lost battle. Death had achieved a huge judgment against Brooke, but remaining was the respect and courtesy due one member of the fraternity to another. There was no question of an arrangement, however, no rapprochement, no forgotten friendship to rue. There was only the baleful acknowledgment that Brooke would plead his case and fight his cause, and that Death would win the judgment and each would thereafter politely nod. Yet, something seemed unfair to Brooke in the deaths of Wim van Euwe and of Jono, and it had disheartened him beyond measure. Death had not only won but had practiced outside the rules, unethically, and this Martin Brooke could not acknowledge with a polite remonstrance for a job well done. This was no accident, no horrible prefigurement of God's will, and Brooke's anger with his colleague was huge.

That night, Brooke had seen shadows on the drapes, mere veiled shapes, undetailed motions against a backdrop of light that circumscribed an arc, then a downward motion, in tones and hues too vague to calculate. The drapes had parted, shafts of light had escaped, and then the boy's arm drifted outside, like a tongue, and then Brooke swore he saw the drapes ruffle ever so slightly behind the boy, even though the boy had passed through, and likewise, he swore, he heard no sound come from the boy, although he was tumbling by then backward over the stone parapet, not quite gone yet, but *there,* seated on the edge of his monstrous fall, and without a sound, a tiny peep, the slightest call. It was unnatural. The quadrangle had been unimaginably quiet, and the boy had fallen in slow motion, or so it seemed to Brooke, first stumbling back through the drapes, the drapes parted as if by a zephyr, the boy's arm uncontrolled as he went over, and then the long moon-swept fall with the stars whispering and the aching tumble as the boy obeyed the laws of nature.

Brooke had spilled his tea, he had grabbed the American's sleeve. He would be able to describe the terror on the boy's face as he approached the window, with Jocko screaming, Jocko calling Wim's name as the boy tumbled and dropped like a plumb with one leg curled under his body and his arms absolutely flying. Brooke had dropped his teacup to the floor, shattering the saucer, and at that same horrifying moment Win van Euwe struck the earth with a muffled thud, and he did not move.

At the moment Wim van Euwe went over the parapet, Brooke thought of his wife. She had died at hospital in Cambridge. He remembered her white face against the pillow, how it had seemed too oval, unreal, bathed in a lick of sweat, her existence dripping away through plastic tubes, the stale sweat of the room, and the fecund, parasitic smell of hothouse roses. When Wim van Euwe fell, Brooke's old heart had jumped, and his eyes had seen his wife, and his son's stone at the cemetery, and he knew he had misjudged Death's proportion, the magnificent ill will, the malice, and he could feel his hands digging into Roberts's shirt, clinging to something, as if he could save the boy by his reflexes. He remembered Jocko screaming and screaming.

He heard Roberts send Jocko away with instructions, and almost instantly he set his mind to a task. Then Brooke was out the door, taking the smoothly worn stairs in the turret house, through which dropped moonlight as thick as wool, striking the cold stone walls and sinking in. Footsteps were pounding in the hall below, Jocko crying for Glenville, his voice an echo in the wilderness halls of the old building, and

Brooke's hands began to shake and sweat. His shirt was wet, and all he could think of then was that he didn't have his black bag of instruments, though deep in his professional mind he knew Win van Euwe would need a surgeon if he were to survive. He was no surgeon, no internist. This was no sprained knee, no cough. Nor was he a priest.

When he reached the door on the first floor, he opened it and stood still. He saw Roberts heave around a corner and disappear through the stone portal that faced the Cam on the west. He had hurried across the quad, his mind blank again, and reached the boy, whose body lay in a fine mist, which had been nearly invisible from the upper stories. Wim was on the stone walk, one arm under his body, a kind of broken X form with a trickle of blood at his ear. Brooke made a pillow from his jacket, tucked it under the boy's head, and then checked for a pulse, felt the boy's forehead, and opened his one closed eye, staggering back when he saw the pupil. He noticed a sawline of light coming from beneath the drapes to Wim's room, he listened for a heartbeat, felt for a pulse, and then he heard Roberts coming back across the quad, breathing heavily. He turned, said "What happened?" to Roberts, who lay in a heap. Then looked back at the fallen boy whose hands were like bone in the moonlight.

Brooke kept a bed-sitter on Emmanuel Lane, directly across from the city hospital, red and gray brick on the verge of Christ's Pieces. In the morning sun, the windows were lemon-colored through to a park, and a slash of green and a puffy fringe of clouds on the horizon above the Fens. Traffic buzzed along the roadway below, and Brooke was playing classical music on the BBC Midlands. When Roberts woke, the doctor was watering some African violets, shuffling around the tiny room in slippers, wearing a baggy Shetland sweater and woolen pants. He propped himself on the arm of a couch and watched Brooke water his plants, a can of water in one hand and a cup of coffee in the other, skiffing noises on the hooked rugs.

"Well hello," Brooke said to Roberts, seeing him awake at last. Roberts tried to push himself up against the arm of the couch, he could see his clothes hanging on the back of a chair across the room. There was a table and a sink, a ring fire for tea and a hot plate. Brooke came across the room and sat on one arm of the couch. "How do you feel?" he asked.

"Terrible," Roberts groaned. He could sense the mass of a blood-soaked bandage on his head, the right ear, the temple.

"You've been sleeping quite a lot. That's good for you in your present state."

"How did I get here?"

"Miles and I carried you here. Actually, we rather dragged you. Had no earthly idea what had happened to you, just saw a huge, ugly gash on your head. We thought it best to avoid English hospitals if you'd any chance of survival without them. Miles sat up with you most of the night while I've been busy."

"Wim?" Roberts asked, bleary, the starkness of lost memory overtaking him suddenly. He had an odd, cracked feeling, an enormous headache. In spite of it, he could remember Wim, the boy's open eye, the fall.

"How much do you remember? Do you remember the fall?"

"Yes, pretty well."

"Do you remember running off toward the Backs?"

"Yes, I made the Trinity Bridge."

"Do you remember returning to the quadrangle and collapsing in a heap?"

"Vaguely," Roberts answered, falling back. "But what about the boy? Is he all right?"

Brooke returned to the ring and made a cup of coffee. He made Roberts have a taste, it was very bitter and strong. Brooke sat down again on the arm of the couch.

"Wim van Euwe is dead," Brooke said. "He was alive when I reached him on the quad. His pulse was very weak, clearly in shock. By the time Miles and the ambulance arrived, he was gone. There was nothing I could have done, nothing anybody could have done. Then I found you behind me on the ground with a bloody gash on your forehead."

Roberts put two feet on a hooked rug, tried to sit up and was engulfed in nausea. There was a wild ringing in his ears. He tried to drink some coffee, but it only made him sick, and he stretched out on the couch. Brooke went to his telephone for Constable Miles, and then returned with a cup of coffee for himself. Roberts was lost in diagonals of thought, the falling boy, the awful silence of the night, at the apex of Trinity Bridge.

"Miles will be right along," Brooke announced. "We may as well save our breath for him. He'll want to hear your story anyway." Brooke had been wearing a small white apron around his waist. He loosed the drawstrings and tossed the apron aside.

"What's being done about Wim?" Roberts asked.

"He's at hospital, poor lad. Nothing to be done. Boy fell on his back and head, suffered massive injuries, I'm afraid. He was terribly injured in that way. Shame he lived at all, even for so short a time as that. We carried you here, then left you with one of the orderlies while Miles and I accompanied the boy to the hospital. I went back to the quadrangle in time to see the ambulance take him away. I hurried to the hospital, but the boy was gone. Miles spent part of the night talking with everyone in Harlow School, then came back and sat up with you. There are still a few boys who haven't gone home yet, but nobody saw or heard a thing. I haven't seen Miles today, but I doubt he's learned very much."

"What were you doing last night?" Roberts asked.

"This time I did an autopsy," Brooke said flatly. "This time I did a thorough examination."

"And the boy's parents?"

"I don't know," Brooke said. "We'll ask Miles. That's his sad bailiwick, I'm afraid."

"Can we trust Miles?" Roberts asked.

"I would say yes, absolutely," Brooke said.

"We can talk freely with him?"

"Why, yes." Brooke blustered a bit and drank some of his coffee. The bed-sitter had moved into shadow, suddenly, it took Roberts by surprise, its nearly perfect square papered in Victorian yellow and white, and the floor covered by gay hooked rugs. Roberts could see an icebox the size of a foot-locker on the floor, under the table, and an electric fire made into the wall. Brooke had a small bed in another corner, and some books on a shelf, the radio. To Roberts it was all very English, and quite lonely. "But I don't really know whom to trust," Brooke said quietly, looking away. He furrowed a brow. "I have no direct estimation about what's happening here. I did not think I'd live to see the day when two children died mysteriously at Harlow, children I know. Now that I've seen it, I'm actually quite useless to deal with it. Your chap Hemingway once wrote that not even the Eskimo have such a small vocabulary as the English aristocracy. He was right. I have no words." Brooke paused and listened to the radio. "I've known Miles for a very long time," he continued. "He has a wife and two children and he lives in a cottage on the edge of town. He's no simpleton, and he's quite independent. He has a good head too, mind you. I don't know what else to say."

"It's just that I'm frightened, and suspicious."

"I quite agree," Brooke said.

"I'm angry too."

"About the boy, yes. I don't see how he could have stumbled and fallen backward off the parapet. It must be three feet from the window to the edge of the balcony. It would nearly require a running start to fall that far forward. I know I've told you that death is circumstantial. A fall. A drowning." Here the doctor looked away at Christ's Pieces, the church and school bearing away small straw-colored clouds, halos of pigeons dancing in the air. "I'm suspicious too, Yank. But I did examine the boy. The cause of death was a massive skull fracture, broken back, and internal injuries. He was crushed in the fall, no doubt. He had some scrapes, normal for a boy who played attacker at Harlow football. Was he the victim of

102

another unfortunate accident, or did he suffer from foul play?"

"Well, which is it?"

"I don't know, but I do know that I found some very peculiar things during the autopsy. I'd like for Miles to be here when I explain them to you, then he can hear them as well, as he must."

There was a tap at the door, which Brooke answered. Miles followed the doctor into the room, pulled up a chair from the table and sat down. He was very trim, athletic-looking in his blue uniform with gold buttons, holding an officer's cap in his hands, juggling it between his knees. Something about him impressed Roberts very much, the gray eyes, the freckled ruddy skin, how he sat very straight in his chair. His hair was clipped short, and didn't seem to have a color.

"Glad you're up," Miles said to Roberts. "You've had quite a go of it."

"Thank you, both of you," Roberts said. He was dressed in a bathrobe, a quilt over his legs. He tried to drink some coffee. Miles continued to play with his cap.

"I want to get your view," Miles said. "Brooke has told me of your interest in Jonathan Smith. I must say how sorry I am about the boy, his death, the rotten mess of things here. I've spent yesterday talking with students, with Glenville, and I've scoured every square inch of the Backs and the bridges with my men. I've even spoken officially with Ambrose Marseden, who you probably remember."

"I believe I do. He probably remembers me as well."

"I'm certain he does," Miles said, smiling slightly. "For your information he is sporting quite an egg on his ear. Looks like a bloody red cabbage. But I also know that both he and his boy were home the evening of Jonathan's death. In fact, I'm certain of it. Brooke here told me of your suspicions and I took the liberty of checking on them thoroughly. I'm in possession of information that shows Marseden and his boy at a football match in the county. There are twenty or thirty people who will vouch for him being there on the night young Jonathan Trench died. I'm afraid that is a blind alley."

"I was thinking so, too," Roberts said.

"But we've got something terrible on our hands, I'm convinced of that." Miles studied his hat for a time, thinking. He declined Brooke's offer of coffee, then ran his hand over the stubble of his hair. "Brooke has told me what he saw in the quad. Now, you tell me what *you* saw."

"I was with Brooke and Jocko," Roberts said, started, and looked quickly at Brooke. "My God, what about Jocko?"

"Don't fret," Brooke said. "I've sent Jocko home to his mother in London. Put him on the train myself, along with all of Jono's things. Jocko was holding together pretty well considering. Amazing chap."

"Good," Roberts said. Miles was staring at him, waiting. "We could all see across the quadrangle to Wim's room. It was a moonlit night, but some clouds too. We were drinking tea, watching the night. Jocko was playing chess. It so happened that Brooke and I had pulled up our chairs right to the window. I remember seeing some shadows, then I was curious. It looked as if there were more than one person in the room. I don't know why I say that, there's nothing I can tell you about except for movement, the shadows. Then we saw the drapes part and the boy's arm appear. Outstretched. Maybe it was limp, I don't know. Then his body just seemed to appear. I would swear he was propelled over the parapet, but I can't be certain how I'd explain the feeling. Then he fell."

"Pushed, you would say?" Miles asked.

"Yes, it seemed that way to me. I saw nothing definite, only a yellow background of drape, and then the boy came through. How could he stumble over such a balcony?"

"How indeed?" Miles said. "Brooke has said much the same thing. But this isn't evidence. At best it is supposition and opinion. But please go on."

"I told Jocko to go to Glenville's and call for you and for an ambulance. He went off fast. I went down the stairs right behind Brooke, and I remember going past Brooke on my way out the stone portals through to the Cam. I shinnied my way down the wall, trying to keep quiet and in shadows, then went west and then back down toward Trinity Bridge."

"Why did you do that?"

"Well, I thought that if my hunch was right, that there had been someone in the room with the boy, then I might see him come out the turret stairs on the other side of the wall. I thought perhaps the person might be on the grounds, and that he could run down the riverbank, or cross into town and go down the High Street. Either way, I thought if I could reach the south wall of the school, I could see for myself if there was anyone there."

"You're assuming in all this that the Dutch lad was in fact pushed. Murdered."

"Yes, it amounts to that."

"Anything else?"

"Frankly, I was thinking about Jonathan. How he was found on the opposite side of the river, near the bank, where it goes uphill into the Backs."

"Yes, I imagine you were. But you believe the death of the Dutch boy and young Trench's drowning are connected?"

"Yes, I believe they are."

"Do you know how?"

"I haven't the foggiest idea. I don't know, I don't even know what happened to me on the bridge. All I know is that I walked through the stone portal on the west side of Harlow. I could see the Clare Bridge to the south along the river, though there was a smudge of mist on the bank. Trinity Bridge was clear in the moonlight, and I thought I saw something move across the bridge, running, a shape, perhaps somebody crouched very low. I don't know, I had the impression of a person wearing a hat. It was just a whisper of movement, and then I ran after the figure and got to the top of the bridge and stopped still to try to listen, take a good look at the Backs in the dark. I stood there for a time, not very long

I don't think. But I do remember thinking there was some-body moving across the Backs, in the willows.

"Somebody? Can you be more accurate?"

"A human form. A blocked hat. That's all."

"Then what?"

"I'm not sure. I was hoping you would tell me. I thought I heard something, like the buzzing of a bee or the whine of gunfire. Then I felt a terrible flash of pain in my head. It was like all of my muscles suddenly had gone limp. It stopped me flat. Then I had an eerie feeling that somebody in the Backs was watching me. I had the notion I was connected to the figure on the hillside, but by then I was feeling like I was going to pass out. Sick as hell. I remember resting on the abutment for a moment, watching the swans in the river. The moonlight was actually hurting my eyes, believe it or not, and I began to become disoriented. I remember thinking how absolutely strange it all was, and then I began to sweat terribly and my heart started racing, it was as if I was having a heart attack. Then I just got sick as hell, it was all I could do to walk down the bridge and hug the wall all the way back to the quadran-gle. I angled toward Brooke, or where I thought Brooke was, and then I blacked out. I had terrible dreams about cities of flame. Then I woke up here. That's all I know."

Miles took a deep breath. He had been sitting stock-straight on his chair, but he sat back, perhaps deflated somewhat by the story. "That's the end of it?" he said, a little sadly.

"The end," Roberts answered.

"You didn't see anything more on the hillside?"

"I think I've told you everything."

"And here we are," Brooke said, across the room. He had been listening with his back turned, looking out the window at Cambridge in the forenoon. "The Yank lost consciousness and slept all night. It's amazing he remembers as much as he does, considering what's happened to him."

"What the hell did happen to me?" Roberts said.

Miles tapped his hat on the chair edge. He continued to do it as he spoke. "We thought perhaps you simply fell and struck your head. Brooke here tells me that you've suffered a fairly severe concussion. It's a wonder that you made it back to the quadrangle in the condition you were in. There is about a five-inch gash in your forehead, above the eye, all the way to the bone. Brooke put in about sixteen stitches, bloody good job too. You'll be black and blue for a few weeks, but you should be fine. What?"

Brooke said, "Right as rain."

"I didn't fall," Roberts said flatly.

"Of course not," Miles said, tapping his hat. "This morning I took five men and went over the bridge piece by piece. There is about a four-inch section of stone missing from the south portion of the rail. It's been chipped away. We found it lying on the pathway. It has some of your blood on it."

"I didn't bang my head. No way."

"I've told you. I quite agree."

"I have the distinct impression that I heard a buzzing noise. Constable, I've been under fire before. I've heard bullets going past. It's not a sound you'd likely forget, once you've heard it."

"I believe you. Brooke and I are assuming that somebody took a shot at you. Missed. Hit the bridge. Depending upon how you view the matter, you had the bad fortune to be struck by a good-sized chunk of flint as the bullet tore it away. Good luck for you the bullet missed you."

"But we can't prove that."

"No, of course not. To find the bullet would be a terribly long chance. One in a million. Not even worth the effort."

"Which leads us to the question, Why?"

"Why indeed?" Miles said, glancing at Brooke.

Church bells had begun ringing noon. There was an overcast sky, like cake frosting.

Miles said, "And what possible motive could anyone have for murdering poor Wim van Euwe, this harmless little boy?"

"And Jono, as well."

"I'm less convinced that Jono was murdered. But I've an open mind. There are certainly numerous questions that need answers. When you're well enough, I'd like to show you something in my office."

Brooke came over to where the two men were talking. "With a good rest, you'll be fine. Matter of sleep," he said. "But I think we should talk about my autopsy of the Dutch lad. I don't make sense of some of it."

Miles stiffened again, tapping his hat faster, making clicks on the surface. "Speak up, Doctor," he said.

"Something had afflicted the boy before he fell," Brooke began.

"Afflicted," Miles said. It was hardly a question, more an expression of complexity.

"Malady, affliction, whatever you will call it. In addition to the trauma of the fall, which was quite evident, I found evidence of a foreign substance in the muscles. Technically speaking, I believe the little boy was suffering from symptoms of locomotor ataxia. A mild form, no doubt, but paralysis nonetheless. This finding is what you'd call anomalous. This means that it is out of keeping with my expectations, though it was not a cause of death."

"Ataxia?" Roberts asked.

"Yes, paralysis," Brooke said dully.

"What on earth?" Miles muttered.

"Yes, I'm certain of it," Brooke continued. "I found evidence of a substance in the muscle tissues of the arm, right arm. Its presence was first detected in the blood samples, an unusual form of paralytic. I would have to say that it would be something like the novocaine commonly used by dentists. This suggests that the poor lad was in some mild form of unconsciousness when he died. I can't be certain of this finding, and I certainly have no idea what this substance is, but it was definitely present in the blood and muscle samples."

"This is outrageous," Miles said.

"There is more," Brooke said. "When I examined the boy further I found what appeared to be a small puncture wound in the neck, just above the right shoulder joint. I can't be certain that this was the method of delivery, if that's what it was, but that finding too is anomalous. A puncture wound, and the presence of a paralytic."

"Bloody hell," Miles said.

"It wasn't much of a wound," Brooke said. "A pinprick. And I'm afraid that as a doctor I couldn't swear before a coroner's jury that this pinprick had anything at all to do with the paralytic. We have here a lot of anomalous facts."

With an effort, Roberts got to his feet, shuffling past Miles to the window. He could see some punters on the river, driving down the water with long poles. The sky was gray, clouds out over the Fens.

"Sit down for a minute," Miles said to Roberts. "This seems rather improbable, but you both need to see something. And improbable is an understatement." Roberts fell back to the sofa, Brooke pulled up a chair next to Miles. They were in a tight circle.

Miles reached inside the jacket of his police coat, unfolding a white handkerchief. He was holding a covered petri dish, which he opened slowly. They could see a thin pin of coral on top of a ball of cotton. There were some dark swirls on the pin, four gray indentions on one end. Brooke had leaned over Miles's shoulder, studying the pin. It looked to Roberts about two inches long.

"Found this in Wim's room," Miles said. "On the floor. Didn't have a clue what it was. Still don't. But I think what Brooke here is saying is important."

"What the hell is it?" Roberts muttered. "Painted swirls, pink coral. Jesus."

"Run your finger along the pin," Miles suggested to Roberts who touched the pin. He could feel the small grooves. "We've had this examined. In fact, I've taken a peep at it under a microscope. The spirals you see aren't painted at all. They've been etched there very carefully in a pattern all the way around the pin. It's just that the shell color is different under the surface. The four gray marks are actually small bits of iron buried in the shell, which below the surface is a different color. I'd say the swirls are like a rifle bore. The iron pieces stabilizers. This bloody thing would be perfectly aero-dynamic."

"Like an arrow," Roberts said.

"A bullet," Brooke added.

"Quite so," Miles said. "Or a dart."

Brooke helped Roberts dress in his lumberjack shirt, his boots. They stood at the window and looked at the city, the river, swans swimming circles.

"Never seen anything like this in my life," Miles said, as if to himself.

WEDNESDAY, DECEMBER 4
LATE AFTERNOON

JACOB Miles snapped his suspenders, smart gray ones clipped to his suit pants by silver buckles. Sitting there in the murky light of the police cafeteria, he was wearing a board-hard navy blue shirt with black buttons, running his finger inside his shirt collar, as if he were about to choke. There were light gray gloves stuck through the epaulets on his left shoulder, and instead of making him seem officious, they made him look to Roberts like a small boy wearing an Easter outfit against his will, as if he couldn't wait to go home and put on some dungarees and play in the mud. In the dim light, his hair had color now, pale sandstone, perfectly trimmed at right angles to his ears. He still bore himself very straight, and very well, though Roberts thought the tips of his ears were strangely crimson. The three men were trying to have some lunch, cabbage and beef, in the basement commissary at police headquarters in Cambridge. Roberts felt light-headed, abstract, and he had a terrible headache. Brooke had insisted he stay in bed, but Roberts had struggled out, he was that worried, confused and frightened as well, in an emotional state beyond noticing the pain.

Some constables and orderlies were finishing their meals, carrying trays, chatting quietly, while across the room two women carried trays down a glass case along metal bars, smoking cigarettes. It was warm and dense in the cafeteria, and the cigarette smoke swam up the staircase, settled in a

111

bleary gauze. There was a picture of the Queen on the wall across from Roberts, he could see her smiling down, looking very self-possessed. One of the charwomen was brooming the floor, Roberts had to pick up his feet, she was smoking and chewing gum at the same time. It made him swoon. It was getting to him, the smoke and the smell of boiled cabbage. He was starting to fade in and out, he could barely hear what Brooke and Miles were saying.

Miles walked to the teapot on the serving line and drew another pot of strong tea, oolong, Roberts thought inconsequentially. Brooke poured himself a cup and ate some apple crumble. On the wall near the serving line was a batch of official-looking plaques, announcements, wanted posters, and regulations, all printed under the sign of the Crown in tiny type. Brooke had changed into a white shirt and shooting-jacket ensemble, but he appeared weary from his long night and day. Roberts stared at his green cabbage, the boiled stringy beef, and pushed it away. Brooke and Miles exchanged glances. "Falling behind, Yank," Brooke said.

"I'm sure the food is good," Roberts mumbled. "But I haven't quite gotten back on my feed."

"Good English beef and cabbage," Brooke said, tapping his meerschaum with an index finger. Miles smiled sympathetically, Roberts noticing that his eyes were quite pointedly brilliant. He picked up a manila envelope and began to tap it on the table top, rhythmically, the way he had tapped his hat on the chair, a nervous habit.

"This document," Miles said, tapping the envelope twice for effect, "is the official report from the toxicologist concerning the coral shell pin found in Wim van Euwe's room, Brooke suggested we send blood and tissue samples as well, to a fellow at the Museum of Ethnology here in Cambridge. So you'll know, he's been at it all day. The museum is connected to the School of Tropical Diseases in London. Quite good, really."

"Tropical d-diseases?" Roberts stuttered.

"The same. Quite a famous institute. I agreed when Brooke here suggested it."

"Remember our perfect world," Brooke said. "The circumstances of Jono's death were unenviably plain to me at the time. I made a simple judgment. Now that I know more about the circumstances surrounding Wim van Euwe's death, the examination calls for more analysis. Right off, I conducted an autopsy. Strange results. Anomalous. But now we have a toxology report. We decided to get this report because of the unknown nature of the paralyzing agent in the boy's muscles and blood. Sent it over to a fellow who has hacked his way around the world's rain forests studying bark or some such bloody nonsense. He's looking for new medicines, muscle relaxants, depressants, stuff of that sort. Knows everything there is to know about toxins, too. Bloody knowledgeable chap." Brooke opened the envelope and took out a document, handwritten in tiny script, about two pages long.

"You can read this?" Roberts said, noticing the dense, nearly indecipherable hand. Miles had gone to the serving line for apple crumble, returning with a plate piled high with custard and pie. He got after it like a bulldog.

"Doctors can read anything," Brooke said. Roberts felt woozy again, thinking about the English and their food, this wonderful people fond of dogs and gardens and long walks, all this barbaric food. Only an Englishman would cook a brussels sprout until it was mush, and only an Englishman would eat sheeps' intestines wrapped in gut and call it a delicacy. Brooke had lit his pipe, put the match out in some custard. He had picked up the report and was studying it closely. "Fellow at the museum is named Winston Carnes. I've known him for years, though he's away from England much of the time. Worked most of his life in tropical medicine, and so he's run up against some pretty singular mysteries in his time, treating huge annelids in the intestine, ameba, skin diseases. I didn't ask him for this report because what happened was so strange, but because I thought he would be interested in the coral pin, the circumstances of its discovery. And because if

I'm right and there is a paralytic toxin present, he should be able to isolate its properties. I've seen him work wonders with some of our boys back from Burma. His pharmacology is first-rate, as well."

"Forgive me, Doctor. What the hell is in the report?"

"Right you are," Brooke said. "Sorry. I'm so used to talking to Harlow boys that I forget how to speak with adults at times." He smiled, tamped his pipe. The char had finished her brooming, and they were nearly alone. "At any rate, to make a long story short, I sent the blood and tissue samples, along with the pin, because I wanted a pure examination. His opinion is as unbiased as you could want. In an imperfect world, that is."

"And what is it?" Roberts asked.

"There was a toxin present. Just as I thought. More properly one should say, a poison."

"A poison?" Roberts repeated, hushed.

"Exactly," Brooke said.

"What the hell . . ."

"Carnes has identified several substances that may be the agent. He is clear that he can't say with certainty right now which one of the substances it was. He needs more of the toxin."

"And what are the possibilities?" Roberts asked. He was thinking that Miles had read the report. The man was sitting over his apple crumble, faintly distracted, lost in thought.

Brooke spread the report on the table, running his eyes over the first page. "Now let me see," he began, laying down his meerschaum. "Curare," he said. "The first toxin Carnes mentions is curare."

"This is Tarzan stuff," Roberts said. "I can't believe you're serious."

"I'm quite serious," Brooke said, annoyed. "But you're off base with your Tarzan opinion. Curare is South American in origin. Carnes writes that it is a substance prepared from the bark of certain trees found in the Amazon basin. Curare would produce mild ataxia, numbness of the limbs, slackness

114

in consciousness as well. Medical science, for example, uses the toxin to treat spastic paralysis and tetanus. In either case, the muscles of the body are subject either to spasms or rigidity, and the curare obviates the symptoms. Carnes knows his curare, he's an expert."

"You said it was only one of the possibilities."

"That's correct," Brooke said. "The poison was found mostly in the muscle of Wim's arm. Apparently this toxin leaves the nervous system relatively untouched. The effects would be helplessness, nausea, disorientation, but no real loss of consciousness. According to Carnes the problem of exact identification is complicated because several tropical organic compounds share very similar chemical characteristics, plant originated, same molecular structure, same symptomatics. The tiny amount is a problem spectrographically as well."

"Let's get to the bottom of this," Roberts said.

"We're all interested," Miles said, looking up from the table. He had begun to tap a spoon, *tap, tap, tap.*

"I'm sorry," Roberts said. "I'm upset."

"Never mind, my boy," Brooke said.

"What other possibilities?" Roberts asked. He had begun to sweat, feel faint, his head banging.

"Some form of the genus *Phytolaca*," Brooke said. "I'm afraid it's all beyond my ken. Carnes indicates that this plant genus is a tropical and subtropical variety found in many parts of the world at those latitudes. Each form of the plant bears a different local name, and each tribe or people commonly use the plant differently, but all to the same end. It is called pokeweed in your Virginia, the pocan, red ink plant, dozens of other names. If you're interested Carnes lists some more of those names in his report. It is crystalline in form."

"How is it different from curare?" Roberts asked.

"The *Phytolaca* is primarily medicinal in use, less astringent and less toxic than curare in the same dosage. Curare is strong enough to be an exclusive poison. The phytolacan is milder, more euphoric in nature."

"But it could paralyze?"

"Most definitely, according to Carnes."

"My God, what else?" Roberts gasped, feeling disoriented.

"Well," Brooke said, "something Carnes describes as snakeroot."

"Sounds medieval."

"Wrong locale," Brooke responded. "Snakeroot is North American. It is the rhizome, or root if you will, of a number of related plants used by Native American tribes. It is a boiled extraction, much like an herb concoction, traditionally used by Indians to treat snakebite. Hence, the name. It acts by producing local paralysis, thus antipodal to the venom. Carnes describes this genus of plant as a birthwort. Bloody helpful, what?"

"Bloody," Roberts said. "So what do we have? A sticky preparation from South America. A crystal from anywhere in the world. An herb used by North American Indians. Do either of you understand any of this nonsense?"

Miles said nothing, tapping his spoon. Brooke sucked on his meerschaum. Finally Miles said, "Brooke and I have tried to think about this all day. We've just felt a need to take stock. If young Wim and Jonathan have come to foul play, I need to take some action. My job is to apply for warrants, make inquiries, bring this matter to the attention of the courts. As for myself, I'm certainly willing to bring this matter to the attention of the magistrate, but frankly I have no idea what I'd say. I have no evidence that these two deaths are linked, and if they are, what links them. I have no real evidence that there was any occurrence beyond a wild accident. The only thing odd is that someone took a shot at you. And even this is only an assumption. But what happened to you on the bridge last evening is most unusual, an assault under very bizarre circumstances. It will leave me with an open case on young van Euwe, but nothing on Jonathan. None of it provides any suspects, any motives, no hint of suspicion, and this is what the magistrate needs to proceed. I simply can't go to the courts without evidence. I presume we know of no motive for anyone to kill either of the children."

"None whatsoever," Roberts said. "Jono was loved by everybody."

"It's true," said Brooke.

"Right, well," Miles said, snapping his suspenders. "I want you both to come upstairs to my office. I want to show you something else which may pertain to the present inquiry."

They carried their dishes to the serving line and left them in a pile for the orderlies. They walked up the stairs to the police station, a single large wood-paneled room with big dirty windows, a waxy smell. Miles had an office in one corner, glassed in, a small desk, some file cabinets and two wooden chairs in front of the desk. You could see out two big windows behind the desk down two side streets of Cambridge. Some white checkered police cars were parked catercornered from the station house, the streets very quiet, the sky ice-white with thin clouds. One young officer was clacking away at a typewriter in the background. Miles hung his uniform coat on a rack behind the desk and sat down. Brooke and Roberts took the wooden chairs.

"Now then," Miles said, reading from a spiral notebook. "Just so you'll know, Mr. Roberts, several of my men spent some long hours scouring the Backs. We didn't find a trace of any footprints. The grass was wet, but it is also quite thick. We think your man, if it was a man at all, probably went across the Backs and had a car. He may have had an accomplice for all we know, or he may have been alone."

"And in your search of Wim's room?" Roberts asked.

"We did a thorough job. We found no fingerprints save those of the lads. Brooke has already informed you about the autopsy. From this end the investigation of the physical facts is complete. Wim van Euwe died in the fall. He was alive when he went out the window, over the parapet. There were, however, some wet spots on the rug in his room. So there may have been someone in the room with him that night, but we found no mud or grass at all. For that matter, the wet spots may have been made by Wim's shoes."

"Did you examine his shoes?"

"Yes, of course. They were wet."

"Then we have nothing." Roberts sighed.

"Perhaps," Miles said. "It cannot be discounted that Wim van Euwe was alone in his room. He had been out in the wet grass and tracked home some dew. He tumbled over the parapet quite accidentally." Miles began snapping his suspenders again. Roberts could see a vein in his neck. "But you see, we have absolutely nothing to connect the deaths of the two boys. Is that how it looks?"

Roberts leaned forward. The bandage bothered him, down over his eye, some of the blood crusting under the brow. "I think they were connected. And I'll be damned if I think Jono's death was an accident."

Miles smiled gravely. Brooke leaned forward too, puffing on his pipe. Miles opened his desk and took out another manila envelope, tied with string. He opened the folder and shook out a green puppet with a triangular head and hinged limbs. An absolutely featureless thing.

"It's Jono's puppet," Brooke said. "How did you get it?"

"No, you're wrong, Martin," Miles said. Brooke had taken up the puppet and was handling it. It seemed a different object to Roberts, of a different color and shape than he'd seen in Jono's things.

"I found this puppet in Wim's coat pocket. It is similar to the one found with Jonathan. Obviously. Of course, both boys may have owned the same toy. They may have seen these bloody things somewhere and gone off with two of them. They were mates. Chums do that sort of thing. I've had a man looking all over Cambridge for a store that sells things like this. He tells me he can't find anything like it in the whole bloody town."

"Neither Jocko nor Amanda had seen the puppet before," Roberts said, taking the puppet from Brooke.

"That's quite so," Brooke added. He glanced at Miles, who nodded slightly, imperceptibly. He put his hand back into the manila envelope and extracted a small piece of bone, two beeswax honeycombs, three black pebbles worn smooth into

118

fishhook shapes, and some cowrie shells strung together on fish line. The objects lay on the polished surface of the desk in halos of light. Nobody said a word for a long time.

"Finally we're at it," Miles said. "These I found on the floor of Wim's room. I made a diagram of the arrangement." He handed Roberts a sheet of paper with some ink markings of the placement of the objects. "I've chatted with Brian ap Rhys, but he doesn't remember the arrangement of the objects found on the riverbank at the time of young Jonathan's death. Of course, there is no reason he should. We certainly didn't make a diagram at the time. Even now, I have no reason to think that these things have even the slightest meaning."

"They must have significance," Roberts insisted.

"Ordinarily I wouldn't agree with you, Yank," Miles said. He picked up the objects from his desk, and put the manila folder back in a drawer. "But one of our rather well known criminal investigators once said that once you've exhausted the obvious looking for an explanation, the explanation must be what's not obvious, it might even be the illogical."

"That's fiction, my boy," Brooke said.

"This is real life," Roberts added.

"Nevertheless," Miles said. The vein in his neck was standing out, slightly red. "The same principles apply. And I'm bloody angry about these young boys."

"We'll get to the bottom of this, don't you fret," Brooke said. He patted Miles on the arm.

"Of course," Miles said, distractedly.

Brooke turned to Roberts. "You're more than welcome to stay with me tonight. I don't think you're hale enough to be out and about."

"Thank you, Doctor. I'll stay in Jocko's room tonight. I suppose I'll go back to London tomorrow. I don't see much for me to do right now, and I think I can get some sleep in Jocko's room. I don't imagine Glenville will mind."

"We'll do our job," Miles said stiffly. He rubbed his temple with his eyes closed. The young officer in the station was pounding on the typewriter. The silence surrounding the steady clicking seemed extraordinarily dense. It was like the end of the world to Roberts, as if all the people in Cambridge had suddenly disappeared and the sound of the typewriter marked their exit. Miles flicked his suspenders one last time, tapped his knuckles on the desk. They were marking time, lost in a miasma of their unknowing. A telephone rang, the young officer answered it, and began to speak in clipped tones, something they couldn't understand through the glass partition. Outside, a blue Ford sedan pulled to a stop, they could see it down the steps, two men got out and came inside the station house. One of the men was squarely built, distinguished-looking in a blue pin-striped suit with flecks of red in the weave, school tie. His shirt was an expensive French cuff job, his hair gray and silky. The man behind him peeped out of wire-rim glasses, wearing a bulky brown overcoat. The tall man in the blue suit walked right into Miles's cubicle and stood in the doorway.

"Clannahan," Miles said dully.

"Constable Miles," the stranger intoned, traces of irony in his manner. Clannahan had slightly ashen skin, dark silver muttonchops, an expensive Swiss watch with an alligator band. Roberts sensed the aroma of limewater, some bay. The man had a flattened nose with broad nostrils, a small scimitar-shaped scar under his left eye, at the corner. It was the kind of scar cricket players sometimes get when the ball takes a rough bounce, cuts open a gash.

"Glad to find you in," Clannahan said. Looking down like a man used to speaking from heights, mild theatrical inflection, the hint of drama, dark bass voice. Roberts noticed that Miles had not stood, his face turning red, the vein pounding. Brooke puffed at his meerschaum, though it was unlit. All the air seemed to have gone from the room.

"What can I do for the Home Office?" Miles said. He was staring straight at Clannahan, his body even stiffer than usual, as if dowels had been driven through his limbs. Roberts saw that the smaller man had retreated to the front door of the station house, standing in a slight breeze bundled in his brown overcoat, hands in pockets, staring outside at the blue Ford. There were two men in the backseat of the Ford.

"I came to inform you," Clannahan said, "as a matter of courtesy—"

"Get to it," Miles said, cutting Clannahan short.

"The Dutch lad van Euwe, we want him in Ipswich. It's a matter of foreign policy. There is a foreign government involved here. Very high-up stuff." Miles bridled visibly, Roberts thought he might fly off his chair. Brooke cut a quick glance at Roberts.

"Bloody hell," Miles said.

"Now, Constable," Clannahan said, smiling wryly. It was a very deprecatory smile, this scarecrow meant to frighten the poor birds away.

"I'm the authority here," Miles said flatly.

"The authority . . ." Clannahan said, his voice trailing. Roberts thought the man had a remarkably snide manner. "The authority is Her Majesty's government." He smiled, revealing capped white teeth. "I can assure you that the Home Office is operating at the very highest levels. The minister himself has been informed and approves."

Miles reddened more. He was cracking his knuckles. The young officer outside had put down his telephone and was listening intently.

"Then," Miles said calmly, "may I ask the cause of all this nonsense."

"Please, Constable," Clannahan said. "We'll need to do an immediate autopsy on the lad. His parents are influential. The body will be returned in a diplomatic channel."

"The bloody autopsy's been done," Miles said.

There was a moment of silence. Brooke nodded at Clannahan, smiled, tapped his meerschaum. Roberts had been studying the man further, the expensive diamond pin on his tie, the opal cuff links, real stones.

"I see," Clannahan said, looking at Brooke. "Then I'll expect to see the report in Ipswich." Brooke nodded, without looking at the man. "Try to see this from the perspective of the ministry." Clannahan seemed to be lecturing the room, affecting a slightly weary manner, explaining the situation to the help. "The death of a foreign boy, especially one whose parents are so important, is a matter of serious concern to the government. You're surely aware of the grave political problems in the Dutch government, the whole colonial mess. Naturally, the minister has deemed this unfortunate affair important enough to assign to me the direct responsibility of returning the boy's body to Holland as a government courtesy. As a matter of respect for the parties involved, what?" Clannahan was snapping his words as if they were salutes. "The Home Office wishes the Dutch government to understand that this is being taken most seriously."

"Surely this is a criminal matter," Miles said.

"In any event—" Clannahan began, taking out a gold cigarette case from his suit pocket, tapping a cigarette with his thumb. "I'd like to see what physical evidence you have, my good fellow." He smiled again, smarmy.

Miles stared at Clannahan. His hands were opening and closing into fists, as if acting independently. The Hands of Orlac. "I'll bloody well take care of the physical evidence. I'll make a criminal case without the Home Office."

"Very well then," Clannahan said in a completely neutral tone. "We'll expect an exhaustive report to review and forward to the Dutch." Clannahan was sniffing a cigarette, an English Oval. "I'll expect written reports of everything you are doing here. Do you understand me fully, Constable?"

"I think I do," Miles said.

Clannahan tapped Roberts on the shoulder. "And you must be the American," he said.

"How can you tell?" Roberts replied laconically.

"Aha," Clannahan mused. "Never mind. If you are Mitchell Roberts, Mitchell Harrison Roberts, then the gentleman standing outside would like to speak to you. His name is Stroke. He represents Her Majesty's Immigration Service."

122

Miles raised an eyebrow. Brooke had stood beside his chair, gripping the back.

"I don't understand," Roberts said, suddenly weary, confused. He tried to look up at Clannahan, but the bandage was over his right eye now, blood crusted. The man named Stroke came back through the police station and handed Roberts a document, red seal, lots of fine print.

"You'll understand this," Clannahan said to Roberts. "Old stick," he said. "You're being deported."

"This can't be," Brooke said. "He's done nothing but look into the death of his godchild." Stroke had gone quickly back outside, standing quite still outside the station door with his back turned. It occurred to Roberts that he was just a messenger, an extra in the wings who acted on cue.

"My visa is in order," Roberts said.

"It's been revoked, I'm afraid," Clannahan said, looking out the window, very removed. "Pity."

"But on what grounds?" Roberts asked.

"Very serious matter," Clannahan said. "Very serious indeed." He leaned back against the jamb, very insouciant, holding his cigarette between his thumb and forefinger, not lighting it, just using it to point. He had taken out a gold lighter, though, something with engraving on the smooth cap.

"Get on with you," Miles said.

"Suppose you tell me the grounds," Roberts said.

"Seems you've breached the peace. Struck and knocked down a chap named Marseden. Quite a serious felony offense. It's quite fortunate for you that the man hasn't brought formal criminal charges." Clannahan touched Roberts's shoulder and turned him toward the door. He had half risen, and he could see the young officer in the next room watching him with wide eyes. Even the cooks and orderlies were bunched on the stair landing, witnessing the fuss. "Stroke here will see to it that you collect your kit and get on the London train. From there you have two days to leave the country. I suggest you do so."

Roberts looked first at Miles, then Brooke, both confused.

He followed Clannahan to the front of the police station and got in the Ford. They drove three blocks down to Christ's Pieces, then Stroke got out of the car and Roberts followed. Together they went down the lane behind Christ's Pieces, a stone church hemmed in narrowly by shops on both sides. All the buildings were gray, windows framed in green with red signs hanging over the entries, very clean and ancient-looking. The sky had cleared and was blue. They walked down a lane beside an Anglican church. Roberts surprised Stroke by walking up the church steps and looking inside. The pews were empty to the nave and sacristy, and a pale light suffused the altar. Roberts studied the gold crucifix above the altar, the candles burning in one dark corner. He smelled calla lillies. Stroke came up behind, on the stairs, looking over his shoulder nervously.

"Come along, then," Stroke said.

Roberts was trying to pray but wasn't having much luck. He turned and looked down the deserted street. He could see a Union Jack fluttering above the museum.

"You know something, Stroke?" Roberts said.

"What would that be, sir?" Stroke replied.

"Right now I'd like to smash your rotten face."

"Yes sir," Stroke said, walking down the stairs, his hands still in his overcoat. "But there's ten thousand more like me in the service."

Roberts caught Stroke at the end of the street. They walked down to Harlow from the High Road. Stroke told Roberts he lived in Ipswich with his "missus" and two children and he loved the game of billiards.

AMSTERDAM

SUNDAY, DECEMBER 8

TWO Dutch officials, young, almost boys, stared balefully at Roberts, this look of hybrid keenness, as if they were donkeys eyeing apples. They wore stiff gray-green uniforms with polished brass buttons, wool half tunics over their shoulders. The shorter of the two had a dropsical eye and a runny nose, both had pale, almost pasty skin, pale blue eyes and a few faint freckles. They had probably been trained to a bureaucratic reticence, but both were youthful and though they didn't seem suspicious, they were having a hard time controlling their curiosity about an ill-kempt American who just then, on a wildly beautiful morning, smelled of whiskey and seemed about to fall over from lack of sleep. Not to mention his rumpled clothes. Roberts was awake enough to notice the taller of the officials, his yellow wispy mustache, his thin lips, which he licked. Roberts knew he looked terrible, he felt that way too, too much liquor, a two-day-old bandage, and an awful hangover. Behind him a tongue of water led from the harbor to the jetties, a customs shed where gulls circled, a few tugs out on the water, and some motorcraft idling toward shore, the docks under a quicksilver sky with azure cracks.

The two young men had examined Roberts's traveling bag, an ornamental portmanteau that he had bought from an Ojibway on one of his fishing trips. The case was framed in light birch, overlaid by maple strips, covered with doeskin, and handbound, then hand-tooled with a forest bas-relief, scenes of fishing and hunting. The shorter youth ran a finger over the hunting scenes and looked at Roberts, probably trying to decide whether to ask for a look inside his pockets. The other had opened some sections of the traveling bag, looking through the contents, a single cheap woolen suit, two pairs of sports slacks, German field glasses, a three-piece breakdown fly rod from Abercrombie's. The short fellow patted down the rubber fishing pants and found a quart of Old Granddad bourbon, which lay at the bottom, under a pair of flattened sneakers. This stopped the officials, who looked at the bottle, then at each other, smiling resolutely, each of them sniffing the contents. The gulls whirled above Roberts, who was in line ahead of a few weary salesmen, tourists, some schoolchildren returning from holiday in England. Everybody was inside a wrought-iron enclosure, the narrow gangway to land over a board walkway, then the city of Amsterdam, dark red-brick and tile roofs, church spires, pigeons.

Roberts could smell diesel fuel and salt, trying to engage the officials with a feeble smile, handing over his passport when asked. He saw the spires of the Neuwe Kirk, the portentious Dam in gray stone, shining windows. The customs hut reeked of chemically treated fir, and below the hut was a railway spur, in the distance a train chugging to an underground station. Steam and coal smoke poured from the depot, depressing black-and-tan billows, but down the avenues leading from the sheds there was a kind of gleaming cleanliness, the burghers' houses with brick and stone facades, shiny black window casings, the sheen of the canals that ringed the city.

Roberts had come across the Channel on Saturday, taking a late train to Rotterdam, crossing the North Sea in stormy weather, which made him very ill, drinking whiskey and trying to keep from passing out. He had been on the international train to Rotterdam, a special closed carriage, which stopped only briefly in the town, then on to the station in Amsterdam. He needed some sleep, a good meal, it wasn't as if Brooke hadn't warned him that alcohol would be terrible for his injury. Now, there was a fat lady behind him, clearing her throat, plainly impatient, and some children screaming, the gulls too, and just that quickly the Dutch lad with the dropsical eye said something in English that sounded like "Goot Rheise," and Roberts heard the other popping a stamp in his passport.

He repacked his case, walked through the iron gates into the open air of the Central Station garden, across a small footbridge, and then followed a narrow canal, looking for a cheap hotel.

The central city, he knew, was planned around the Neuwe Kirk, a commercial district of quiet shops, big hotels, the streets deserted in the early morning except for old couples strolling, students feeding the gulls and ducks. All the banks were dark and the stalls of the Central Market shuttered. He walked around a series of waterways, which radiated from the harbor in a snowflake pattern, tight radials around the big church. On the fringes of the central district were the parks, canals narrowing to bands, lined by tall town houses, and beyond that the green wilds of the Oosterpark and the enormous Rembrandtpark. Roberts was supernaturally weary, pausing in a milk bar for some ham and cream cheese, walking for another hour before discovering a simple pensione on a side street near the university library. He liked the musty feel of the place, its long hallways with a dignified, intellectual mein, and it was near the flower market too, he could smell the tulips, the irises. He rented a room on the third floor in back, with a tiny window that looked down on the flower market stalls, a canal, and far away the spire of the National Monument. The sky was a soft haze of blue and gold and when he lay down on the bed he covered himself with an enormous down comforter and dozed, rising to open the window for fresh air, finding it almost impossible to sleep.

He took off his rumpled clothes and bathed in a tiny stall at the end of the corridor. The water was heated in a porcelain gas-fired urn above the tub, the fixtures of brass, steam dusting the tile until it dripped. He rested in the water, thinking about Wim and Jono, his mind stalled in a quagmire of contradictions. He found himself studying the bubbles of water in the bath, drinking a small glass of whiskey he had brought from the room, considering the boys, how they had died, was it murder, how it had all happened. He kept coming back in his mind to the "toys," these strange things that seemed to link events, the cowrie shells, the beeswax honeycomb, black pebbles smoothly rubbed into rounded shapes, a single animal bone, remnant of a small creature. He tried to form a picture in his mind of the meaning of all these objects, but he kept returning to the strange green puppets, hinged and feature-less, the running shadow on the Backs, but above all the face of Clannahan as he had tapped his shoulder, looked down from his frame of silver hair, the expensive Swiss watch hammering away in Roberts's face. It was boundlessly absurd, why would Clannahan have transferred Jono's body to Ipswich, all the way across England? He found sense in his explanation for wanting to take Wim to Ipswich, all the formalistic folderol, it was a diplomatic thing for sure, but why all the deliberateness and malice? How had Clannahan heard of the Marseden incident?

Roberts had traveled to London from Cambridge, stayed with Amanda. He had told her there was no real evidence in regard to Jono, partly because there wasn't any, partly because he was beginning to have real fears. He knew that Miles could be trusted to continue the investigation; Roberts had an innate belief in Miles. Before leaving, he had telephoned Miles and they both vowed to continue until they had found out the truth. They were certain that these deaths were no accident, but they couldn't say why.

Miles had promised never to abandon the case until a satisfactory answer had come. None of them had them slightest notion of how to proceed, not Brooke, who had done an autopsy and had turned in his report to the proper authority, not Miles, who was left with his "toys." All Roberts could suggest was that he make a trip to Amsterdam, where he would try to speak with Wim's parents, where he would attempt to discover the origin of the puppet, the beeswax honeycomb, all the rest. He sat in his bath, nearly stunned, because of the concussion, the whiskey, the overnight travel on rough seas, but when he felt the water growing cold, his skin puckered, he went down the hall and used a phone to call the van Euwe home. He spoke briefly with a butler. Herr van Euwe would welcome his guest after evening Mass.

Roberts tried to sleep but rose after two hours just as tired. He left the hotel and walked along a winding trail that paralleled the Marrits Kade, a broad avenue of cobbled stone leading directly into the big Oosterpark on the eastern edge of central Amsterdam. A beautiful little canal called the Singel Gracht crossed the avenue and its blue water caught and held the shadows of the clouds and the tips of the burghers' houses. He was warm in his lumberjack shirt, but he could see his breath. To the north was a nature park, its tall firs towering above the houses and the zoo, and he could see a domed conservatory shining in the sun. Rail lines hummed far away. The houses along the canal looked as if they had been carved from amber, it was that time of day when the sun fell behind the trees, each window catching the last rays, the cobblestones shining like polished cedar.

The Singel Gracht was flat and still, but an occasional bus boat chugged down the canal, ruffling the water so that it splashed against the stone walls, waves slapping back, bumping, all the images jumbled. Each of the houses had the same characteristics, a single flight of stone steps, a small stoop, two window boxes on either side, huge ebony doors with knockers carved in shapes that symbolized the family coat of arms, its business, its profession, the generations. The windows were framed in green and black piping, on the roofs were pulley towers used to haul furniture directly to the upper floors. It was quiet, ghostly silent, and Roberts could hear monkeys chattering at the zoo, the silky rustle of the boats along the canals, gulls honking while the wind whisked the fir trees. Roberts imagined by the sound that he could be back in Colorado, high up near an alpine lake. He walked up Oosterpark Road, found the van Euwe house on a corner across from a mirror lake in the park, orange light flooding its huge surface. He noticed the knocker on the door had been carved into a rope strangling the head of a snake.

He rapped three times and he heard the echoes fading down the halls of the house. A butler opened the door, nodding, a dour old man in a black coat with a weathered face, nodding dumbly again when Roberts said his name. Roberts went inside a narrow entry that led to a hall hung with mirrors. The butler pulled a cord on the wall, looking at Roberts with his rheumy, uncomprehending eyes. The woodwork was burnished mahogany, molded plaster ceilings dulled by candle smoke. Roberts couldn't hear the monkeys anymore. Then a long shadow appeared at the top of the stairs.

Maximillian van Euwe strode down the stairs, stooping at the waist to avoid cracking his head on the canted roof, extending his hand, which Roberts shook. He was a surprise to Roberts, this very tall person, his skin burned red from the sun, cracked above the ears, his forehead a welter of peeling skin and blisters, his eyes puffy. The butler disappeared down the hallway and Roberts found himself telling van Euwe how sorry he was about his son, they had met briefly in Cambridge, then apologizing for coming at such a time. Van Euwe nodded politely, looking grim and distracted, mumbled his thanks, whisking his finger and saying "Yes, yes," evoking with much effort a small smile. He was thin and middle-aged with a dome of yellow hair cut short around his head. His eyes were steadily blue, like a flame, made more so by the puffiness. Even his eyebrows had been bleached nearly white, and all the swelling had made his lips seem pinched. Suddenly Roberts noticed that the man was wearing black batik pants, a creased cotton shirt sewn with intricate designs in blue and red silk, an abstract pattern. He was wearing a necklace of jade beads, figures of fish and warriors and monkeys. But when he moved back up the stairs he seemed very frail to Roberts too, a ballet dancer at the twilight of his career, yet there was a precision in his form. The sandals he was wearing flopped.

132

Roberts followed the man into a study on one side of another narrow hallway. It was like a garret, with two sloping ceilings, except that a west window looked down to the street, the Oosterpark and the canal. The room was furnished in rattan and wicker, van Euwe's teak desk a marvel of intricacy. All of the bookshelves were stocked with bound volumes in red leather. The books were tomes on history and geography. There were models of sailing ships all around, on stands in the corners, even one hanging from the ceiling. On one side, the walls were covered with batik and geological maps. Van Euwe sat down behind his desk, lighting a cigarette, giving a huge globe a spin, the continents hazily sketched, the seas full of monsters, leviathans. Roberts refused a cigarette, and they both sat in the gray diffused light while van Euwe turned on a single desk lamp. Roberts watched the Oosterpark turning gray in the background, all the gulls circling. There were still a few people in the park, strolling along the wide promenades, one couple rowing a boat into the center of the mirror lake. Roberts looked at van Euwe and he recognized an enormous grief.

Van Euwe smoked furiously.

"I don't know how to begin," Roberts said.

"Of course," van Euwe replied without expression. The line of his jaw seemed to support his entire face. His English was correct, spoken with a pronounced accent, but with a practiced schoolboy manner. "You must forgive me," he said. "But this is a most difficult time for my wife and myself. I could not have imagined I would survive my only son. This is too horrible to contemplate." He crushed the stub of his cigarette and lit another immediately. Then he opened his desk drawer and took out a silver flask. With one hand he took down two goblets from an upper shelf on his right, opened the flask, and poured a yellow fluid into each of the glasses. It had a slightly whitish luminescence, spreading like smoke. "Anisette," van Euwe said. "Have you tasted anisette?"

Roberts sipped the liquor, an aromatic licorice. "I'm afraid not."

"An elixir made from the old-world carrot. This is a distillation of the flower. Imagine it. What do you suppose prompted ancient man to discover such a thing?"

"I'm grateful even if I don't understand," Roberts said. The taste was very strong, the burn even stronger in his stomach. The butler appeared in the doorway carrying a silver plate of cookies and black rolls, some butter. He looked quickly at van Euwe, who nodded. The butler placed the tray on the teak desk and left as quickly as he had come. Van Euwe took another glass of anisette and pointed at the plate.

"These are *speculoos*," he said, pointing to the cookies, "and what we call *poffertjes*. The cookies really are like your gingersnaps. These are like pancakes, heavier perhaps. They go quite well with anisette. I hope you take pleasure in them." Van Euwe paused to smoke his cigarette, staring at Roberts, perhaps trying to locate him in the realm of his thought. Roberts tasted one of the gingersnaps. It was rich and sugary. He sat there, unsure how to begin, sipping anisette, while the Oosterpark took on another shape, black lace with tiny fires breaking out, the trees hazing to a web. Van Euwe pinched his eyes, closing them. "Forgive me," he said. "I've just come from Mass. My boy has been committed to God, but somehow I find no comfort in that." He sat there, grief-stricken, studying the smoke from his cigarette. Roberts remembered what Amanda had said. She had cursed God, and still there had been no answer. Roberts was distracted, the room seemed to glow. "Do you have children, Mr. Roberts?" van Euwe asked.

"No, I'm sorry I don't. Perhaps someday."

"Yes, perhaps. You'll find no greater love. Nothing in philosophy or art rivals it. Such a simple thing, really." Van Euwe finished another cigarette. The room was filling with the heaviness of anisette and tobacco. Roberts felt his headache returning, the weariness. "Are you familiar with Erasmus?" van Euwe asked.

Roberts relaxed with his anisette. He felt as if he had settled into a trance. He had been looking at the park growing dark. All of van Euwe's books. "He was your Dutch philosopher. I know his thought well."

"Amazing," van Euwe whispered. "I have studied Erasmus all my life, Mr. Roberts. I have believed his thesis that there is no greater good than the intellectual love of God. I have believed that man was destined for enlightenment and progress in his material life. That even moral problems have completely logical destinies." Van Euwe smiled self-deprecatingly, irony creeping into his tone. "I have been a scientist by profession, a rationalist all my life." He paused to smoke. "I've lost my faith," he said flatly. "The world is a bestiary, Mr. Roberts. There is no room for intellectual love, no room for God. We have gone beyond the machine age. We live in the age of greed, solipsism, a retarded jungle."

Roberts finished his anisette. He leaned forward and tried to catch the man's attention. It was as though van Euwe had drifted away in a lifeboat, wide ocean behind, this wall of water. "I've come to discuss Jono Smith, and the death of your boy. I'm sorry to be so insistent on having this conversation, but really I have little time. Amanda is relying on me to find something out about her son."

"Yes, Amanda," van Euwe said. "Jonathan was a fine boy. I know Wim and he were great friends. I was out of the country when Jono came to Holland, but I know my wife loved him very much. It is hard to believe they are both gone." Roberts could see van Euwe fighting the tears. The room was heavy with smoke. "I don't see how I can help."

"I think the death of Wim is connected to the death of Jonathan. I can't prove it."

"Oh." Van Euwe moaned. "I don't see how that is possible. I saw Jonathan last Christmas, just briefly when I returned from the colonies. We were shocked by his death, Hilda and I. But what connection could there be? Jonathan drowned in a river. All we know is that Wim fell from a window. You must not create connections where none exist."

"Have the authorities contacted you?" Roberts asked.

"The English, yes. I'm told he fell."

"Nothing more?"

"The autopsy results." Van Euwe had covered his face, he was spinning the globe absently. "May I ask your profession?" he said.

"I train horses," Roberts answered. "Run a ranch."

"And you know Erasmus?"

"I'm a failed philosopher. I suppose *lapsed* is a better word. I found horses and dogs easier to understand and love than either people or history."

"Well said," van Euwe muttered.

"And you, Herr van Euwe?"

"No, please," he answered. "May we finish with you? Have you known Amanda long?"

Roberts could see some stars, an edge of the park gone totally black, Holland flat and watery in the background. He told van Euwe all about himself while the man listened intently. When he finished, van Euwe poured more anisette.

"And I am a petroleum geologist," he said. "I specialize in reservoir dynamics. It only sounds specialized. Actually, I make guesses about the behavior of oil in a pool beneath layers of rock, how it might behave, how it can be tapped. I examine the reservoir after I locate it, tell the company if it can make any money, how much, how long. In that sense, I am an extremely well paid alchemist. This has been my entire life."

"I take it you travel a great deal."

"Constantly," van Euwe said. "I have been in Southern Africa, Zanzibar, Angola and Nigeria. For the past eight years I have gone again and again, exclusively to the Indonesian islands, all over the archipelago, looking for oil."

"And you were away when Wim was killed?"

"Yes," he said absently. It was clear to Roberts that the man was having a hard time concentrating. "I'm so sorry," he said at last.

"Yes, I understand," Roberts acknowledged. "But I still must be very direct, if I may."

"Yes, all right."

136

"Do you know anyone with a reason to murder your son?"

"Murder," van Euwe said.

"I think you said you haven't heard the particulars from the authorities."

"Not all," he said. "You saw my son fall. Is that quite correct?"

"I was in Jocko's room across the way. I could see your son's window. Yes, I'm afraid I saw him fall. I have some reason to believe that he was pushed. I'm sorry to tell you this news."

Max van Euwe closed his eyes again, covering them with his left hand. He sat that way for a long time, the smoke from his cigarette drifting into the half-light of the room, his shoulders pinched together. He looked as if he were sitting in a pouring rain, helpless. He raised his other hand, rubbed it across his forehead, through his hair.

"The English government has sent back my boy's body with its sincerest condolences. They indicated he had fallen accidentally from his room at school. They forwarded the autopsy report. What more would you have me do?"

"You've studied the evidence?"

"No, of course not," he snapped.

"I saw the fall, sir. Someone ran from your son's room immediately afterwards. I followed the person into the shadows across the quadrangle from the room. When I was near a bridge, someone took a shot at me. Broke off a chip of stone. You can see my head." Roberts touched the bandage that covered his stitches. The wound was black and blue. "Please help me, Herr van Euwe."

It seemed in that instant as if all the light abandoned the sky above the city. The Oosterpark lake had become a deserted oval and Roberts heard the chattering of the monkeys again in the zoo, their echoing cries. Van Euwe seemed to have fallen into shock, his face pale, even above the red sunburned skin. He barely moved, he just sat staring at the globe with its dull yellow glow, the continents and seas illuminated by a bulb within the circle. He seemed hypnotized.

"To the extent," Roberts said, "that there is some reason

for your son to be murdered, it might help me understand Jono's death. I've told you I'm being honest. The reason is that Jono's family has suffered terribly as well. If there is any connection at all, I must know it." Roberts remained motionless, hoping van Euwe would recover.

"I assure you," he said. "There is no connection."

Roberts had a leather bag tied around his neck, inside the lumberjack shirt. He got out the bag and untied the leather thong that bound it, tumbled out the green puppet, the black pebbles and the cowrie shells. They snicked against the teak desk, the only sound except for the faraway monkeys, the globe creaking on its axis. Roberts felt he could hear his own heart. "Do these objects mean anything to you?" he asked.

Van Euwe opened his eyes, pinched his nose. "Let me see," he said wearily. "Where did you find these?"

"They were found with the boys."

"What other connection do you have between these two children?"

"Nothing at the moment. They were friends. They were little boys. They shared a room at Harlow School."

Van Euwe breathed deeply. He leaned forward over the teak desk, trying to concentrate. "Let me reassure you, Mr. Roberts. There is absolutely no connection between these two deaths. This may be no comfort to Amanda, but I am absolutely certain there is no connection." He sipped some anisette.

"But how can you be so sure?" Roberts asked.

"Let me assure you—"

"I don't want your assurance," Roberts snapped, aware he was losing his temper, that he shouldn't. He was tired, his head was banging, perhaps it was the anisette too.

"All right," Van Euwe said, obviously exhausted as well. "If I make an explanation, will you go back to England?"

"Probably so," Roberts said.

"Then let me explain. I've told you that I'm a petroleum geologist. In the modern world, the search for oil is the equivalent of the search for El Dorado. Only more so. You cannot compare Spanish gold to the tremendous wealth there is beneath the earth, in oil and gas. I work for the Dutch national company, very large, very rich. This company has interests in many parts of the world." Van Euwe had relaxed, he spoke with his eyes closed, leaning back in his chair with his head nearly against the windowpane. His cigarette was burning in his fingers, smoke curling, obscuring his face. "Most recently, for the past eight years, I have been in Java and Sumatra. It is a very isolated and primitive part of the world, and it is my belief, and the belief of my company, and my government, that there are enormous reserves of oil and gas under the seabed. The technology of exploiting such reserves, buried offshore, in angry seas, is very expensive. But, make no mistake. It is available. And as the price of oil increases, the technology becomes relatively less and less expensive. Still, the risk is enormous, as is the potential profit. Billions of your dollars are currently at stake. My job is to make the geologic and seismic maps and charts that make possible a reasonable scientific analysis of that risk. There are also political risks as well. I'm afraid, though I can't be sure, that this political risk is what killed my child."

"I'm sorry, I don't understand," Roberts said.

"Have you not wondered why I sent my son, a Dutch boy, to be educated in England? In a language not his own? Away from his mother, his friends? His own home?"

"Not until now," Roberts admitted.

Van Euwe laughed. Roberts hadn't expected it, it came as a surprise. "These islands are beset with civil unrest. Many groups seek independence from the Dutch government. Some groups are wildly anarchic, some communist, some nationalist. Of course, these are hardly optimum conditions in which to search for oil, to contemplate spending millions and millions of your dollars. As for me, I have absolutely no interest in these political matters. My sole concern has been the search, the beauty of it, its precision. I have always loved my work, nothing else has mattered to me but it and my wife and my son. This and nothing more. But, frankly, most groups in

Indonesia oppose the Dutch. Everything. Their government, their companies, their social customs. They don't want the Dutch national company searching for its fortune in Indonesia. Some time ago, my company received a threat against its employees, wherever they may be. It was a general kind of thing, but the threat included family members. Since that time, I have not traveled much with my wife. I sent my only son to school in England. He wished to remain in Holland, but he went nevertheless, and he adjusted quite well. Oh, he missed his mother, his friends. But your Jono made him see the possibilities, as well. I did not see his leaving as something altogether negative."

"You ignored the threats on your own life?"

"Of course. I am a grown man, with principles, judgment and pride. I am capable of taking such risks for my work. But I could not ask my wife and son to take them as well. I could not be threatened into giving up my life's work. I hope you understand that."

"Yes," Roberts said. "So you believe these threats were carried out against your son."

"Perhaps," van Euwe said, slumping again. The speech had worn him out. "This was probably a political deed. There is a West Irian movement to attach Borneo to Indonesia as a free province. This is where my most recent posting has been. If my son was murdered, and I'm not saying he was, then he may have fallen victim to one of these movements. These toys you have are Indonesian, perhaps a message. These people do not want the Dutch national company to have an oil concession. Don't you see, Mr. Roberts?" Van Euwe had begun to stare at the globe again, looking angry, then puzzled and defeated. It was as if his whole life were whirling before him, the continents, the sea dragons, all the leviathans. "In that case, the English will be responsible for pursuing the criminal. The authorities here in Amsterdam can only seek to assist them, and at that, there is nothing very hopeful. So you see, my son's death may have been an act of political violence. It's likely. But you see there can be no connection to young Jonathan's death. That would not make sense. I hope his mother can rest with that knowledge." Van Euwe drained his anisette.

Roberts sat back, disappointed, while van Euwe twirled the globe again. He was transfixed, observing the globe's rotation, these great exposed surfaces. "So you see," van Euwe said, as if he were talking to the room, "my son has been killed, perhaps, by the impersonal forces of men who oppose my company and my government." Roberts thought the man had become almost wistful, his eyes blank. "There was a time," he continued, "when this terrible earth was thought to be inhabited by monsters of the deep, demons in caves, dragons in forests. Every event was deeply malign, spirits inhabited everything, every object. Each man was dominated by psychological ignorance. In those days, explorers faced their own terrors, almost more than they faced physical hardship. You can imagine how it must have been to be a seafarer setting out on a journey, across the oceans, what splendid dangers!" Van Euwe paused, spinning the globe ever faster, clicking it with his fingernail, his eyes reflecting the motion, around and around. "And now," he went on, "we discover the truth. The monster is inside ourselves." He laughed, almost painfully, like a wracking cough. "Oh, my son," he said, holding his head.

"I'm so sorry," Roberts whispered, leaning forward over the desk. "But I wonder if I might speak with your wife?"

"No, p-please," he stuttered. "She's gone for a walk after Mass. I don't know when to expect her back. I would rather you didn't wait. I'm so very tired."

Roberts touched his arm, stood up. "I'm staying at the pensione Herren Gracht, opposite the Flower Market. If you think of anything else, please contact me there." Roberts gathered the toy objects, put the bag around his neck. Van Euwe had nearly collapsed, holding his head in his hands, trying not to break. For a moment, Roberts thought van Euwe had reached for the cowrie shells, the puppet, he couldn't be sure. It was a miracle that Miles had let him bring them across the Channel, Roberts knew he was taking a big chance doing it.

"I don't see what . . . ." van Euwe said, his voice trailing away. Roberts walked to the door, looking back at van Euwe, who had begun to stare at the globe again. He looked to Roberts like a man in a photographic negative, colors fine grained, almost sooty brown. Outside a fog had risen from Oosterpark.

"Another time," Roberts said, going out the study door, standing on the stair head.

He walked down the narrow staircase, bending down to keep from banging his head. The butler appeared and opened the door.

There was fog over the Singel Gracht. Roberts walked down the stone street toward the park portal. He could see the lake through the trees, and there were still some people on the gravel walks, walking dogs, an old couple pedaling a tandem bike. The houses formed a narrow frame to the park, all the windows lighted. He was surprised when someone touched his elbow, he was that lost.

She was a trim woman wearing a plain black dress and a fox stole. Her hair was pinned back in a bun. There were black pouches under her eyes, as if she hadn't slept, sadness in them too, she reminded Roberts of a Rembrandt portrait.

"Excuse me, sir," she said. "Are you the American?"

She sounded German. It was a clipped accent, very careful and precise.

"I'm an American," he said. Roberts was studying her doe eyes, the blond hair going gray.

"My name is Hilda van Euwe," she said. "I'm Wim's mother."

"I'm so sorry," Roberts began. Sensing instantly how wrong he was, he wondered what he should be saying, but he couldn't start over.

"Yes, thank you," she said huskily.

"I met your son in Cambridge." It was starting to get cold. Roberts zipped his bomber jacket.

142

"I know," she said. She looked nervous. She kept glancing at the portal to the Oosterpark. Suddenly she grasped Robert's arm and led him across the street, through the portal. A gravel walk branched in two directions. They were standing in foggy light. "I must hurry," the woman said. "I must go home soon."

"Have you got some trouble?" Roberts asked.

"No, but I must explain." She was breathing heavily, tears forming at the corners of her eyes.

"I was hoping to speak with you," Roberts said while she caught her breath.

"Quickly," she said. "Quickly, why did you come here?"

"Only to make inquiries into Jono's death. I wanted to see if there was any connection between your son's death and his. I wanted to help. Jono's mother is very distraught. I'm sure you can understand."

"What did my husband tell you?" she asked. She had put her gloved finger to her lip, she didn't want Roberts to interrupt.

"He said there had been threats against his company. The families included."

"Did he say what form those threats took?"

"General threats. We didn't discuss it."

"Please," she said, tears rolling down her cheeks. "You must speak with someone else before you leave the city. Will you meet me at the entrance to the aquarium at noon tomorrow. Please say you will come."

"The aquarium?"

"Here," she pointed, "at the zoo. In the Natura Magistra. A cabman will take you there."

"Yes, of course," Roberts said.

The woman took two steps away, then turned to look back over her shoulder.

"How did you know I was here?" Roberts called.

"The butler gave me your message. It was intended for my husband, I know. I've been waiting outside for you."

She walked across the street, leaving Roberts in the fog. He

143

walked around the Ringwalk, through Oosterpark and back toward the Singel Gracht, where he caught a water taxi back to the pensione. It had grown much colder, and there was ice on the water.

MONDAY, DECEMBER 9

THE early morning was crystalline blue, though later the clouds blew in from the sea, bringing cold weather with grains of snow spitting down. Roberts had been out walking, aimlessly, along the Heren Gracht, watching the water taxis hauling passengers up and down the canals, taking people from the train station and depot, toward central Amsterdam, tugs loaded with freight, food and flowers and cargo, great wings of cheese, flats of mushrooms. The streets were crowded with businessmen and shoppers, some students from the university playing musical instruments, guitars, tambourines, drinking beer in the taverns, all together a polite riot of color and noise with the policemen, like conductors, directing traffic from white boxes in all the squares. At noon the snow stopped, the clouds broke, and the sun slanted down on the slate roofs, the firs in the parks, the huge evergreens dripping with melted snow. He ate a quick lunch in a café near the big canal beside the horticultural gardens, a sandwich of gouda and ham, milk, he watched the boats going along the water, tried to listen to the people talking, admiring the women in their smart wool suits. There was diesel smoke on the horizon above the harbor.

Three wide lanes led east into the Oosterpark. The bells of the Dam struck twelve as he walked down Midden Laan directly into the center of Oosterpark.

Hilda van Euwe was standing near the entrance to the

aquarium. Beside her was a distinguished-looking man in the traditional Dutch suit of green with black lapels, a light gray dress shirt and silk tie. He had wavy white hair and ruddy skin. There were some children playing in the park, running circles around the two, shouting. Hilda motioned to Roberts, embarrassed, and when he approached her she said, "Thank you for coming," with her eyes darting nervously. She turned quickly to the other man and walked inside the entrance to the aquarium, two wide glass doors.

Roberts followed them into a foyer, where he found three dark portholes on his right opening into fish tanks, the fish swimming in halos, silently, one great blowfish puffing up bubbles from the tank floor. They walked down a long corridor amid the tanks, in the dark, and then up a flight of stairs to an outside arena above the aquariums, into the sudden glare of an atrium surrounded by glass, trees waving outside in the winter wind. There were tables and chairs covered by gay umbrellas, people having lunch. Some waitresses bustled back and forth from a kitchen. Roberts realized he was viewing the monkey house outside, part of the zoo, there were dozens of monkeys combing the trees, swinging wildly, setting up a racket.

They sat down at one of the tables. The man extended his hand to Roberts and they shook. "Hubert Lind," the man said, smiling wanly. "Hilda does not speak English so good. She prefers that I translate. Does that suit you?"

"If it suits her," Roberts said, looking at her.

Hilda said, "I'm so sorry. Speaking English makes me feel stupid. I hope you understand."

Roberts tried to smile. He was self-conscious about his bandaged head, the black wound, his lumberjack shirt and boots. "English makes me feel stupid too," he said. Hilda laughed quietly, Lind smiled. The waitress came and Lind ordered an Advocat with herring and pickles, one for each of them. The waitress hurried back with their drinks, a concoction Roberts thought tasted like eggnog and gin, the pickled herring a dull blue on a white plate, eyes wide open, covered in a dill sauce, surrounded by tiny pickled gerkins.

"I have not much time," Lind said.

The atrium echoed with conversation. The snow had begun again, bits of it cracking against the atrium glass. The trees seemed to have turned gray.

"Hilda tells me you are an American," Lind said.

"She knows who I am," Roberts said. "But I don't know who you are."

"Of course," Lind said. He had jowls and his eyebrows were luxurious, overflowing his face, with black-specked eyes. He seemed to speak a diplomatic English, clipped but without much accent. "I have known Hilda and Max for many years. I have been the friend to Max, very close."

Hilda was speaking agitated Dutch. Lind listened gravely, following her motions with his eyes while Roberts nibbled a herring. He had slept a little, but was feeling sick and tired.

Hilda leaned across the table, nearly knocking over a glass. She spoke quickly to Lind, almost exasperated. Some schoolchildren had come up the atrium steps and were busily jousting for chairs, shouting happily, their screams filling the hall with echoes. Lind listened to Hilda and said: "Hilda is explaining our friendship, she and I." A lion roared from the zoo and the schoolchildren screamed. "You see, Mr. Roberts, I have been in business with Max for many years. Since Max married Hilda, I have been a friend to them both. You must not think me disloyal because I am speaking to you behind Max's back."

"It is true. It is true." Hilda crossed herself.

"I have no reason to doubt you," Roberts said. He was beginning to feel this had gone far enough. "The important thing is what you have to say." He nodded at Hilda, who was trying to smile, exercise some control over the situation.

"Ah, that is good," Lind said, leaning back in his chair, tasting the Advocat. The drink had been served in a tall tulip glass. "It is good that Americans are so direct. It must come from your notion that time is money. I'm afraid if it were up to us Europeans, we would chat all day." He took a gerkin and chewed it. "I will tell you who I am."

Roberts listened to the monkeys, the children. He didn't know why he wasn't concentrating, perhaps it was because of the sounds of the kids.

"For many years," Lind said, "Max and I worked for the Dutch national oil company. The company was organized after the war to exploit the resources of the East Indies, which had returned to Dutch hands after the Japanese occupation. I was an engineer. Max was an explorer. It was a little like Livingstone and Stanley. Together we shared many hardships, the terrible climate, making our way around the world for the company, living in jungle huts, on the edge of steaming swamps. Ah, there were mosquitoes, disease, the unfriendly people. The hardship made our friendship very strong. We had met during the war, fighting the Japanese. Together after the war, we continued to fight, only this time in the name of science. I was the technician, the practical man, ever an eye on the probable. Max was the dreamer, the man of mysteries, ever an eye on the possible. Together we became like one man."

"An Erasmus," Roberts said.

Lind smiled slyly. "Yes, if you wish."

"And you, Herr Lind. What are you now?"

"In time I became influential in the company. After so many years, there is almost no distinction between those who worked for the company and those who worked for the government."

"You work for the government now?"

Lind bit his lower lip. "Here is where I must trust *you*, Mr. Roberts. May I ask for your confidence?"

"You have it, Herr Lind. My trust is in Mrs. van Euwe, and through her to you."

"Very good." Lind sighed. "Perfectly understandable." Hilda nodded. She had ignored her Advocat and herring, but was listening raptly. "Yes," Lind continued, "I am a diplomat. I serve as a go-between from the government to the company.

148

There are many areas of mutual interest, many in the government who wish to see the company succeed, and many in the company who need the support of the government."

"I know how it works," Roberts growled.

"Yes, perhaps you do," Lind said. He had parted his lips to reveal pure white teeth. His skin was like paper, reddish in hue, unwrinkled, with neutral features. It seemed to Roberts that the man's white hair was the only clue to his age, which he guessed was near fifty. Another wave of schoolchildren came up the stairs, jamming the corner of the atrium, watching the monkeys. Suddenly they made a scattered dash for the tables. Roberts sipped some Advocat while the noise settled. "Yes, perhaps you do," Lind went on. "But do you have any idea what fortunes are at stake in Java and Borneo? How much money can be earned in oil there?" Hilda had broken in, speaking excitedly again, Lind looking at her while she spoke, very patient. He turned to Roberts. "Hilda was saying that she hopes you know who killed her son, that you will do everything you can to bring the person to justice. She is very frightened for her husband, who probably has no intention of leaving his profession. Hilda is concerned that because you came on behalf of Jonathan, that you will forget Wim. She wants you to know that she is very sorry for the English boy, that she loved him, and mourns for him. She does not know how or why Jonathan died, but she thinks you are her only hope for Wim." Lind paused and looked at Hilda, who was leaning forward in her seat, near tears, wringing her hands. Lind smiled at her, trying to ease the tension. He looked back at Roberts. "I'm afraid she thinks you can avenge Wim. You are her Angel." Lind speared a herring. "But we are perhaps ahead of ourselves."

Roberts drank more Advocat. He was growing more and more concerned that his energy was dissipating, that the focus he was trying to maintain, on Jonathan, the drowning, was being blurred. He was drawn to Hilda van Euwe, he wanted to help, but he didn't know what he was expected to do. "I'll not mislead you, Madame," he said, looking at the woman. "I

149

saw Wim fall, and I believe he was pushed. But I have no proof, and no likelihood I'll have any, of who did the killing. I have only a bare motive, this notion of political threats. Your husband made it all seem vague. He assured me there was no connection between the death of Wim and that of Jonathan. You see, that's why I'm here. About Jonathan."

"Vague threats," Hilda intoned. She took a deep breath, looking at Lind.

"Now, Hilda," Lind said. "So it is what I thought."

"What do you mean?" Roberts asked, looking at both of them.

"She means," Lind said, "that the threats were very real. Concrete."

"Real threats by whom?"

"By a leftist group here in Amsterdam."

"Why would Herr van Euwe not tell me?"

"He is very loyal to his company. He believes in the whole system. He believes that the authorities will find the killer and punish him."

"And you do not?"

"Quite frankly, no. I believe the company and the government would prefer that this matter go unnoticed, that it get lost in the bureaucratic maze. The company is engaged in delicate negotiations with the government of Indonesia on an oil concession. Any hint of political turmoil, ill will, could hinder the process. The company has millions at stake. They could lose the whole thing to an English company over something like this. I'm afraid this is something that Max does not understand. Perhaps he knows it inside his heart, but he refuses to believe it. As I told you, he is a dreamer, an idealist."

"Perhaps you should tell me the whole story."

Hilda nodded at Lind, who folded his hands on the table and studied them for a while. The schoolchildren were eating and the waitresses scurried about with trays of sandwiches and milk. Hilda had composed herself and was sitting with her face in a patch of brief sunshine. Roberts thought she was very striking, almost beautiful, with a great dignity of bearing. She had taken off her stole and was tasting some herring with a tiny fork. He noticed the deep blue veins running along the back of her hands, the narrow white fingers, the delicate wrists. Lind bit his lip, trying to begin, tasting some Advocat. Hilda nodded again.

"I began my work for the Dutch company after the war," Lind said. "I had served with Max in a construction battalion in the Far East. The Japanese had ruined much of the infrastructure of the old Dutch East Indies, leaving nothing in its place but a bastardized colonial administration. You know the types, seedy officials in white suits, drunk on gin and bitters. A few tribal leaders taking bribes. The nationalists in the jungle making war on the whole system. It was as corrupt a situation as you're likely to find, and there was little or no real government, no health care, no schools, no post. The company, in my opinion, became one of the stabilizing influences in the race against starvation and disease. Others would say they exploited the country. Who knows? When order was restored, the Dutch government was fully in charge and the company began the search for oil in earnest, throughout Sumatra, Java, Borneo. Max and I began to travel extensively. We mapped wild regions, we walked up and down mountain trails, we sailed around almost all of the inhabited islands. Max caught malaria, he has suffered from it on and off his whole life now. We've had amebic dysentery, worms, heat prickle, snakebite and fungus infections on our feet and hands. I have had a tiny prick on my hand fester into a monstrous infection overnight. No doctors, no hospitals, monkey meat to eat. But when we had completed the job, we had discovered one of the largest oil deposits in the history of the world. Fabulous wealth, untapped, billions of barrels of oil and gas. You can't imagine the wealth. There are deposits offshore in Borneo, near Sarawak, and in West Irian. There are other resources as well. Gold and diamonds, bauxite, wood and timber of all kinds. The islands are zones of enormous possibility, and whoever gains a foothold there will

151

make millions of dollars in profit. The English would love to have a foothold, they are close to making a deal. It is very close, indeed."

"And what does this lead to?" Roberts asked.

"Things have changed in Indonesia."

"How is that?"

"This must be strictly confidential."

"You have my word," Roberts said. Lind looked at Hilda and they smiled.

"At any rate," Lind said, "my work began to involve more than reservoir engineering. After the finds were made I began to study the people and their social structure. I kept an eye on local political matters. I negotiated with the local movements for peace. Frankly, I began to gather intelligence for my government."

"With the company's knowledge."

"Oh yes," Lind said. "They knew all about it."

"It isn't uncommon," Roberts said dully.

"Yes," Lind said. "I take it you disapprove. But I did not do it for the money. I did it because I believed in my government and my company."

"But Herr van Euwe didn't know this."

"Never, sir, I regret to say. There was never any reason to share this information with him."

Lind ordered another Advocat, some sweet cookies and coffee. The waitress brought the cookies and coffee, and Roberts sat drinking a cup. "You must understand," Lind said, "that the political situation in Indonesia has changed drastically."

"Herr van Euwe told me there was civil strife."

Lind raised an eyebrow. "This is an understatement. The precise term is 'civil war.' My government prefers to call it unrest, but there is a war raging, I assure you. Dutch troops are engaged. The government hides this fact from the public. This is an old story. There are troops in a foreign country to keep the peace."

"There is a war of liberation," Roberts said.

"If you wish to call it that."

"I don't see why you're telling me this."

"Please be patient," Lind said. "Max is very loyal to his employer, so he kept the whole truth from you. It is certain that he believed Jonathan's death is uninvolved, so he probably believed he was doing no harm. I only wish you to understand the entire picture. Max is also a very private person with great pride. You are a stranger to him, you come to his home, you ask questions, he can think of no connection, there is probably none, so he is polite and reserved. In his own way he was being quite truthful with you. He loves his son, he is caught in a terrible web of contradiction. It has overpowered him. He is a dreamer and an idealist in a world gone mad with materialism. You must find it in your heart to forgive him."

"And you will tell me the exact truth?"

"Yes, I am going to do that."

"But why, Herr Lind?"

"We will come to that presently."

"Then go ahead. I'll wait." Roberts drank some coffee. It was very sweet, doused with cream.

"Good enough," Lind said soberly. "Two years ago a Marxist national movement centered in Sarawak made direct threats against Max and myself. They made other threats against local managers, but they singled me and Max out. I must tell you, horribly, it was probably because of my activities, more than those of Max. They wished to terrorize the employees, drive out the company. They want nothing to do with the Dutch. In this the English have a certain complicity, I'm afraid."

"Money."

"Money, perhaps more."

"So Wim was sent to England."

Hilda said, "Yes, we thought it would be safe." Big tears had appeared in her eyes. She looked as if she might break down completely. "Please understand," she said haltingly, "my husband is not a political man. These threats he could not understand. He loves Indonesia. It confuses and puzzles him.

153

He does not understand this violence." A big tear tumbled down her cheek. "He does not understand who would harm an innocent little boy."

"Yes, Hilda," Lind said. He looked at Roberts. "Max is a dreamer whose love is minerals and sailing ships. What is this modern world that such a man should lose his only son, that he should fear for his life?"

"I'm afraid terror isn't new," Roberts said.

"But it is so perfected now," Lind said.

"I'll agree it's reached a new level of perfection. In modern life, it is the projection of total terror that is so astonishing." Lind sighed, sipping some coffee. Roberts was beginning to feel quite discouraged, seeming to be no closer to the cause of Jono's death, but being led into an investigation of Wim's death. He still sought the connection between the two, but was no further in learning what it might be. Even the "toys" were an enigma to him, just pieces of junk.

"Yes. To be terrified in one's own home, thousands of miles from the real battlefield. It is a hideous ordeal."

"But I don't understand," Roberts protested. "Why are you telling me all of this?"

"Please, please," Lind insisted, putting a finger over his lips. "We have reached the critical stage. The most important place for you, and for Hilda." Hilda had wiped her face with a handkerchief, but there were still tears in both eyes. The waitress had brought more cookies and coffee, and the school-children were making an orderly exit. An eerie silence descended with the faint chattering of the monkeys in the trees, dishes clinking in the kitchen. "As I told you," Lind continued, "the risk in terms of money is great. Any company which commits itself to exploit the continental shelf of Borneo, or West Irian, may realize a great profit. Not to mention assuring its government of a steady supply of oil for many years. The stakes in this enterprise are beyond the imagination. The English companies, and the English government, would like to see this whole area open to competition. It would suit the English if the local war in the Dutch East Indies

154

resulted in an entirely nationalist government, one that could be exploited by the English. Then their companies would have the oil. It is politics."

"My God," Roberts said. "You're intimating that the English would look the other way if someone came into their country to kill Wim."

"It is possible, I'm afraid," Lind said flatly, looking away.

"Why doesn't your government inquire?"

"I told you," Lind said, waving a hand. "This is not diplomatically possible. We cannot make any accusations against people with whom we must deal. It is a sad fact that the life of this one little boy is but a grain of sand to these people."

"And so you need outside help."

"A catalyst, if you wish."

Hilda began to speak in rapid Dutch, her eyes brimming. She spoke for a very long time, looking at Roberts, then at Lind, locking in on her grief and anger.

Lind said, "She has said that she needs your help in England and here. I am afraid she is asking you pointedly to assist in finding the person who killed her son. There is, she thinks, some person in England who made it possible. She says that only English justice can assist her. It is a terrible thing to ask, she knows, but unless you act for her, her only son will be a casualty of this new world order. She asks, 'Do you know anyone in England who will help?' I'm afraid she is begging you again, Mr. Roberts." Lind sat back, seeming exhausted as Hilda began to cradle her head and cry again.

Roberts closed his eyes, thinking. He knew he had no choice. He reached inside his lumberjack shirt and got out the leather bag, untied its thong. He tumbled out the cowrie shells, the beeswax comb, the puppet. Lind sat in stunned silence, studying the objects, placing a fingernail on the shiny puppet face, Hilda leaning forward, her tears falling on the table. A wind had come up, banging the atrium glass. All of the sun had gone away and it was a dull gray day, without luster. Roberts could see the firs move in the wind.

"My God," whispered Lind. "Where have you found these things?" Lind's voice had taken on an electric urgency.

"These particular objects were found in Wim's room on the night of his death. An English police constable allowed me, at great risk, to take these out of the country. We have no idea what they might mean. An animal bone. A puppet. The smooth black pebbles. A beeswax comb. None of this makes sense."

Hilda appeared perplexed and frightened. The objects lying on the shiny surface of the table had taken on a metaphysical aspect, you could tell she was becoming upset by their arrangement. "It is a strange logic," Lind muttered, looking up at Roberts.

"Tell me what the hell you mean," Roberts said.

"This is the doing of *obat*," Lind answered. The foreign word Lind pronounced sharply, two crisp syllables like hammer on flint.

"Never heard of it," Roberts said.

"Magic," Lind said, stonily. "You must understand," Lind said in hushed tones, "that I have spent nearly eight years in the jungle. I have studied the people of Borneo, their customs—their prejudices, if you will. In these isolated places, there is much belief in magic, in potions, charms, incantations. These are a pantheistic people, many objects are either holy or malign to them. The magical objects, the ones with power, are called *jeemat*. The individual who possesses these magical objects and knows how to use them is conferred the power from the objects. These objects may be simple seedpods, crushed insects, these circular pebbles," Lind fingered one of the black stones. "The people believe in them very strongly. They are used to cast spells."

"The pelvic bone?" Roberts asked.

"That is an easy one," Lind answered. "The uplanders believe that the center of the body is the liver. The pelvic bone symbolizes that organ."

Hilda began speaking Dutch again. She had touched Roberts's hand, holding her own over his while she spoke, her gray eyes full of tears. When she had finished, Lind said: "Hilda must return to the house. She blesses you. She prays for you. And for Jonathan. Again she says he was a lovely boy." The woman smiled at Roberts and put on her fox stole. Roberts watched her descend the stairs.

"I can tell you what happened in England," Lind said when Hilda was gone.

"Please do," Roberts said.

"The murder of Wim was a ritual. It was committed by a person from Java or Borneo. In his own culture this person is called a *bali saleng,* an evil spirit who takes the blood of its victim. The *jeemat* left in Wim's room symbolizes the accomplishment of his task, a kind of message or warning, the symbolic taking of blood and liver from the victim. This *bali saleng,* whoever he was, probably believes himself invulnerable."

"This is utterly insane," Roberts said.

"Oh yes," Lind answered. "Quite insane. But these items seem quite authentic."

"And you have an idea of who this person might be? This *bali saleng.*"

"I can only make generalizations," Lind said. He had taken out some money and was reckoning the bill. "He is, of course, from Indonesia. He is a new immigrant, probably a student with political connections to the leftist movement. I would say he is caught between cultures, probably being used by the movement to commit this political murder without being able to free himself from the deep animism he harbors."

"What would he look like?"

"Probably an uplander. He'd be short of stature with dark black hair, dark skin, a broad flat nose. The Indonesians of the Java region are thinner, lighter and taller."

Roberts was feeling the Advocat, a lightness in his head, objects growing halos. Part of his sensations were swimming. "What about the puppet?" he asked.

"Ah, the puppet." Lind sighed. "Its use is widespread in Indonesia. It is part of the *wayang.* When placed before a lighted curtain, the puppet is made to dance, creating a shadow on the curtain. This dance symbolizes the play of spiritual forces, good and evil. It is a way of coming to terms with the ever-present contradictions of the human soul, the human condition. By seeing the shadowlike nature of these puppets, all men come to be amused by their own folly, by the folly of history, shallow cravings, their desires—something like that. Among Hindus you will find similar conceptions in the doctrine of Maya, appearance and desire. I am afraid the island has a moral code very different from our own. There are no absolutes in Indonesia, only a constant interplay of forces. There is no single God to arbitrate, validate one's soulful experience, no repentance and sin, no sainthood. As human beings, we are at war only with our own visions, our illusions and strivings, and the *wayang* is the artful symbol of the war."

"There *is* something I don't understand," Roberts said.

"Yes?"

"The *jeemat* you've talked about, the objects, what I've been calling 'toys,' are apparently symbols of evil."

"Yes. The *bali saleng* left them in Wim's room at the English school to symbolize the taking of blood, the taking of the liver organ. They are symbols of revenge and retribution. They are used to provoke fear. In this case, they are trying to convince the Dutch oil company that it is too dangerous to continue to deal in Indies oil."

Roberts leaned forward, trying to concentrate. Something had wedged itself into his mind, and he was able to focus again despite the headache, the swimming sensation. "These same *jeemat* were found on the riverbank near Jono when he drowned. There was a puppet in his jacket."

Lind sat stunned, his face drained of color and expression. "This is quite impossible. This would not make sense." He sat tapping his fingernail against the table, like Max and Miles, Roberts wondered where the gesture came from. Finally he said, "No, it is impossible. These *jeemat* are vengeful. They make sense only in connection with Wim's death."

158

"And the puppet," Roberts said. "What kind of sense does that make? You speak of it as if it were not a symbol of evil like the *jeemat*."

"The puppet is different," Lind said. "The whole *wayang* is in reality an attitude to be expressed toward death itself. The island people create the shadow dance in which great battles are fought. There are great misdeeds, great acts of cowardice and heroism. There is sacrifice and selfishness, love and hate, pettiness and honor. In the shadow dance all men are equal, both the noble and the peasant, the warrior and the worker. In this way the people laugh at their own folly, at their own misfortune. The *wayang* teaches humility and humor, for it shows that good fortune is as fleeting as bad. The noble who slaughters a thousand peasants one day dies of an infected toe the next."

"A Danse Macabre?"

"Nothing so medieval, or European. It is an ancient belief that has none of the odiousness of sin. There is only gaily and acceptance, a kind of worldliness, a giving in to power."

"Then if the *bali saleng* is such an evil spirit, why would he leave behind the puppet?"

"It is good you ask," Lind said, "very perceptive. At the answer to this question I can only guess. But it is a good guess, because all of these objects show a kind of logic. The beeswax comb to show the deviousness of the thing, its many corridors, the pelvic bone as a liver, the cowrie shells, a necklace of vanity. So you see."

"Go ahead, Herr Lind."

"Very well. I think I know these people. This man may well be a Kenyah, or another islander. These people are quite fond of children, they love them, dote on them, worship them. It seems to me that this man, so far from home, forced to kill a child, may have left the puppet as a kind of apology, an expression of sorrow, as the *jeemat* were an expression of anger."

Roberts tried to drink some coffee, but it had gone cold. He thanked Lind for his help, and they sat in the atrium while the wind banged the glass, the monkeys chittered in the trees. "I don't know what I can do," he said finally.

"There must be a way," Lind began. "In my present position I can help you with information, some money. But I know you are the only one who can help presently because my government is not likely to act until it is forced to act. Right now, this government would like the matter to stay hidden, until the oil concessions are granted."

"And Jonathan?" Roberts asked, as if to nobody. It was an empty question, addressed to his own anger.

"I cannot imagine why the *jeemat* were left near the boy. It makes no sense." Lind buttoned his coat. "But there is a further logic in the *jeemat* for Wim."

"Further logic?"

"Yes," Lind said sadly. "You noticed the door knocker on the van Euwe house?"

"Yes, a rope with the head of a snake."

"It symbolizes medicine and herbs. The van Euwe family has a tradition in business of importing spices and potions from the Indies. It was their trade, many many years. Another meaning in Indonesian for *obat*, or magic, is medicine. Powerful medicine. The genius of this message will not be lost on my government. This is why you must act, where I cannot. If you can find the murderer, then the government will have to take action."

"All right." Roberts sighed. "What group are we talking about? Where are they found?"

"They are called New World. Their leader is a man named Bok Demal. He is a doctrinaire, very hard-headed and practical, but also immersed in ideology. He is very well educated, at the Hague. He is also very careful and very clever. The police have had him under surveillance for quite some time without being able to learn much about his contacts. It is impossible to deport him, as he has broken no law and holds a valid Dutch passport. He holds forth in a *rijstafel* on Prince Hendrik Arcade, near the harbor docks. I don't know how it can be done, but there must be a way to bring this matter to a head." Lind had taken out a small silver case, and was pinching snuff. "I'm sorry this doesn't bring you any closer to the killer of young Jonathan, if indeed he was murdered."

"Oh, he was murdered," Roberts said angrily. "I think he was killed by mistake. I think your *bali saleng* telephoned the school for Wim, expecting him to come downstairs and answer. But Jono took the call, because Wim was bathing."

"Oh my God," Lind said quietly. He had covered his eyes with his hands. "My God," he said again. "I am so sorry for this I cannot tell you. I know only that children should not die for the troubles of others."

Roberts said, "I agree with you, Herr Lind."

"But I can help you, my boy. You may rest assured that I will watch over your every move. I can help you, but I cannot move myself because of my diplomatic function."

"I understand," Roberts said. "Perhaps you can help in one special way."

"Anything," Lind said.

"I've been deported from England. A silly matter of an argument and fight. I'll need to go back. But it will have to be *arranged.*"

"Yes, I quite understand," Lind said. "I believe I can be of quite a bit of help to you in that regard." Lind had stood and was walking around the table. "Let me leave first, if you don't mind. It would be discreet." He had put on a pair of doeskin gloves. "Perhaps you could enjoy the zoo or the aquarium." He took two or three steps and stopped. "I'll be looking after you," he said.

"Herr Lind," Roberts said. "You're doing all this for Hilda and Max?"

Lind walked back to the table and put his hands in his coat pockets and looked down at his shoes. He seemed moved, unable to speak. He looked up at the atrium, where the sky had grown flecked again with snow.

"Wim was my godchild," he said.

TUESDAY, DECEMBER 10

A NORTHERN gale had broken loose the clouds. They tossed across the harbor like flotsam, the air dense with the sea. Roberts could smell the sea in everything, an undertow of diesel fuel, the flecks of spray tipping over the jetties and quays, ruffling the tide, white pockets of foam on the waves. Gulls hid under the docks. There were a few small boats in the Oosterdok, and along the Het Ij, some tugs and scows chugged toward the vent in an open sea. Roberts could see this from the Prince Hendrik Arcade, a smooth macadam road of four lanes, which led from the city to the depot, running beside the train tracks eastward, toward the harbor.

The quayside was barren and gray. Roberts was standing in a warren of warehouse waste, worker's cafés, loading docks, where men were busy working in the foul weather loading trucks, crating machine parts, chemicals. Some Indonesian bars were across the way, their glass windows explosive with yellow light, around the corners, down the alleys, all the cul-de-sacs with their cheap hotels for immigrants and stevedores.

Roberts had gone up to the Hague on the train, spending nearly a whole day at the national library, prowling around the university periodical desk, perusing every English-language document he could find, every article, monograph, pamphlet that had anything at all about the Kenyah people, the cultural and social life of Borneo, the political struggle

162

over the future of Indonesia, the geography of oil, the story of magic, sorcery, belief. He had come back, deathly tired, sick, his head banging worse than ever, tried to sleep. Now he was standing on the lonely windswept quay, on the corner of the Prince Hendrik Arcade, trucks roaring by along the wet stone, in the diesel fumes and salt spray while the wind howled around him. He stared across the street at the dull stone facade of an Indonesian *rijstafel*, its leaded windows sweating, the frames cracked and dirty, all its strange aromas and sounds. He was thinking about the name Bok Demal, which meant "liver spirit," his group, called New World, which was said to be the leading liberation movement in the chain of eastern islands. He felt as if he had learned a great deal about the *bali saleng*, the Taker-of-Blood, and about the tremendous superstition that surrounded the beliefs of the forest people.

He walked across the Arcade, between trucks, stood on the quay beside a concrete seawall, watching the surf pound the docks, sending the gulls spinning, the fishing boats and moored tugs bobbing violently with the waves. Across the Arcade, the lights in the *rijstafel* seeped through the dirty panes in smudged waves, wet with sweat and spray, and he could see a dark Malay standing in the café window, his jet-black hair tied in a ponytail. The Malay came outside in the wind and tied down a piece of awning that had broken free in the gale. He stood, staring out at the sea, just as a shard of sun stabbed through the low clouds, glinting on the black macadam, the cigarette in his hand streaming smoke, his hands cupped around the cigarette, some workingmen passing along the sidewalk. Then he went back inside the café, stood behind the cash register, smoking, leaning forward on his elbows against a glass case. Roberts could hear a din of music coming from the open door, its character marred by the howling wind, the crash of the sea against the walls. Trucks continued to roar down the Arcade.

Roberts felt very stiff and old. He had changed into his rubber fishing pants, some long johns, the bomber jacket

163

zipped around a flannel shirt. He felt he should have been prepared by his long day of study, but he wasn't, all he felt was a hollow fear, his heart had gone cold, he wanted to wail and cry, to strike Bok Demal, to kill, but he knew he couldn't, which was making him crazy. As he stood in the salt spray, the bulk of Amsterdam visible over the warehouses, all the firs limned by spray, the bell towers dark, he thought of Jocko and Amanda, then Jonathan, of the green English countryside before the war, when Death was a stranger. And now, he had confronted the most terrible thought of his life, *that Jonathan had been murdered by mistake,* that his death had no more meaning than a fleck of lint. He felt as if he could die from the thought, it was paralyzing him. How could money and domination mean more than life? What was this world that it should be so cruel? Roberts walked across the Arcade.

The air inside the restaurant was thick with cardamom, tobacco smoke. He could see two musicians in the back of a narrow room, standing on a pedestal bandstand, both thin islanders in white cotton shirts. One was playing a *sapeh,* a flat stringed instrument from Java, a kind of guitar that emitted cat screeches in unharmonic jumps. The other had a *gampon,* a zylophone, balanced on his knees. The music was just a roar to Roberts, dense as jungle, strangely unsyncopated, this atonality that had a richly hypnotic tone, like an advanced jazz improvisation that produced a wave of sensation, as if one were surrounded by predators. There were rows of crude wooden tables down each side of the café, the ceiling low, the kitchen in back through swinging doors. Benches had been built into the side walls, and on the other side of the tables were wicker chairs. A dozen fishermen and stevedores were sitting at the tables eating fish and rice, smoking Indian cigarettes, drinking coffee and lager. Some had looked up at Roberts with interest, their faces withered, going back to their meals when they'd finished looking.

A waiter hurried past Roberts carrying a tray of rice, curried tomatoes, potatoes, small gobs of boiled pork, red peppers and peanut sauce.

Roberts collared the Malay and asked for Demal. The Malay was an ugly fellow with yellow teeth, nasty hairs on his chin. He was older than Roberts had thought he was going to be from his brief glimpse across the street, the guy had watery, jaundiced eyes. The Malay walked around the counter and spoke with a man in a gray double-breasted suit sitting in the back of the *rijstafel* near the musicians. The man in the suit had a baby face. From what Roberts could tell, his suit was very shabby. The man crooked his finger, and Roberts walked to the back of the *rijstafel*, passing the Malay, who glared. He felt as if he had gone underwater, moving in slow motion through an aquarium filled with strange fish, the music and all the smoke, the strange din from the kitchen, were making his head light. The fishermen watched him as he walked. The waiters had stopped, holding their trays on their shoulders, looking at Roberts—he felt as if he had lost his clothes. He felt as if everyone was waiting for something terrible to happen, the trapdoor to fall, the hanged man to appear under the scaffold, his tongue exposed and drops of blood in his nose. Roberts could hear the wind. Bok Demal was eating boiled fish, some yellow rice. He sat calmly above his plate, dipping his fingers into the peanut sauce, the shrimp. Roberts was impressed with the limpid quality of his gaze, the black hair slicked back from his high forehead.

"Sit down, sir," Demal said without looking up.

"You speak English," Roberts said. He sat at the bench table, in a rattan chair, directly across from the man. Demal smiled at Roberts, drinking some beer, which left a froth on his lip. He looked no more than twenty years old though he was probably older. He had to be, Roberts thought, a Javanese with coffee-toned skin, black hair making a V far down his forehead. Up close, Roberts could see how really threadbare his suit was, the white shirt he wore ragged at the collar and cuffs. Demal reeked of fish smell and coconut oil, cinnamon and clove. He looked like a little boy dressed in his father's clothes.

"I speak English," Demal said, "and Dutch, German, French, even some Japanese. Does that surprise you?"

"Nothing surprises me."

"I'm a little brown boy with a doctorate from the Hague." Demal discoursed in a monotone, staring now at the front of the café, where the wind was banging the windows.

"I've skipped college," Roberts said.

"An American?"

"Mitchell Roberts."

"American," Demal said, smiling, like he was rolling the word around in his mouth, tasting it. "I should have known from your clothing. It is very odd, but you are the first American I have spoken to directly. English, yes. This is like finding a polar bear on one's sofa." He emitted a childlike giggle. "You will become, perhaps, a specimen."

"There are lots of Americans around."

"Not so many as us Indonesians," Demal said. A waiter had come by, Roberts ordered a beer. The waiter came back with a tumbler of flat lager. Demal lit one of his black Indian cigarettes and began to blow smoke. The musicians had stopped the serenade and the bar filled with the clamor of foreign conversation. Outside the wind was really howling, smacking the docks, sweeping along the arcade. Roberts watched as a quilt of foam roared over the quay. Demal was smoking, pushing his fork around in the yellow rice.

"And who is Mitchell Roberts?" he asked.

Just then a young man in a white cotton robe walked to the table and stood behind Roberts. Demal looked up at him with those limpid black eyes. Roberts turned and looked at the man, who had an angry scar behind his right ear, running to his chin. Like Demal, he smelled of fish sauce and sweat. He began a chatter directed at Demal, very high-pitched and nervous. Demal listened patiently and spoke to the young man, the same swelling vibrato.

"He thinks you are from the government," Demal said. "He wants us to take you to the kitchen, where they throw the fish bones. He wants to kill you. He has a *pareng*, a jungle

166

knife. I am afraid he is very violent in his approach. What do you think I should do?"

Roberts turned back. "Tell him if he does that, if he touches me with his goddamn grubby hands, if he even makes a move to threaten me, I'll take away his goddamn knife and then I'll cut out his liver. Tell him once I've done that, I'll eat his liver." Demal had broken an impish smile. "Tell him," Roberts said loudly. The smile left Demal's face and he spoke briefly with the young man, who walked away. Roberts watched him out of the corner of his eye, the young man staring at him, his face frozen.

"I told him you were an American," Demal said.

"Did you tell him the other?"

"No," Demal answered. "Your speech would have provoked the young man. I am surprised that you know about the liver cult. But right now I'm more interested in talking with you than seeing you murdered in the kitchen. After all, I don't even know why you're here, what you want." Demal sipped some beer. "But you must have a knowledge about our people, I do admire that, it interests me. I know you're not from the Dutch government. So I sent the boy away."

"I'm not here from the government. For myself."

"Then like all Americans, you are selfish."

"Like all ideologues, you generalize."

"Come now, Mr. Roberts." Demal was frowning, intrigued and impatient both, playing with the last of his cigarette, rolling it around his yellowed fingers. He bit his lower lip and pushed away the rice plate. The café door had opened and a gust of wind blew in, followed by some spray. The sky was growing a fringe of purple over the harbor where a string of lights blazed, shining in the fog. Only a few trucks passed, you could hear the roar of the ocean far out to sea, the foghorns honking, like geese, the sea moving up and back in long lonely moans. The musicians had begun to play, the *gampon* sounding like a hollow log in the room, struck with a cloth-covered mallet. "I suppose we could trade these clever asides all day," Demal continued. The Malay banged shut the café door. "But

I must insist that you come to the point. You've taken the trouble to seek me out, there must be a reason."

"All right, Demal," Roberts said. "There was an English boy killed in Cambridge last month. His name was Jonathan Smith. I want to know why he was killed, who killed him."

"But my dear sir," Demal said, his eyes alive. "Why would I have that information?"

"And Wim van Euwe?" Roberts asked.

"Ach," Demal said, waving a finger. "You may as well say history killed the Dutch boy. I certainly didn't do it."

"Nonsense," Roberts snapped.

"What do you know of the struggle?" Demal said. His tone had become harsh, this shrill whistling question winging at Roberts through pursed lips. The waiter returned to the table with a dish of rice pudding, Demal tasting it with a spoon, his face red. He had set down some black coffee, and Demal took a sip. "Our world is changing," Demal said, calmed. "We are all caught up in the change. Life is being purged in great contradictory tendencies, stages in the flow of historical dynamics. Your own imperial culture is dying, Western Man, its death throes are violent, there is great destruction. This culture which has created you is a beast whose epoch is closing, the dinosaur. As an individual, Mr. Roberts, you count for nothing. The tide is the historical tide." Here Demal paused, as if he had been lecturing and now thought had interrupted. "You individuals are ghosts of the past. When your capitalism dies, your imperialism will be swept away too, and your greed and your exploitation will be destroyed. It will be as if a typhoon had cut through your towns and cities, and you will be buried by the debris of history, transformed by your own contradictions, engulfed in the heap of your silly convictions, your shallow morality. The end of colonialism is near. But for my people, your end is our beginning, the end of colonialism, the beginning of freedom and self-determination. What do you Americans know except materialism, conquest, power? Who killed Wim van Euwe? You may as well ask who killed the mastodon. It was nature that killed the mastodon, Mr. Roberts. And it will be history that kills you."

"A pretty speech," Roberts said.

"The truth," Demal shouted. He pounded once on the table.

"You haven't answered my question."

"Yes, your question. Quite honestly, I don't know who killed Wim van Euwe. And I've never even heard of Jonathan Smith."

"You made threats against Max van Euwe."

"Yes, his company is an imperialist conspiracy."

Roberts sat back. His head was spinning, the smoke had made him dizzy. "I've just come from London," he said. "At Battersea there is a cemetery. In that cemetery is the body of a young boy, barely twelve years old. I loved that boy, and I think your organization had him murdered, perhaps in a terrible mistake. He was mistaken for Wim van Euwe, but he's dead. I don't know what earthly good you think it does to murder children, but I think you did it. But these boys were flesh and blood to me, they had mothers and fathers, futures to explore. They knew nothing of historical process, ideology. And so I say to hell with you and your forces, your excuses for murder and mayhem. To me you're a snot-nosed brat, a monster hiding behind slogans, using your pretexts to murder innocent children. I've seen your historical forces on the march. I've seen it in newsreels, storm troops marching through the streets of Berlin, crowds roaring at Nuremberg. I've seen history in the forests of Ardenne, my friends dying. It was history that took the Jews to slaughter at Auschwitz. It was history that covered the Soviet peasants with lime. This history you talk about has the stench of death about it, millions of deaths. You smell of death, you reek of it. But it is the single soul that matters, the child. To hell with your history if it means the deaths of innocent children."

"A pretty speech," Demal said. He looked dreamy, still the limpid black eyes. "You lack a philosophy." He sighed. "It is people who murder people, but those brownshirts in Nazi

Germany were the sons of wealthy burghers, makers of steel, petrochemicals." Demal had broken a thin sweat, which made his face shiny. The music had swollen the room, Roberts ears were ringing. "Oh Mr. Roberts, you are rootless in a dangerous world."

"You're right about one thing," Roberts said. "It is people who murder people. I've killed, but not in the name of history. If we do that, we're no better than the brownshirts. I do have a philosophy. It's by way of Tom Jefferson."

Demal sipped some coffee. "I know what your philosophy amounts to." The *gampon* was clomping away, like a forest falling, crashing. "You Western men are like pirates with a treasure map. The map is history. You want the map to lead you to the treasure. You scour the world, using the map to search for treasure. Your hidden gold. You seek to make the map reveal its secrets, its symbols, until finally one day the pirates begin to quarrel over the map itself. You destroy yourselves in the name of the map until ultimately you've lost sight of the treasure, you are locked in combat to see who will control the map. This individualism of yours is like the map. It is the abstraction, not history. But I've killed no one, had no one killed. If Wim van Euwe has been murdered, perhaps it has been over one of your own abstractions, who knows?"

Two Malays had come from the kitchen and were busy nailing a sheet over the opening in the swinging doors. Somebody behind the sheet had lit a bank of candles, the waiters had turned off the overhead lights and a hazy dark settled on the room, smoking candles, tobacco smoke. A steady rain washed down the awning, fell on the streets. It seemed to Roberts that the *sapeh* and *gampon* had increased in intensity, a counterpoint to the sound of the rain.

Demal motioned to the waiter for more coffee. He brought two tiny saucers of the sweet steaming liquid. Roberts could smell tapioca, boiled fish, coconut oil, he was barely able to breathe. Then there was a crescendo, the musicians ceased and there came a piercing shriek from behind the ambient sheet. Two shadows appeared on the white surface of the

170

cloth, thrust up from the glow of the candles, one large puppet who seemed to be in armor, with a long-shafted spear, another puppet with a sack tossed over its back. The puppets began a rhythmic dance, in circles, as the musicians played softly. The audience began a chant, and there was some laughter and applause.

"*Wayang golek,*" Demal whispered. He was puffing steadily on a cigarette, his black eyes glowing, eyebrows arched in pleasure. Outside, somewhere, a church bell chimed, the sea was slamming against the quay. "This is the great moral struggle," he said. "This is how we display the forces of life, the play of shades, perhaps you can understand the analogy. To my people, this performance brings great solace and pleasure."

Roberts watched the performance, the warrior chasing the peasant, thrusting his spear. The peasant was jumping, dodging the blade. With each thrust, the men in the café shouted, clapped loudly. There was a steady tinkle of coffee cups, muffled conversation.

"The noble warrior," Demal said, reflectively. "He wishes to steal the rice from the peasant. They lead each other a merry chase. When the noble finally closes in, he stabs with his spear. But what happens?" Demal smiled. "The rice sack is punctured. The rice spills to the earth, ruined. It will be a long season without food. The noble and the peasant will both starve." Demal crunched out his cigarette in the pudding. "It is a charming story, don't you think? It is the drama of *wayang.*"

The music had stopped. A young boy walked onto the pedestal dressed in a cotton tunic. He began to clink a pair of brass cymbals. The *gampon* caught up a back beat, terrible and hollow.

"Now the great battle," whispered Demal. "The nobles must select their king. It will be accomplished through war, the ultimate test. War is the ultimate *wayang.*" The sheet had filled with whirling shadows. The men in the café set up another chant, hunched forward over their coffee and ciga-

171

rettes, a murmur. The music had risen to a single indistinguishable beat while the armies marched and fought. One by one the puppets fell, were silent until the entire sheet was a rumple of bodies, crumpled. At the edge of the scene, through the carnage, a single puppet began to walk, a peasant slowly picking his way across the field of battle, sack on his back. The workmen in the café began to applaud and the waiters lit the overhead lamps again.

"The peasant is constant," Demal said. "Are you amused?" Demal had lit another cigarette. "Are you not delighted to witness the poor peasant walking among the dead nobles? The battle was over the right to steal his rice. Don't you see? The peasant survives. This is the march of history, this is the real lesson." He sat back, pleased.

Roberts felt damp all over. "Listen, you bloody intellectual," he said. "You sent a Kenyah to England and he murdered Jonathan Smith. I'm going to find the bastard and then I'm going to make him pay. I don't mind debating you about the individual and history, but the debate is finished."

"So be it," Demal said. "The world can no longer afford your kind of individualism." Demal's voice had become hysterical. He seemed to relax then, leaning forward so Roberts could hear above the music. "I tell you the absolute truth. I've sent no Kenyah to England. I've had no children murdered."

"Then what happened?" Roberts asked.

"I assure you I do not know."

"You threatened Max van Euwe."

"Yes, certainly. He was a tool of the Dutch company. And his friend Lind."

"I think you're lying," Roberts said. "Both boys were killed in Cambridge. *Jeemat* were found near them. A *wayang* puppet in their clothing."

Demal slouched, his face broken finally into some emotion. He shook his head, crushed out his cigarette and looked around the room. "This is why you think a Kenyah did the murders."

"Yes. I'm sure of it."

172

"But it can't be." Demal seemed lost in thought.

Roberts pulled out his wallet. He had a picture of Jonathan which he handed across to Demal, who sat studying the photograph, a callow boy in a cricket uniform on the steps of a museum, smiling, the trees in bud. Roberts thought he detected a break in Demal, true emotion. Demal got up from his bench seat, touched Roberts on the shoulder and asked him to remain. He walked back through the kitchen doors and returned holding a leather notebook. He sat down and opened the notebook, rummaged through its pages, a loose collection of documents, photographs, diary entries. He handed Roberts a black-and-white photograph. Roberts saw a white temple in jungle, the sky full of fleecy clouds, on the steps of the temple bodies of women and children, priests in robes, even dogs. He felt sick, looking at the scene. Demal was observing Roberts, registering his reaction.

"A village in Java," Demal said. "The Dutch came through with an armed force and slaughtered the villagers who had gone to the temple for shelter. These were innocent children as well. There are thousands of dead children for every Wim van Euwe. Thousands. My struggle is for these Indonesian children. I would give my own life to save theirs. You see, I believe that even my own life is nothing against this historical necessity." He seemed shaken, Roberts slid the photograph back across the table. "But I must tell you, I could not kill a child. I say I could. Perhaps in some circumstance I could. But I did not order Wim van Euwe murdered." Some fishermen were leaving, paying their bills, waving good-bye, walking out along the windy arcade. The waiters were collecting plates. Roberts felt suddenly cold and shocked, almost impotent.

"How can I believe you?"

Demal looked surprised. He studied Roberts in the smoky café light. "I'm through talking," he said.

Roberts shook his head. The rain had stopped and there were traces of fog over the seawall. Roberts was about to stand when the café door came open again. In the entry stood a dark man, maroon in color with a flat nose and black hair cut

173

close around his face. He had long arms, his shoulders square and thick. Roberts caught his eye and held him, seeing the confusion, the trace of panic in the expression.

"That's a Kenyah, isn't it?" Roberts asked Demal. Without waiting for an answer from Demal, Roberts continued. "That wouldn't be your man in England, the one who killed Jonathan, Wim van Euwe too?"

"Don't be ridiculous," Demal snapped harshly. "He's an illegal from outside Jakarta. He hasn't been in Holland six weeks. He probably thinks you're from Immigration or the police." The young Kenyah disappeared from the restaurant doorway. Demal touched Robert's arm. "You must believe me, Mr. American, there hasn't been any murder in England done by me, or by anyone in my organization. Our battle is strictly against the Dutch, against the colonialism that is strangling my country."

Roberts didn't acknowledge Demal; he turned and headed toward the door and went outside. He stood under the soaked awning while the rain pelted down. He could hear the sea thundering along the quay. Far away it was smashing against the dikes, blowing spray over the docks. Beyond the Oosterdok and the Nordzee canal, in the Het Ij, tugs' foghorns moaned. Fog was mixing in the sea spray, creating a grist of floating vapor that suffused the air, obscured the railway tracks, the black warehouse buildings and cheap hotels of the district. Roberts remained silent, trying to listen for the sound of the Kenyah's footsteps receding in the night. He could see a form down the darkened street, turning a corner at the war memorial. Roberts hurried across the street, past the Arcade, with the wind behind him now. He was being soaked by the driving rain.

Out of the darkness a sleek Mercedes pulled to a stop by the curb where Roberts was waiting. He was startled for a moment—the car was like an apparition from the fog, hood steaming. Then a back window was rolled down and he saw the face of Herr Lind. "Please get in, Mr. Roberts," the man said, opening the door. Roberts fell inside the car, utterly exhausted. He closed the door and immediately sensed his own fever in contrast to the warmth and closeness of the Mercedes. His wet skin was sticking to the plush seat. Lind had made room for him and now motioned for the car to move. It was being driven by a big-shouldered man in a gray suit and topcoat. Roberts closed his eyes, too tired to speak.

They drove across the city, past the flower market, to a bar and café near Roberts's pensione. It was late, nearly closing time, and the barman was wiping down the zinc bar. The place was deserted except for an old woman who was mopping the floor in back, smoking and having her final free gin. They sat away from the door and ordered brandy while Roberts caught his breath. The bar was a baroque setting with beamed ceilings, dark mahogany furniture and maroon *fleur de lis* carpeting. Roberts felt as if he was burning; he took off his bomber jacket and sipped some brandy. He was trembling from the cold. Outside it had already begun to sleet. Perhaps it would snow as well when the air got colder.

"Suppose you tell me about your last two days," Lind said.

Roberts closed his eyes. The brandy was burning in his throat. "I've been at the Hague, in the anthropological library reading about magic, sorcery. About the *jeemat*. I thought it might make a difference. Then I decided to drop around the *rijstafel* and talk with Demal, make him think I knew more than I did. I was having an ideological discussion with him when a fellow came in the café. When he saw me he became terrified and ran away. I don't know why, but I had an insane notion he might have been one of Demal's agents, that he might have been the man who went to England and killed Wim."

"Very resourceful," Lind said. "But I'm afraid it isn't so."

"How do you know this?" Roberts asked.

"The man driving the Mercedes is Josef," Lind replied. "He is not a policeman, but he is connected with them. We've spent our last two days trying to see if Demal could have been responsible in any way. We've traced his movements over the

175

past several months. I'm sorry to say we don't believe any of his organization went to England. Not even secretly."

"And the Kenyah," Roberts muttered.

"Just another illegal. There are thousands like him in Amsterdam right now. You probably frightened him."

"That's what Demal said too." Roberts slumped back in his chair. "Demal denied everything. He had no explanation for the toys. I suppose he could be a practiced liar, but he was convincing."

"In this case, he may be telling the truth."

"How did you ever find me tonight?" Roberts asked.

Lind smiled wanly. "I've been keeping an eye on you, Mr. Roberts. I told you I could not intervene directly, not until the matter had become one for the police. So, I've kept you under my wing, so to speak. I was nearby when you came out of the restaurant."

"Can't you arrest Demal," Roberts said.

"On what charge?" Lind asked.

Roberts blinked.

"And besides," Lind said, "after tonight you can be sure that Demal will be very careful. He might even leave Holland."

"But where could he go?"

"Ach." Lind spit. "He has many contacts. He could return to Indonesia. He could go to England."

Roberts felt a clutch in his throat. "You can't mean the English would help a man like that."

"I've told you," Lind said. "There is a great deal of money at stake. If the Dutch company loses its grip in the East Indies, the English companies have much to gain. The murder of Wim could drive a terrible wedge between the Dutch and the Indonesians. The English would like to see such a thing." Lind dropped some coppers on the polished table. Roberts noticed the barman staring at the clock, putting on his suit jacket. The old woman had gone and they were alone in the bar with the wind banging the windows, the streets aglow

176

with rain. Roberts could still hear the foghorns, they reminded him of animals prowling the mountains.

"And Demal showed me pictures of a temple massacre. He said it was Dutch soldiers who did it."

"There is a struggle," Lind said. "Children die. Men and women, too. Years ago I fought the Japanese and the issue seemed clear. Now the world is a much more horrible puzzle."

They put on their coats and went out to the Mercedes. Roberts got in back with Lind and they drove down to his pensione, about six blocks, across from the flower market. The windows steamed up and Roberts could barely see the streets. They parked in front and sat for a long time. Roberts was filled with foreboding, he thought he had come a long way, but that he was doing something wrong. He recalled the look on Demal's face when he showed him the picture of Jono, how the man had seemed truly moved. Something inside Roberts had rebelled. Why would Demal leave *jeemat* when he was a college-educated ideologue? It didn't make sense to Roberts, but he couldn't tell why.

"Have you ever heard of an Englishman named Clannahan?" Roberts asked, suddenly, sitting in his seat trying to see out to the street, where the snow was bunching in the curb.

"English Home Office," Lind answered, not looking at Roberts.

"Ties to oil?"

"Naturally," Lind said. "Just like mine."

Roberts slid his arm over the back of the seat. He could smell rosewater on Lind, the brandy. "I want to go back to England," he said. "Can it be arranged?"

Lind thought for a moment. There were beads of reflected light on his forehead, the windshield, sleet hitting the metal hood of the Mercedes. "It can be arranged," Lind said. "Tomorrow, the next day. Stay at your pensione. It will be something of an undertaking."

"I'll wait," Roberts said.

"Do you have a clear purpose?"

"Find the man who killed Jono." Roberts swiveled, looked at Lind, who was staring out the window. "And Wim, too."

"You'll inform me?" Lind turned to Roberts. "For Hilda?"

"Of course," Roberts said, touching Lind's arm. He got out of the Mercedes. Lind turned the car into the street and Roberts went up to his room, where he tried to sleep.

LONDON

SATURDAY, DECEMBER 14

THEY had trained at High Wycombe, going on maneuvers in the midland gorse fields, long marches, bivouacs in Yorkshire, where the land was damp with snow, motoring back and forth in trucks from the barracks. When spring came, talk of the invasion was everywhere, on every tongue, it was in the pubs, at chow, an undercurrent to every thought. But the weather had been dazzling, high slate skies, or clear blue, with white puffy clouds drifting over from Ireland, a mild breeze blowing through the wildflowers, then rain, mostly at night, stopping by midmorning, leaving the air clean and shot with sun. There was palpable excitement in the air too, and nobody spoke of death. The invasion was something grand and proper for men to do.

Sometime in early May they had their last leave, Smitty and Roberts going by train up to Ipswich, met by Amanda, the three of them renting bicycles. They pedaled across the old city, beside the estuary bridge, the low river sliding green toward the sea, the tide tugging it back, gulls squawking for food, the stalls full of flowers and leeks.

Joseph loved to go fast, his head back, trailing a white scarf, they had all wanted to be airmen, this American singing at the top of his lungs some nonsense ditties, "Mares Eat Oats," all the townspeople laughing, pointing, some waving at the young people, crazy with life in the middle of a bad war. And Joseph was a fool for fun, for showing off, but his heart was so good, and his manner so gentle, he could not be blamed. Amanda rode in the middle, hair streaming back, Joseph rounding the High Street turn with a whoop, nearly falling, regaining his balance, making for the open country. Roberts lagged, content to go slower, watching the people, seeing their faces, enjoying the birdsong, the chase.

They were in East Anglia, wheat fields the color of honey, the stacked hay, narrow lanes bounded by flint walls, in the distance Norman churches, huge stands of oak, chestnuts emerald green, their white spring blossoms. They stopped to pick blackberries coming ripe, and everywhere the green English countryside falling away, bees buzzing. They rode and sang and drank ale in pubs, making for the North Sea coast at Norwich.

Then, one late afternoon after they had come swooning over a rise, they saw the first sick rabbit, then another, and soon they saw fields full of the sick creatures, wobbling in the wildflowers, legs swollen, eyes protruding. They lay dead in the ditches. They were black with decay. As soon as the bicyclists stopped for lunch, someone in a pub told them about the disease, the rabbits were helpless, it would run its course.

They had gone on, pedaling south after a day on the North Sea, but something had stalled their spirits, though they continued to visit the ruined churches, pick berries in the clutch of lanes and fences. Somewhere, he couldn't remember now, Roberts had heard Joseph skid around a turn, careening, a soft cry coming out of him in a rush, and then a curse. He and Amanda stopped around the curve and saw that Joseph had struck one of the helpless rabbits, that Joseph was lying in the road, his knee skinned and bleeding, a stricken look on his face, a bloated rabbit crawling off into a ditch. Roberts could hear the thing making a peep, he thought it sounded like a baby bird fallen from a nest.

Amanda was off her bike, going to Joseph, kneeling beside him, and in that instant Roberts could feel the two of them come together, something about their eyes, that single universe of shared pain, that wholly absurd and silent torment.

He stopped, sitting on his bicycle on the brow of a hill where curves coiled downhill in loops, the sunshine, a village far away and the music of the wind through the rye and he believed that if he had fallen, that he would have been loved, fate had that kind of gravity, chance had that kind of seriousness. He often thought of it, later, after the years had fled and none of it mattered, what circumstance had thrown Joseph down from his bicycle? What fool cause?

"You silly," Amanda was saying, "I loved you both."

She smiled, looking down from the head of the stairs. Roberts was carrying a bowl of cornflakes, he didn't know if it was morning, afternoon, he had been deeply asleep, just getting up and into a blue bathrobe, coming up the stairs.

He had taken the Dutch diplomatic boat overnight to Portsmouth, disembarking unnoticed while the weary English customs crew stamped papers without a glance, they were used to meeting the exempt boats. Going through without inspection, he took the two-hour train to London, had a hot bath in the Kensington Park house, and collapsed onto the cramped daybed in the cellar, warm as a mouse. It was as if he were shedding some skin, this new life he thought he was getting, coming back to England with so much on his mind, his head had stopped throbbing, the black bruise was fading, he thought maybe he could help Amanda, but first he had to sleep.

They went around the corner to the big upstairs room. Amanda had made some coffee, a pot of it steaming on the window ledge, and Roberts collapsed onto the sofa, bound in an afghan, sipping the hot coffee. He could hear the heavy Saturday traffic going up and down the Portobello Road, where the antique bazaar was probably flooded with crowds, the pubs already busy, he thought it must be just afternoon, the beginning of the real day. Amanda was looking lovely with her hair freshly washed, tied back with a white ribbon, Roberts couldn't take his eyes off her, he was beginning to stare, her auburn hair, the full lips, he knew how he felt and it had stupefied him. Finally, he began to explain himself, how he had gone to Amsterdam after being deported, it was something he'd done on the spur of the moment, right at the station. Amanda was smoking, biting her lip, the sun flooding through the room, this fire in the windows, arcs of pearlescence. The sky looked as if it had been brushstroked, pigeons, red buses down below. You could hear the hawkers, organ music too.

"I've been so worried," Amanda said.

"I'm afraid I didn't find any answers in Holland," Roberts said. He arched back, trying to see down the street, south Kensington, Portobello, brown diagonals and soft pastel.

Amanda moved across the sofa, sat on the floor with her elbows on the coffee table. She played her spoon in the coffee cup, thinking, looking worried. "I've telephoned Martin Brooke to come over."

"Good," Roberts said. "I'm glad."

"I didn't know where you'd gone."

"They gave me two days to leave England. Chap named Clannahan. Had to get my things together, talk with Brooke and Jacob Miles. When I got here I didn't know what I was going to do. I was too sick to worry about it, so when I got to Victoria, I headed for Holland."

"This has to do with Wim, doesn't it?"

"Yes, I'm afraid so."

"Still, it was terrible for Jocko, for Brooke. We didn't know where you'd gone."

"I took a chance."

"But we didn't know if you'd come back."

"Well I did. I'm here illegally. If the immigration people get me, they'll throw me in the can. Jail."

Amanda brushed back her hair. For Roberts the room had a calming sense of peace, coal smell, old books, the sun streaming down on Saturday, he didn't want to move, he wanted perfection. "Nevertheless," Amanda said, "Jocko was absolutely beside himself. He has hardly slept. He telephoned Harlow constantly to see if Miles knew where you were. I've never seen him so obsessed. Two or three times a day he telephoned, for Glenville too. It wasn't something he'd talk to me about either. It was as if he was trying to grow up overnight. No matter what I said, he wouldn't open up to me. I think this is the first time he's shut me out of anything in his life."

Roberts returned from his reverie. It wasn't fair, there was so much to do. "It was my fault. I asked him not to bother you with what I was doing. I didn't think he'd take me so literally. It was a stupid thing to do. Forgive me?"

"Of course," Amanda said, breaking a smile.

"Still, I don't understand what he'd be so obsessed about. He doesn't really know very much."

"Well, whatever he knew, or thought he knew, it was making him very upset."

"Perhaps it was just about me. We've made plans."

Amanda moved over, sitting under Roberts now, looking up at him. "I don't know," she said. "I could hear him up all night, pacing his room. He begged me not to bother him." She drank some coffee, forced a pause, as if she were trying to hold the thing away from her, distance it. "When he got up in the morning, he was back at the telephone."

"Why Glenville?" Roberts asked. He was beginning to worry. He didn't know why.

"Don't know," Amanda said, clipped. "But I can tell you Jocko spent the whole afternoon yesterday with Martin Brooke. Then he didn't sleep last night again. I've tried to tell myself that with all that's happened, he's just having a difficult time dealing with Jono. We all are." Roberts explored the room in his mind, like a ghost, the wool smell of sage in the rugs, the sun like lemon rind. "Of course," Amanda was saying, "I told myself he was worried about you, too. Without you, I'm afraid we'd be lost."

Roberts pondered all the calls to Glenville. "But why Glenville?" he whispered to himself, looking out the window, chestnuts in Kensington Park with dark armatures.

"He wouldn't say a word," Amanda said. "He was on the

telephone last night. I had the feeling he was talking with Glenville then. I don't know why. But when I went downstairs he had begun to shout nearly. He seemed to be shaking, it appeared as if he might cry. But when I tried to talk to him, it was as if he didn't know me. He put down the phone and went to his room without saying a word."

Roberts knew what he was doing was wrong. He was seeing the young English nurse, dusty freckled face, maple eyes, the wild poetic smile. So much youth.

"Perhaps if I talk with Jocko," he said.

"That's just it!" Amanda muttered. "He's gone away to Cambridge. He left on the early train before you arrived. There was a single-line note in the kitchen. Don't worry—be home late. That sort of rot."

Roberts sat up. He felt a surge of fear. "Have you spoken to Brooke about this?"

"Just telephoned. Thought you should be here. All of us talk this thing over. When I told him Jocko had gone, he was upset as well. He'll be right over."

"This is all my fault," Roberts said. "I encouraged Jocko to feel a part of doing *something*. I also encouraged him to keep you out of it. Trying to protect you. What you'd call a lot of tommyrot." Roberts put his hand on Amanda's.

"He trusts you," she said. "There's no harm in that. I'm only worried he's in over his head."

Roberts changed his clothes downstairs. He was terrified, guilty for not telling Amanda that Wim had been murdered, it would lead to Jonathan, then what? There was somebody out there killing children. He didn't think Amanda needed to know that right now. Not right now, anyway. When he'd dressed, he used the telephone to call Glenville, but there was no answer and so he found some croissants in the refrigerator, went back upstairs. Amanda had changed into a long dress, high boots, a sheepskin sweater. He took a cup of coffee up the narrow stairs to Jocko's room and looked around for a scrap, something, anything, a clue to Jocko's behavior. It was making him crazy, so he took a short walk around the Portobello market looking at books and maps. When he came back, Brooke and Amanda were upstairs drinking coffee. Brooke was wild in appearance, red face, garden pants with soil on the knees, a Harlow cardigan in green and oak.

Brooke sat stiffly, playing with his pipe. "Now, what's this about Jocko?" he asked Amanda.

"Gone to Cambridge." she said.

"Bloody hell," Brooke swore. "All my fault. Boy should never have gone."

"Never mind that," Amanda said. "Do you know what he's up to? Where he's gone exactly?"

"Quite," Brooke said emphatically. Amanda exchanged a quick glance with Roberts. "The lad," Brooke continued, "has a notion that Master Glenville is involved in Jono's death. He's been working the notion over for the week. Came over to see me, and couldn't stop talking about it, but I didn't see how the notion could be true. For one thing, there couldn't be a motive to murder poor Jono." Brooke had looked at Amanda, who was staring wide-eyed at the doctor, both of them locked in the terrible embrace of his words. "Like an old fool, I coddled the lad. Now, I'm afraid he's taken the matter into his own hands. He's probably gone 'round to see Miles." Brooke patted Amanda on the shoulder. "I shouldn't think there'd be cause for worry, dear."

"But you said he had a theory," Amanda said.

"Yes, the theory. Told him there must be an explanation. Glenville wouldn't harm Jono."

"Go on, for God's sake," Amanda said. She was flushed, Roberts could see her tremble.

Roberts suddenly sensed how cold the sunshine really was, yellow light like clear ice. Amanda had let the coal fire go out, and there were drafts too. Away in Richmond church bells chimed, crisp notes in the air. Roberts hated what was happening, all of it.

"Do you remember the night Wim fell?" Brooke asked Roberts, who nodded, Amanda holding his hand now while she began to breathe heavily, smoking her cigarette.

"Clearly," he said.

"Glenville came to the room that night. We were all there. He said he'd answered the telephone the night Jono died. Someone wanted to speak with Jono. He didn't recognize the person. He didn't pay much attention, he said. When he spoke to the three of us at Harlow, Jocko thinks Glenville was lying, that the call was for Wim. And that's not all."

"What else?" Amanda snapped.

"Jocko thinks there was something odd." Brooke had grown flustered, trying to think. There were tears rolling from Amanda's eyes, Roberts wanted to touch them, hold them back, he could feel how cold the room was and he wanted to organize a defense against it. "You see," Brooke went on, "Harlow boys receive their calls on a phone in the main hall. There is a monitor on duty who takes the calls, runs and gets the chap. That is, only in the evening between certain hours. And on holidays, it isn't normal for a telephone call to come in. I told Jocko it could have been that the monitor wasn't there, Glenville took the call, doing the lad a favor. But even so, he was troubled by the Sunday call, during a holiday, and then for the master to run upstairs. And what Glenville said about the boys receiving many Sunday calls, it isn't true. It is all unusual, I have to admit."

"Glenville said he'd taken the call."

"Well, yes, that is a bit of a bother. Jocko thought it bloody unlikely he'd do something like that. It certainly would be out of the ordinary. But I told him it was possible that Glenville would answer a phone. Jocko even thought the bloody thing was unplugged during holidays. That's what had him so bonkers. I told him to go easy. But he vowed to call Glenville until he had all the answers. He didn't know where you'd gone, when you'd return, and he wanted to do this for his brother."

"My God, Mitchell what's he gone and done?" Amanda sobbed.

"Does Miles know what's going on?" Roberts asked.

"Well, no," Brooke said, haltingly. "I'm afraid I discouraged the whole business. I didn't see why anyone would have a motive to murder Jono."

Amanda got a train schedule from her letter desk. She sat down on the couch and studied the microscopic row of figures, times and trains, tracks, horrible English script. Roberts's heart began to pound. Amanda stabbed at one of the rows. "I'm going to Cambridge right now. I'm going to find my son. There's a train from Liverpool Street Station on the hour." She turned, tipping over her coffee cup. "You'll come?" she asked Roberts. He nodded and she went downstairs to pack. They could hear her in the hall, rummaging in boxes, drawers.

"Now then," Brooke said, knowing Amanda was out of hearing. "What's this all about, old man?"

"Wim was murdered. It probably has political overtones. When Jono went downstairs that night, the murderer thought he was Wim."

"Oh dear God," Brooke said. He closed his eyes.

"The paralytic. The toys. We're supposed to believe that an independence group in Amsterdam is responsible. Trying to drive a wedge between certain Dutch interests and the present government in Jakarta."

"The bloody idea," Brooke muttered. "Killing children." He bounced his pipe off the coffee table. "But how could Glenville be involved in something like that?"

"I don't think he could."

Brooke studied Roberts, powerless for a moment against his ideas. "Well, good," he said. "At least Jocko is off on some wild-goose chase."

"I don't know," Roberts said. "I have a feeling that it is me who's been on the wild-goose chase in Amsterdam. Somehow I don't think the group is responsible."

"But the toys?"

"Yes, about the toys," Roberts said, thinking more out loud than anything else.

"You mean Glenville may be involved?" Brooke asked. "What a ruddy old fool I've been. I should have taken Jocko more seriously. You'd think after all these years . . ."

189

"You couldn't have known. It was only my trip to Amsterdam that started me thinking along this line. I think we should hurry up to Cambridge and have a chat with Glenville."

Brooke hurried from the couch, down the stairs. Roberts followed, standing at the front window, watching people on Kensington Park Road while Brooke used the telephone in another room. He could hear Amanda in the cellar locking up. The hand-tooled suitcase was by the door already, Roberts hadn't even unpacked, he was ready to go. Standing there, shoulder against the doorjamb, he could see that the sky had flaked away in the late afternoon, like old paint, its surface flat with cold where the sun had gone. Some children were gathered on the corner watching an organ-grinder, laughing as a monkey scampered around with its cup. He had so much feeling, he could hear the sound of the children, scampering, the monkey tapping the cup on the street, it all had a metaphysical ring, like the church bells that had been chiming in Richmond. He sensed he was just behind something, motion obscured by shade, Jocko was gone, Glenville, he had no idea what he was going to find. It frightened him terribly. It was awful.

Amanda came up the stairs from the cellar. She had a small case, her hair tucked in a bun. Brooke had come back from the kitchen. "I've telephoned Miles," he said. "But his wife told me he's been gone all morning. Taken their boy to the football match."

"We'd best hurry," Amanda said. Before Roberts could move, she was already out the door, down the steps, standing beside the iron gate. She was waving at the black cabs speeding by. Roberts could discern the desperation on her face.

Brooke had gotten just behind Roberts, where the door opened to the stoop. "You don't think any harm could come to Jocko, do you?" he whispered.

"Oh God," Roberts said, "it's possible."

Brooke glanced at his watch. "The boy will just be getting to Cambridge now. Perhaps he'll try and wait for Miles. Let's hurry along, we'll be there in less than two hours."

Amanda had found a cab, standing in the open door with her bags tumbled inside, looking stricken, motioning for them to hurry, hurry. The traffic was thick in Notting Hill Gate, you could smell the ale and the broiled sausage, all the people on the streets, the cinemas just opening for business. Roberts had almost forgotten, it came as something of a shock to him, but it was nearly Christmas, he could hear the music from stores and shops, there were some trees in the windows, old guys asking for pennies on the corners, in the underground entryways. He couldn't get over it, the season, how it had slipped away from all of them. They went toward the roundabout at Hyde Park, Martin Brooke stabbing at his pipe, staring out the open window with a cold wind snapping at his hair, all of them quiet while the cabbie drove toward Liverpool Street Station.

Central England lay under a drab sky, flinty gray stone landscape with gulls and pigeons slashed in the clouds, pubs and shops with sharp black roofs. When they went across the High streets, all the children would gather and wave with their cheeks ruddy in the cold, dogs snapping in fun. The fields were fallow brown, dun yellow, all the stone fences wet and shiny. All the way Amanda said nothing, sitting in the carriage, near the window, her face pressed against the glass, smoking one cigarette after another while the terraced fields fled. Brooke had a long conversation with an Anglican priest until the priest fell asleep in midsentence, slipping down in his seat, his bifocals tipped against the end of his nose, snoring, his head down on his breastbone. Roberts was trying to think about Glenville, watching the tiny Lancias and Fords speed down the lanes, far away, and then suddenly he would think about Jocko, then Jono, and his eyes would tear up, and he began a long prayer, silently. Brooke had purchased a pot of tea from a concessionaire and was drinking it from a paper cup while the Anglican snored.

At Cambridge they hired a cab, driving through the city on the High Street, down past Trinity, all the bridges where a

191

few students were walking in the cold, reading on benches, feeding the swans. Brooke got out at the Trinity Library and hurried down a side street, headed toward police headquarters to wait for Miles, call his wife again. Amanda and Roberts went on to Harlow School and across the quadrangle toward the administration wing, where Glenville had his digs. Amanda was walking very fast, Roberts had to hurry to keep up, looking at Wim's window, the memory of that night coming back, the figure on the Backs running, the way Roberts had experienced a sudden convulsion of pain, and then nothing. Once inside the building, he could smell the wax and cherry wood, and he could hear Amanda pounding on the door to Glenville's small apartment. He saw her lurch inside, and then scream.

When he got to the room, inside, leaning in the doorjamb, panting heavily, he saw Glenville prostrate, nearly spread-eagle, on a cot in the corner of the room. Dark blood had pooled on his chest, his stomach, it had seeped into his clothes, turning black. The ashen face would have been beatific, this holy ring of white, but the lips were blue, beads of sweat on the forehead, and the eyes nearly blackened. Roberts thought he looked like an old man with sunken cheeks, someone you might find in a nursing home, all the life seeping away, eaten from inside, just skin and bones, and it shocked him, but Roberts could tell the man was breathing, he could see his ribs rising through the sweat and blood-soaked shirt, he could hear a stertorous rasp. Amanda was standing beside the dirty bed, hands over her mouth, she looked frozen, staring wildly at the dying man.

Roberts pulled her away, back toward the center of the room so he could have a look. There was a sour smell coming from Glenville, something vile and distinct, and the room smelled too, of bacon grease, bachelor grime, all the years of dust and despair. Soot had collected on the walls, like a factory, English bed-sitter-style. Roberts tossed away a sheet that covered the man's legs and took a look at him. He had been gutshot, terribly, perhaps twice, there was blood on the floor near the bed, a smear along the doorjamb on the inside, you could tell he had dragged himself to the cot, tried to pull up the sheet. He had forged himself a shroud, a death mask too, all a piece of work. It was an agonizing wait, bleeding to death from inside, capillaries, veins, the organs drowning. Roberts lowered his head until he could feel an icy exhalation. The stink was death. Amanda had gone outside, trying to use the phone, but Roberts could tell it was no use.

Glenville's eyes fluttered open. "No time," he said.

Roberts moved his hand, he could see the wounds below the sternum, a dark crust of slime. It was stone cold in the dingy room, dim gray light sifting in from nowhere. There was a moment when Glenville's fingers twitched, touching Roberts's wrist, like a cadaver. "He took Jocko," Glenville said, "it couldn't be helped. He did this, and took the boy." Amanda was banging on the telephone. Glenville tried to lift himself, his head fell back. "Quickly," he breathed. "They told me no harm would come to van Euwe. They said they wanted to frighten him. I didn't know it would come to this. But I needed the money so terribly." Roberts was looking directly at the dying man when his face relaxed absolutely, like a shade had been drawn. And Roberts felt something indecipherable move. "Look what I've done."

Roberts understood it then. Poor Glenville, failed humanist, the shabby suit, shuffling away his life in a schoolful of boys, the dank dim room, life blooming around him while the days grew colder, Glenville, dying embodiment of small greed and large disappointment. He felt a tremendous sorrow for the man. "Tell me who did this," Roberts said, close to the dying man's ear.

"A man, I don't know," Glenville coughed.

Roberts heard footsteps in the hall, then Brooke was at the door, Amanda behind with her face over his shoulder. Brooke kneeled down beside the cot, taking the man's pulse, shaking his head as he looked at Roberts, touching Glenville's forehead.

"Brooke," Glenville whispered. "For God's sake, listen to

me. I've set it all down in a letter, posted it to you. He's taken Jocko."

"Don't try to talk," Brooke said. "Miles will be along soon. We'll take care of you."

"No use," said Glenville, eyes closed.

Amanda had wet a rag, begun to wipe Glenville's face. She looked at Roberts and said, "There was no answer at Miles's house. I didn't know what to do."

"Telephone for an ambulance," Brooke said.

Amanda had given the rag to Brooke when the telephone rang, bursting the silence, it was like the sudden tear in fine fabric. Roberts went into the hall. He had to get away, he couldn't stay and look at that white face on the soiled linen, sweat dripping. He picked up the telephone.

"I've seen you come up to Glenville's room Mr. Roberts," a voice said.

"Who is this?" Roberts asked. He had expected Miles. There was no context for his experience now, it was like a hall of mirrors, this strange voice, the nacreous light in the hallways, wax smells, all the filigreed light seeping through the faraway windows.

"Come now, we have serious business."

"What do you want?"

"I want that letter."

"I don't have any letter."

"Glenville said he mailed it. I want it back."

Roberts felt himself sinking into a subregion of grave clarity. There were things he now knew, without knowing how he had come by the knowledge, things had peeled away to reveal other things, one thing. "You have Jocko?" he said.

"Naturally," the voice said. Calm dead tone, almost luxuriant.

"You can't get away with this. It's gone too far."

"This is not an American movie."

"Of course."

"We'll kill the boy."

Brooke had come out into the hall, wiping his hands on the

garden pants, blood on his Harlow cardigan. He frowned, spreading his palms in resignation. Glenville had gone away, there was nothing to do.

"Now listen," the voice said. "Be at Ealing Common train stop tomorrow in London. Precisely at ten-thirty at night. Bring the letter and come alone. Please do not involve the police. The boy will die. You give me the letter, I give you the boy. We can let this matter end there. Anything else would be far too risky for everybody. Do you understand?"

"Yes, I understand."

"Please, no weapons. It would be too difficult. You'd never be able to do it."

"Of course," Roberts said. Brooke had cocked his head, puzzled. Roberts found himself standing stupidly with the line dead in his hand.

"Is it about Jocko?" Brooke said.

"They have him."

Brooke returned to the room and came out with his arm around Amanda.

"Miles will be along," Brooke said.

They were vectored in the groaning twilight, a wine-dense haze, with the sound of the swans honking on the Cam.

SATURDAY, DECEMBER 14
EVENING

JACOB Miles sat in his glass cubicle, chewing the stub end of a pencil all the way down to wood, spitting out the eraser, while Amanda sat slumped in one corner of the office, a tam in her lap, face pale with worry. Brooke had gone up to hospital at Christ's Pieces with Glenville, the ambulance crew. He wanted to hold off an investigation of the death, they didn't know what else they should do. Roberts had been trying to explain Amsterdam, what he thought it meant, Miles sitting and chewing on his pencil stub, snapping his suspenders nervously while the dark evening gathered in the streets outside. The day had become bone cold, an English cold that suffused itself with dampness, the kind of cold that wore you out with wetness, interminable, sapping. There was an electric heater in the corner, snapping on and off, a thin glow against the blank slate sky, the tiny flakes of snow that had begun to fall in regular patterns on the shoppers who were out on the High Street. You could hear traffic, and some Christmas carols, the church bells of the city, and the sound of the students starting to fill the pubs. They were alone in the station house, trying to decide what to do, Amanda grim and angry, frightened to death, Roberts overtaken with fury until he could barely think.

Miles made some tea on a heating ring, he was sipping it without pleasure. Roberts had urged him not to make an official report of the crime, he thought there was something extraordinary happening, but he was having a hard time explaining it. They were locked in the frigid room, all alone, with a bleak night falling outside and all the songs of Christmas swimming down the street.

Miles tapped the pencil on the desk. "Just so we understand one another. You'd best tell me the whole thing. How you feel. What you think I'm supposed to do if I don't make an official report. I don't give a damn about my bloody job, it's the lad I'm thinking about."

"Jocko," Roberts began. "He's the one I'm thinking about also." He glanced at Amanda, who returned his look, blankly. She had no color, no formal structure to her expression, it was like paste. "Suppose I give it to you one thing at a time?"

"Please do," Miles said.

"My feeling from talking to this Demal fellow is that his group isn't responsible. His people have a reverence for children. He seemed genuinely shocked when I told him about Jonathan. He's a very intellectual sort of guy, I can't see anyone associated with him playing mumbo-jumbo with these puppets and cowrie shells. Poison darts, for God's sake, and Hubert Lind doesn't believe it either."

"You think his group was set up, nominated for the blame?"

"Yes, I do. Precisely."

"Why would that be?"

"Some person wants the Dutch oil company to fail in their efforts to get a huge concession. Trouble between the Dutch and independence groups would be just the ticket for another oil company."

"That is very crass."

"There is a lot of money at stake. Millions and millions of dollars."

"I have to have more," Miles said.

"Listen to me," Roberts pleaded. "Does it make sense to you that this tribesman would come to England, stun a young boy with a toxin, a poison from the tropics, then leave around all this *jeemat* nonsense, a *wayang* puppet, and then take a shot at me and damn near kill me? It isn't that easy to get a gun here, not easy at all to bring one into the country. It doesn't make sense."

Miles frowned, checked his watch. He was worried about his official position. "I agree with you," he said dully. "That part of this matter has always bothered me."

"There's something else," Roberts said.

Miles poured some more tea. "Well?" he asked.

"Didn't you think it odd that Jono's body was transported to Ipswich immediately? Brooke didn't have a chance to look at the boy. Bingo, he was gone. Then just as swiftly Amanda arrives in Ipswich and she takes Jono back to Cambridge where he belongs. All overnight, all very hush-hush. It is absurd, even Brooke thinks so."

"It is absurd, I quite agree."

"I think I know why it was done."

Miles snapped his suspender. "Please tell me."

"They wanted an autopsy. You've heard yourself that Brooke would never have conducted one on Jono. There was no forensic reason. The boy had drowned, it was an accident, there were no witnesses, no bruises, no signs of foul play. But if there was an autopsy, the doctor would discover evidence of the toxin. The Dutch government is informed, there is a scandal, the boy's death is attributed to Indonesian groups. The Dutch oil concession is in danger."

Miles closed his eyes. Amanda had begun to cry, huddled in the corner where Roberts couldn't touch her, it was a slow soft cry, matching the snow outside. "God forgive me, but I think you may be right. That means they thought Jono was . . ." Miles looked at Amanda, stopped speaking. It was too terrible, and she was sobbing. He walked around the desk and stood beside her, just off her shoulder, trying to think of some way to help. "I can't believe Clannahan . . ." he said, stopping again, his face filled with confusion.

"Perhaps not, I don't know. Perhaps he got his orders from the Home Office as he said. They thought Jono was Wim, wanted it handled officially."

"How do you explain your deportation?" Miles asked.

"Yes," Roberts said bitterly, "there's that."

"Let me see if I can guess." Miles had turned, one hand on Amanda's shoulder, staring outside, framed by the dusk, a few cars going down the street. The snow was like dust, luminous. "You think if I make an official report, alert the Home Office, that Jocko will be endangered. You think this is connected to the government."

"I think there is a risk of that. Yes."

"And right now, the only evidence that there is an English connection is Glenville's letter."

"Yes, for now."

Miles opened his desk. The letter had come to Brooke's Cambridge flat in the afternoon. Brooke had retrieved it that evening. Glenville told his story in it, what he knew, that he had agreed for money to transmit a false telephone message, get Wim to come downstairs. The man begged forgiveness, he was horrified that the boy had been killed. He knew that an Englishman had made the arrangement, all by telephone, he couldn't supply a name. In a soft, almost feminine hand, on soiled school stationery, Glenville expressed the emptiness of his life, how he wanted the money so badly. Whoever hired him had called again. And Glenville had admitted he'd written the letter, mailed it to Brooke. Miles was standing in the window, in near dark, reading the letter, looking at Amanda then, sighing audibly. Roberts felt light-headed, he hadn't eaten since early morning, a bowl of cornflakes in the sunny London room, it seemed an eternity ago, miles and miles, so far away in his memory it hardly existed.

"Ealing Common tube stop," Miles said, when he had finished with the letter.

"That's what the voice said."

"Devilish clever."

There was frost in the windowsill, a tiny formula of water webbed in one corner. The room seemed small, exhausted.

"If I remember my London tube stops," Miles said, "Ealing Common is above ground. It is a very busy stop, ordinarily. The station is a raised platform, iron stilts and stairs at either

199

end. Late on Sunday night, though, it would be nearly deserted, and only a few trains would come through. Anybody coming in on one of the trains could have a bloody good look around. They could see anything. You couldn't very well have the place crawling with bloody coppers."

"What do you think he'll do?" Roberts asked.

Miles paused. "I think this person will arrive after ten-thirty. He won't come up the stairs. This whole affair is designed so that he can come and go on the train. It would be too bloody risky to walk down the Uxbridge Road in plain sight with the lad on his arm. My guess is that he'll probably ride a train into the station, have a good look around. If he sees coppers, then he continues on. Nothing we could do. I think he'll be on one of the trains. Maybe ride through the station, get off at another stop, then come 'round again, satisfy himself that the coast is clear. There are many trains, he could come from anywhere."

"All he wants is the letter," Roberts said. He wanted this over, he wanted to take Amanda away, do what he had to do. "They don't know what's in the damn thing and it is the only evidence outside that would prove the Indonesians aren't involved."

"Bloody hell," Miles exclaimed. He put his head down. "My duty is to turn this letter over to Scotland Yard. Alert London right away."

Amanda said, "Is that what you intend to do, Miles?"

"I don't know," Miles said quietly. "We could have police on all the trains. We could try to see that no harm comes to Jocko. If you're all wrong about this, we won't have another chance."

"Oh look, Miles," Roberts said. "If he gets the letter back there would be no reason to harm Jocko."

"I don't know," he said.

"He may not release Jocko," Amanda said.

"Perhaps," Miles said. "Certainly if he sees police anywhere we have a serious problem." Miles turned and stared at Roberts. "I'll be honest. I don't think he intends to release Jocko. I'm sorry, Amanda, but that's what I think."

"Goddamn it," Roberts muttered. "Suppose we switch letters."

"Fiddle," Miles said. "If you're right, Mr. Roberts, and this is an Englishman, then he won't give you Jocko at any bloody rate."

Rage threatened to overwhelm Roberts, a high-towering anger, fueled by his despair, all the lost years, and even his loneliness. He could feel himself shaken, he felt naked against this cold room, all the absurd Christmas music filtering through the snow-blown sky, the sound of Amanda crying, like tiny bells. He went to her, put his arms around her, felt her quaking on his shoulder. Miles had appeared in his vision, back turned, staring out the frosty window, looking at the gray buildings, a swale of glossy lights on the Fens, far away.

"I want my Jocko home," Amanda cried, wild, amid staggering gulfs of sobs. Roberts thought she might collapse, lose consciousness. "I don't care who is dying in what nameless country. I don't care what company is making money from oil. I don't care about your bloody duty as a constable." Miles had half turned, his face lit by an inauspicious shock, brows furrowed. "I just want my only son. I want to be left alone." Her tam dropped to the floor and Miles stooped to pick it up. He had forgotten the kettle and it began to hiss on the electric ring.

"I've my own son," Miles said softly. "He's seven years old. Just so you know."

"I'm so sorry," Amanda sobbed. Roberts was holding her now, he thought she might fall down if he didn't.

Miles stiffened, leaned back against the sill. He announced in a loud voice: "I think you're bloody well right, Mr. Roberts," he said. He caught Roberts in a stare, hard, brilliant, it was like a clarification. "It's the way they took Jono to Ipswich, your deportation, that's what isn't right. I feel like Amanda does here, it's Jocko that's important." Roberts nodded as Miles took the kettle off the fire. He poured water over some leaves, steam rising, a puff of cloud in the cold room. "I've seen a film," Miles continued. *"High Noon,* it was called. Bloody good, too. A sheriff is being hunted by some gunfighters. There are several of them, only one of him. The citizens of his town have turned against him too, cowards to the man. They think he should stand up alone, because he's the sheriff. The point of it is that there isn't any togetherness against evil." Here Miles smiled gently, bringing the teacup to his lips. "At least, that's what my wife says. She fancies herself a movie critic, reads the *Observer,* all that. For a simple chap like me, it just means that there are some things you do alone. You keep bloody quiet about it and you do it alone. Looks to me, Yank, that this is one of them."

Roberts was trying to get Amanda back into her chair. Miles handed him the tam, he eased her down. She had stopped crying and was sitting with her face in her hands, sinking away into her quiet grief, the fear.

"That's not the only thing," Miles said. "As a practical matter, I think you and I have just as good a chance to get Jocko back as the whole bloody London constabulary. I'm not saying there isn't any risk. There's a hell of a lot. But you know what happened in *High Noon?* The sheriff tried to handle all those bad fellows, but in the end it was his wife, the Quaker woman, who had to save him. Bit of a surprise it was too." Miles had chewed into the pencil again, spitting out some wood shavings. "Perhaps we'll have a bit of our own surprise, as well."

A bell tinkled over the station door and Brooke came inside, shaking himself, some flakes of snow falling off his collar, making his way between the forest of wooden desks, the Victorian maple railing. He was still in his Harlow cardigan, the garden pants, shivering with cold. His jowly face was wet, crimson, his hair wild. Roberts was surprised that he didn't look more tired.

"Did you manage it, Martin?" Miles said.

Brooke smacked his lips. "Right you are," he said. It was his clipped, professional tone, Indian army, stiff upper lip. "For now we're saying Glenville died of gunshot wounds which were self-inflicted. On this cold Saturday night nobody around the hospital much cares, shove the bloody beggar in the refrigerator and go home to the egg and sausage. What?" Brooke patted Roberts on the shoulder, mustering a good smile, nodding his head.

"For now," Miles said. "The chief constable agrees with the coroner." Brooke leaned against a filing cabinet, staring at Amanda, giving her a smile of encouragement. "I want you all to listen carefully," Miles said. Roberts had gone to stand behind Amanda, lightly touching her shoulders. "The Ealing Common station is above ground. I want Mr. Roberts here to go to the station at precisely ten-thirty with the letter. Walk to the middle of the platform and stand there as if you hadn't a care in the bloody world. Don't concern yourself with anything at all except the safety of Jocko. I want you absolutely prepared to hand over the letter and do nothing else. I want your mind focused on the one thing that's important—that you hand over the letter, and you don't make any suspicious moves."

"Suppose I take a gun," Roberts said.

Miles shook his head. "We'll have none of that."

"But—" Roberts began to protest.

"Absolutely no weapons," Miles said.

"All right," Roberts said. "No guns then."

"Right we are," Miles said. "Now that's settled. You take the letter and go to the platform. Wait until our friend gets off the train, whoever he is. When you see him he will have Jocko. If he doesn't, then we'll know we're in trouble. But I have that thought out as well. Put the letter down on the platform about two or three feet in front of you. I want you to make him come for the letter."

"Make him come and get it," Roberts repeated.

"Precisely," Miles said.

"But look, Miles," Roberts protested. "I can't jump this asshole. I mean I could jump him, but if he's got Jocko it would be too dangerous. I guarantee you *he'll* have a gun."

"Of course," Miles said. "I agree, quite. But hear me out." Amanda had lifted her head, she was looking at Roberts with a look of hopelessness he had never wanted to see, it was like reading the skeleton through her skin, all the pale luminosity of her personality had gone, she was living in the death of her children and he was aching with her pain. "When our friend gets off the train try to be calm. Don't look for anything, or anybody. Just attend to your business."

"Which is?" Roberts asked.

"Place the letter on the platform and ask Jocko to step aside while our friend retrieves his evidence. This is one thing you must attempt to accomplish."

"You're going to shoot him. Hide out. That's much too dangerous."

"Please don't think. Concentrate on opening the slightest distance between Jocko and our friend."

"But my boy," Amanda said.

"I'll be frank," Miles said. "I don't think he'll return Jocko at any rate."

Amanda stared at Roberts. Her face was blank with anxiety. He could see the bones, all the structures drained of form, like white rock.

"He could," Miles said, "quite simply step off the train and shoot you, Mr. Roberts. We can hardly control this kind of thing."

Amanda went limp in her chair.

"It's a risk I accept," Roberts said.

"Right, then," Miles replied. "What about you, Amanda? Do you accept this risk for Jocko?"

She looked at Roberts. "Yes," she whispered.

"And you, Miles?" Brooke asked.

"Trust me," Miles said to the window, engrossed now in the falling snow, how the soft blue light had suffused the city, the countryside now like the outline of whales in a phosphorescent ocean. Miles sighed deeply, more a moan that had a cavernous effect. "Trust me," he said.

SUNDAY, DECEMBER 15

ROBERTS had never felt so alone. Amanda had insisted on driving her Cortina across London, coming along, and there had been a brief irrational quarrel, strongly bitter and surprising to both of them, it was like breaking a family heirloom, seeing the horrid shards on the floor, trying to patch it back together. And now he could see her reflection in the wet glass windshield, jaw set, a look of wild desperation that was almost feral, an expression that he had never seen on her face before, beyond him to explore. They had made up, Roberts in the cellar, sitting in the dark with his thoughts, trying to relax, rest his eyes, make his head quit throbbing, when she had come down the stairs very quietly and placed her fingers along the back of his neck, calculating the depth of his estrangement, then kissing him gently on the cheek. He knew, or felt he knew, that she was without responsibility. It was stupid for him to insist that she stay on Kensington Road while he and Brooke went down to Ealing Common, he apologized, still staring at the dark, and he heard her go back upstairs and it was settled. Still, he was amazed at the darkness of the city of London, where were the ten millions?

Brooke was in the backseat, one hand on Amanda's shoulder, his overcoat draped on the seat. They were going down the yellow-lighted Cromwell Road through the huge funnels of official London, dark-rimmed stone, bits of fog whiskered in the streets, Earl's Court topcoat gray in a windy rain. Roberts could not accept the utter stillness of this Sunday night. The streets could have been the scene of some kind of monstrous devastation, an absolute emptiness on film, unwinding slowly backward without aim. It was as if they had been locked inside a toy city by some magical devil, alone, wearing their collective exhaustion like a skin. You could hear faint music from the clubs and bars, but it was a plague sound, not for the living, as the shops and flats and museums fled away. Roberts thought he might touch Amanda, demonstrate his solidarity, but then he didn't couldn't bring himself to offer her the slightest hope. He could hear Brooke wheezing in the back. He probably had a cold. Once in a while they met traffic drifting down Cromwell Road, or crossing over to Shepherd's Bush, or on the roundabouts, little darts of orange fuzz on the rain-slick streets.

The great green expanse of Acton Park unreeled, Amanda going far too fast now, her hands bound to the wheel, down the Vale and then to Uxbridge, miles and miles of gray row houses and playing fields under clouds of fog, across the river all the factories, power stations, their huge stacks visible in the distance. Brooke's face appeared on wet glass, a shank of wild white hair, like Einstein, bejowled in a universe of diamond light. They hadn't slept, none of them. They had been up all night, drinking coffee, pacing the floor, Brooke sitting at the window with his eyes on the park across the street, Roberts browsing through the Hobbes and Locke, the Laurence Sterne, Amanda welded to the kitchen chair in a clear cold haze of cigarette smoke.

Uxbridge became big and ugly, an urban road as functional as a hammer, blocks of flats rising two and three stories, anonymous brick and mortar, all dark. Pub lights shafted down the rainy tunnels, it was making Roberts heartsick. They came to a roundabout and Amanda slowed, taking the turn, stopping briefly, then pulling forward again along the near edge of a football field. There were fog lights ahead cutting through the dark, you could see an elevated platform, an iron stilt webbing structure, a slipstream of trash and newspaper blowing underneath. There was a welter of bill-boards advertising ale, toothpaste, cornflakes, keen smiling faces with white teeth, frowsy looks of joy, peeling paint and paper. Roberts tried to clear his head, make his heart stop beating. It was thumping so that he thought it could be seen through his bomber jacket, he felt like someone was beating him with a bat. A train rumbled across the platform and halted in a shower of sparks and steam, groaning, creaking as the boards moved, the rails crying. It was an explosion of shapes and forms, and then the doors whisked shut and the train began to pick up speed again, away from the platform. Roberts could see the brakeman in back standing forlornly in his tiny compartment, his dark blue uniform, the shiny cap. Amanda cut the engine and they were in absolute dark.

Finally, Amanda relaxed, leaning her head against the seat, touching Brooke. Brooke clapped Roberts on the shoulder. "Godspeed, my boy," he said. Roberts could see in the dim light that there were huge salty tears rolling down Amanda's cheeks, they were awash, a torrent of silent pain.

Roberts zipped his jacket. "I'll be right back with Jocko," he said. "Take it to the bank."

"Right you are," Brooke said.

Amanda opened her eyes, cocking her head slightly, smiling curiously. She bit her lip and kissed Roberts, leaning over, brushing his cheek. He remembered then that she had kissed him that way once before, when he had gotten on the train at Ipswich, after their tour of the East Anglia country, going back to the base, they wouldn't be seeing one another again until after the war was over. It was like a cloud shadow passing over his face, warm to cool, sienna to lavender, the passing of enormous architectural forms, sand castles washed by wave. For a while he had remembered the kiss, and then it had been overwhelmed by the din of battle, until, red-eyed and cold, hungry beyond any visceral acknowledgment, bur-ied in a snowy foxhole beneath a fir forest of frozen branches, he had forgotten the kiss. And now it had come again, another shove into battle, lips with the frost of love and death.

Roberts got out of the car and started up the Uxbridge Road in the mist. He was in a huddle of commercial buildings, banks, grocers, agents. Trudging under the dim fog lights, around the traffic circle, uphill along a branch, until he came back to the Uxbridge again, he kept his eyes on the raised platform, the two flights of iron stairs and the unbelievable forlorn emptiness. It was like laboring through Arctic snow, a tundra wilderness. In his anxiety he would stop, start to breathe again, seeing his breath icy blown away. There were surfaces to his fear. He was amazed by the many facets it had, deep gut-wrenching anxiety, a gnawing loneliness, despair, tension, a limitless and unbounded anger, this sheathless sword that cut and slashed in all directions. At one point, he swore he could feel his own blood circulate. He went up the stairs to the wooden platform as if he were dragging an anchor.

The platform was oddly lighted, halos every ten yards for a hundred yards, like beads into the fog. Holding her grocery sack, stalks of celery, a cabbage, one bunch of lillies, an old woman hunched on one of the near benches. And there was an old man too, down the way, with stiff bristly gray hair, sideburns like brushes, standing against a green iron pole, smoking, while three red-haired teenage girls giggled in a clutch farther away. Roberts was alone, cut away, and he knew it. It had sunk in like the cold, all the way to his vital organs. His mouth felt dry.

While Roberts walked down the platform, one Circle Line train rolled in, surprising him, he staggered back in the harsh glare, expecting something to happen. Some pub drunks poured out of the car in front of him. He could smell the ale and tobacco, but they laughed and rolled away, slapping backs, cursing, until he could see them go down the stairs, the sound of them only an echo in the vastness of Uxbridge Road. There would be more trains, he knew, lines to south Ealing, Heathrow, each lumbering away to another dark place, unloading more pub drunks, old women with grocery sacks and tired legs, all these luminous souls bound for home. At the end of the platform the clock read ten-thirty, he was right on time, and so he sat on a bench, alone, watching the red-haired girls leave on the Circle Line, heading for the West End, the hands on the clock crawling slowly uphill.

These minutes, like film spewing from a projector. Roberts found himself daydreaming, he saw Smitty's face in the shiny dial of the clock, he could feel the cool brush of Amanda's lips, her cheeks salty wet, the steam from each train rose into an abrupt cloud shape above the cliffs of Normandy where the Germans were firing. Details emerged, receded, smudges of ghostlike memory, but always Amanda, Jocko's face across the tennis net as he skidded and winged his shot. He saw that most of half an hour had gone in reverie as two trains came into the station, a Picadilly Line, nearly empty, another Circle train with two or three anonymous bodies walking tiredly into the night. Then Roberts saw a blind man tugged onto the platform by a black German shepherd, the man in dark glasses, carrying his cane, enfrocked in a dirty black coat, rubbers unbuttoned to his shins, sloppy and confused, lurching down the empty platform. It made Roberts shiver.

Rounding the curve, down five hundred yards, he could see another Circle Line train, one of the last, nearly empty, except for one or two forms in the brilliant light of the compartments. The cars were rocking on the tracks. You could see the ads overhead, the gray straps bobbing as the train swayed, the motorman in front with his red face and gray stare. The blind man was tapping forward now, hunting an empty bench, only ten yards from Roberts, the dog with ears pricked, as the train whooshed past in steam and a horrible clanking, like someone dragging chains through broken glass, the sudden hiss, mechanical muscles aching in the undercarriage. "Circle Line," the blind man was calling, tapping, flat cap covering his face and his blind man's glasses frosty with mist. "Circle Line," he called again, hopeless.

Roberts wanted to help the man. His skin was prickly with the need, just walk down the platform and stand in the cold and announce that the Circle Line was standing in the station, help the old man, pat his dog on the head. He remembered Jacob Miles, his face to the window, warning him to keep a clear head, focus on the thing that needed doing. And here he had been in a deep reverie. And now he was going to help a blind man. Roberts knew there were imperatives he would have to ignore. The blind man said, "Circle Line."

The thing that halted Roberts was a man on the platform who had come out of one of the cars. He seemed enormously tall, bundled in an expensive camel's hair coat, brown cashmere scarf, Roberts could see shiny stars on his brogues, a soft fedora pulled over his face, just a wash of white hair over the ears, sharp jaw, a flash of wristwatch when he moved his arm over the boy's shoulder. Coming out of the steam and glare it seemed to Roberts that a Mephistopheles had snapped into existence. It shocked him, he could feel his heart stop, in the background the blind man calling "Circle Line." The tall man smiled, showing a beautiful row of white teeth, they were gleaming in Roberts's mind's eye, catching a glimpse of the train windows full of rain, and the boy between the man's arms with his head folded in scarf, flat cap pulled down over his eyes. Roberts recognized his freckles, one line of earlobe, that was all. He thought he could see a pair of glasses on the boy's nose. They had made Jocko wear glasses, he thought, an enormous magnification of reality. The boy couldn't see. The blind man was tapping away from the bench, his dog on a chain. Everyone is blind.

"Please, no names," said Clannahan when he had come close. His lips had pulled back unnaturally. Roberts thought he could smell rosewater. Clannahan was holding a gun behind the boy's ear, pointed at Roberts. It looked like a .25 automatic, silver with an ivory grip. "One name and the boy has to die. I'm sure you can understand that."

"I know your name," Roberts said.

"Just the letter," Clannahan replied coldly.

The Circle Line train began to move, creaking away in a roil of steam and light. Clannahan watched it go with the windows limned in a cluster of reflections, the platform, the halo of lights progressing along the wooden boards, a few bored passengers, the blind man standing confused with his dog. The brakeman passed and the train was gone finally in one gasp of bilious exhaust.

"What now?" Roberts asked.

"We have exactly five minutes," Clannahan said. "The next train will be along." Jocko was directly in front of Clannahan, who had one arm around his chest. The gun was leveled at Roberts. "Please give me the letter."

"And then?"

"I'll be popping along, old stick."

Roberts knew he was going to die. It was funny, but it made absolutely no difference to his emotional state, it was as if he had known it all along, his own death on the tip of his tongue, like a forgotten name. Glenville was dead, who had known Wim's death was murder. And now there was Roberts, who knew a name. Clannahan would take the letter and put a bullet in his chest, and it would all end in a dull bureaucratic inquiry, sound and smoke and interminable speeches in the House of Commons. He wondered if Clannahan would harm Jocko. The boy knew nothing. The only thing he knew had died with Glenville in his bed-sitter bachelor digs. This knowledge came over Roberts like icy mountain water in a stream, seamless pain, a brief interval of throb, then numbness, almost pleasure.

"How could you do this?" Roberts asked, stupidly.

"For the money, old man."

"Killing children."

"I assure you, young master Jonathan was a tragic mistake. It was supposed to be Wim all along."

"You must be insane."

"I assure you that isn't the case." Clannahan glanced down the platform. There was only the blind man in his black frock coat. "There is just so much money to be made in business. One slight twist of fate and millions of pounds fall into my hands."

"I want to see the boy's face."

Clannahan looked at Roberts, his gaze hard. He took off the boy's cap. Roberts could see the huge bottle glasses, curly black hair, a maze of freckles, his coat collar all the way around his neck, over his mouth. Clannahan tightened his grip, holding the boy's neck so he couldn't turn. Then he pulled down the cap. Roberts nodded, then explained that he had the letter in his jacket pocket. He was told to get it with his right hand. There was a brief moment when Roberts wanted to vault the distance, take a swing at Clannahan, give his anger a chance to succeed. Instead he dropped the letter to the platform.

"Now step back a bit," Clannahan said.

"Circle Line," called the blind man. "Circle Line, please, gentlemen."

Clannahan surveyed the platform, the clock at the end. Roberts thought he could hear a deep rumble from far away across the vale, all the dark chestnuts, row houses, the empty blocks of flats.

"How does a monster like you get loose?" Roberts said. Clannahan had nicked around Jocko, he was kneeling for the letter. He shook his head.

"You're behind the times, old man. Shiny morals and badges of courage, what a lot of rot. You're coming into an age of bottom lines. Business and government, all the same. Your Herr Lind isn't much different than me."

"Herr Lind?" Roberts said, feeling surprised and distracted. He kept looking for a glimpse of Jocko's eyes, but he couldn't see them. They were covered by his coat collar, the hat, big bottle glasses. "What's he got to do with all this?"

"Nothing at all," Clannahan said. "It is just that he's very much like me. A spy. A double-dealer. A government official."

"He doesn't kill children," Roberts said angrily.

"Only a matter of time," Clannahan mused, smiling now with his white teeth, more a low scowl, waving the gun. He gripped Jocko tightly about the neck and leaned down for the letter. With one hand he popped open the envelope and read the contents. "This is very disappointing," he said dully. "I had expected much more. It looks to me like this whole affair could have been avoided." There was another dull rumble, lights flickering between the buildings in the near distance. Roberts felt the platform give a quick shudder. "Ah," Clannahan muttered, stuffing the letter into his overcoat pocket. "Our people were surprised when you went to Amsterdam. We watched you. Meeting with Lind at the zoo. It was that meeting that prompted us to watch Glenville. I'm not surprised you've returned to England. Though how you did it is a bit of a puzzle." He had lurched back toward the track, dragging Jocko in a vicious stranglehold. "Circle Line," shouted the blind man, making for the edge where the wood dropped four feet to the electrified line. "Circle Line!"

"For God's sake, Clannahan, let the boy go," Roberts pleaded. He could hear the train clearly now, the Circle Line, rounding a corner, its horrible rickety clomping. Its headlight caught the fog, made a million bars of shredded light.

Clannahan carefully lowered Jocko to the platform, made him lie flat, placed his brogue on the boy's neck. "Stay there, boy, don't move."

"Do as he says," Roberts said.

"Too bad," Clannahan said. "You've used my name. You've sealed his fate."

Roberts was staggered with his own stupid duplicity. One word and he had killed Jocko. He was cold, his hands like ice. It was too far, he'd never make it.

The blind man stumbled toward the edge of the platform. "Circle Line," he called. "Help a blind man!"

Clannahan raised the gun just as the blind man's German shepherd rose in a burst of snarling teeth, arching, its back humped in a solid blur. Roberts felt time stop. The train had reached the platform and was boring down the line and all Roberts knew was a momentary silence, pieces of existence breaking all around him, and then a sooty roar, he couldn't tell if it was the train or the sound of a gunshot. They were transfigured in a single transcendental second, boy, Clannahan, silver flash of fire, the huge dog ascending against Clannahan, who was falling backward, screaming. Roberts wasn't sure, but he thought he called Jocko's name when the mirrored gum machine behind him exploded into a hale of glass. And then he saw Clannahan go over the platform edge in a pool of demented glare, the train grinding away, the blind man on his knees while his dog barked viciously.

Roberts lay on his back. He could see the train doors whisking open and the dog standing with its legs spread just on the edge. All this light was pouring out of the compartment, smiling billboard faces, gum ads, some old men in black huddled on their seats, staring out with glum looks of astonishment. The blind man had thrown away his cane. He was kneeling over Jocko, taking off his dark glasses and the dog was licking his hand.

"Miles," Roberts called, on one elbow.

"Right you are, Yank." He smiled.

Jocko was on his stomach now, trying to get up. The doors to the Circle Line train had whisked shut, the train was beginning to move. Roberts thought he could afford a small prayer, but he couldn't think of one, and before he had time to think again he could hear Amanda's voice at the end of the platform, growing stronger as she ran down the wooden length of it, calling her son's name, while Jocko rose and ran toward her with his arms wide.

WEDNESDAY, DECEMBER 18

THEY were in the main room of the London house. Miles was in front of the coal fire with his son, Dennis, watching the big German shepherd play with the shadows. His wife, Anne, would tease the dog with hand signs and it would bound around the room, ears perked. Brooke and Celia were eating fruitcake, finishing the last of the eggnog.

Miles squatted beside Roberts. "For a minute there I thought you were going to do something silly. Thought you might try for Clannahan."

"It crossed my mind," Roberts said. Clannahan's gunshot had shattered a mirror behind his head and he was wearing another bandage, just behind the left ear on the neck.

"Funny," Miles mused, "how people seem to ignore blind men. Noticed it quite a lot. Somehow don't count them as proper human beings. Thought it might somehow work."

"You had me worried."

Miles grabbed his shepherd by the neck. "Zack here is the best trained bloody police dog in England," he said. The dog was backpedaling. Amanda had gone downstairs to the kitchen for coffee.

"Has Clannahan said anything?" Roberts asked. "As badly as he was hurt?"

"Singing like a canary," Miles answered. "He was working for the oil company. Thought if he could create a rift between the Dutch company and the Indonesian people, that the concession would go English. Clannahan took money to arrange it so the Dutch would lose. Shameful business, really. But we've got the letter, the gun, rounded up his fellow who did the killings. I suppose as a diplomat Clannahan was exposed to all sorts of temptations to earn huge sums of money. In this case he succumbed to an oil company that hired him to arrange some sort of scandal which would influence the granting of the concession. He knew that Wim and his family had been threatened by terrorists, so he decided to use that to his advantage. If he could make it look as if Indonesian terrorists were going to kidnap and murder Dutch oil company employees or their families, then the English company might get the concession. This matter of the puppets and cowrie shells and black stones was intended to incriminate the terrorists and leave the impression that a Dutch company exploring for oil would be severely hampered. Of course we know that the telephone call to the Harlow School was meant to lure Wim downstairs where he would be stunned with a poison, then drowned, or perhaps kidnapped. It's a sad business, and poor Jono took the telephone call for Wim, and we know the rest. I'm afraid the Home Office is in for a bit of a blow in Commons. But we know the whole story now at least. I feel so bloody sorry for Amanda. I hope she makes it through all right."

"She will," Roberts said. "How about Clannahan?"

"Lost his right hand. Broken back."

"Too bad," Roberts said, zipping his bomber jacket. "Thank you, Jacob," he said. Miles gave him the thumbs-up, hugging his dog.

Roberts said his other good-byes and went out on the landing. He could smell coffee brewing. Amanda was standing there in the half-light.

"I've got to go home," Roberts said. He heard Celia laugh, the dog bark. Amanda was wearing a bulky sweater and corduroy pants.

"Yes, I know," she said. Amanda touched Roberts with her fingertips, gently, tracing the line of his jaw. "Thank you for my son," she said quietly. He kissed the tip of her finger as it passed.

"Amanda—" Roberts managed to say before she stopped him, placing a finger over his lips.

"I know, darling," she said. "I've so much adjusting to do and I need the time." She paused, trying to gather herself. "I've decided to go back to acting. Maybe take some workshops. All of this is so much more complicated than sick rabbits on a road in East Anglia." Roberts had no words, he was struck by the airy senselessness of all he was feeling. Smiling, Amanda said, "I understand you have plans with Jocko."

"I meant to t-tell you," he stammered.

"It's fine," she said. "He so admires you. My American cowboy." She was holding Roberts's lumberjack shirt, peering up into his face. He wanted to kiss her more than anything.

"I'll be waiting for him," Roberts said.

"Will you come next Christmas?"

He nodded and picked up his hand-tooled suitcase, marched down the stairs. He didn't want to look back, he just wanted to go home, remember things. It seemed to be his way, his head was full of the past, Smitty on the boat, bouncing the baseball off the boiler plate, the taste of cheddar Amanda had served when they were both in training, riding a horse through a cold autumn gloom in the Sangre de Cristo mountains, all the aspens shedding gold leaves. He was in love with so many things that gave him pain. He knew it couldn't last, he wanted it to change. When he had gone from the house he took one last look at the place, its big windows glowing, shadows inside from the coal fire, Amanda looking at him through the open front door.

Snow had been falling. The flakes were circling down, powdering the street. He could smell roasting chestnuts, a dusky smell of coal. The roofs were covered with snow and seemed surreal. He walked up Kensington Park Road, past Ladbrooke Gardens, more people now, Christmas bulbs in the shops, music.

He reached the tube, its entrance bathed in an orange

glow, the white tiles sheened with light. Jocko was there, squatting on a rug holding a straw effigy, an old man in a frock coat, eyes of coal, battered top hat. There was a tin cup on the rug.

Jocko smiled, "Penny for the old guy, mister?" Smiling again. "Penny for the old guy!"

Roberts put a penny in the cup. Snow had blown down the tunnel, a fine white loam on the concrete. Smoke from an open brazier had blown down too.

"You'll show me the lakes?" Jocko asked.

"A volcano in Oregon filled with blue water."

"And horses?"

"Horses, too. And Dodge City and wild Indians and purple mountains."

Jocko got up and put his arms around Roberts. They embraced while the people passed by.

"God bless you, Jocko," Roberts said.

"God bless you, Mr. Roberts."

Roberts pulled away from Jocko and walked down the long corridor, where the air was damp. The light had a livid quality. He sensed a wind rise from the tunnel and he was drawn inside, down to where there was only steam and the awful sound of machinery.